Franco and Anna Gennusa

THEIR JOURNEY

by

Mary B. Patterson

D0885695

PUBLISHED
BY
BRIGHTON PUBLISHING LLC
501 W. RAY ROAD
SUITE 4
CHANDLER, AZ

FRANCO AND ANNA GENNUSA

THEIR JOURNEY

BY

MARY B. PATTERSON

PUBLISHED
BY
BRIGHTON PUBLISHING LLC
501 W. RAY ROAD
SUITE 4
CHANDLER, AZ
WWW.BRIGHTONPUBLISHING.COM

PRINTED IN THE UNITED STATES OF AMERICA

COPYRIGHT © 2013

ISBN 13: 978-1-62183-089-4
ISBN 10: 1-621-83089-6

Second Edition

COVER DESIGN: TOM RODRIGUEZ

Acknowledgements

How do I thank my sisters for remembering and giving me their memories of our best and worst times? How can I express what I feel when listening to stories of our past? How do I say thank you for giving me the material to write this novel, for remembering, and lovingly giving me the insight into what life was really like growing up in a different land, for remembering my history, for protecting me as I grew into adulthood, for giving me so much love and attention? To all of you, my special sisters, I give my love and this wonderful story.

To my oldest and most special sister, Teresa (Terry) Mitera; you taught me that family always comes first. Thank you.

To Giuseppa (Jo) Balboni Romano, who is no longer is on this earth and for whom my empty heart aches; for your exceptional beauty, I describe your character as Pina in this novel. Thank you.

To Vincenza (Holly) Clark, many, many thanks for the new shoes I received for the first day of school every year, and for our life-long friendship. I look into those bright eyes of yours and know that God put you here on earth as a constant reminder of the brighter parts of my life. Thank you.

To Francesca (Franny) Clark, who looks down at me from heaven with those big dimples. They were so deep when you smiled, but they also showed when you cried big tears for our grandparents in Sicily. Thank you.

To Innocenza, (Nancy) Gatto for taking all the punishment from our parents that I solely deserved for being such a mischievous child. Thank you.

To my parents, Anna and Francesco Gennusa, who are no longer on this earth. You lovingly showed me how hard work and determination would make me a survivor. Thank you.

Lastly, I want to thank my deceased husband Dennis C. (Pat) Patterson who also treasured my sisters' many stories. Thank you, my love. I will love you, always.

Introduction

My oldest sister Terry was telling stories about our early life in Sicily during World War II during dinner one evening in her home. This was the subject of so many wonderful evenings we regularly spent together.

"Mary," she said, "you were just a baby on a cold autumn day, riding in our cart, going to our village home from our country farm. Suddenly, father abruptly stopped the cart. He screamed for us to get out. Mother jumped at his command, and the rest of us did the same. Father demanded we run to a tree that stood alone a short distance away. I heard a loud roaring sound and looked up to the sky. A German plane was coming toward us. Mother was holding you in her arms as we all ran together. We got to the tree, and father yelled for us to climb to the highest branches."

My sister told that story filled with fear, a bit of humor, and so much confusion. She looked at me, puzzled, and asked, "What was father thinking? Did he really think that the tree was going to protect us?"

That story rooted itself in my heart. As I contemplated it over and over, I felt so much emotion, and was compelled to write this novel.

In another desperate and confusing time during the war, my parents did not realize that my sister Nancy was very sick. Terry sensed that she was dying, wrapped her warmly, and carried her on a cold winter day to the village doctor. Terry, unconcerned for her life, and the Germans around her, bravely saved Nancy's life.

The characters and situations in this novel are fictional. However, some of the stories, as told to me by my sisters, were taken from true events that happened in our family. The characteristics and personalities of the Gennusa girls are true to my sisters and me. Our strong bond and deep devotion, to each other and to our families, is also accurately represented in this book.

My parents had a marriage of convenience, "arranged" by their parents when my mother was a young woman. Both my mother and father had much to give to each other and to their families, which made for a rich marriage.

My father was a successful olive farmer who leased his farmland from the Monastery, Muccune Di Povire Tarucco (Mouth of the Poverty Farm). He owned a home on the land, located in the village of Bisacquino.

My mother, an American Citizen, had lived in the United States during the early part of her life, and was bilingual. Her first language was Italian, although she spoke English very well. After moving to Sicily, she spoke English to the American soldiers during World War II when they passed through our farm en route to their next destination.

It was my father's decision to come to America to work, save money, and then return to Sicily; the money he made would be saved for our dowries. But living in an American society with high-heeled shoes and bright red lipstick hidden from our parents, turned Sicily into a distant memory for the Gennusa daughters. Unwilling to travel back and repeat our unbearable and long, uncomfortable overseas trip, my sisters never wanted to return.

The Beginning

It was September 8th, 1943, and World War II was still under way. The fascist dictator, Benito Mussolini, was unable to control or improve his country's disastrous condition. Italy, under Mussolini, had persistent problems—unemployment, organized crime, corruption, and low economic growth. Still, he was unwilling to give up his power. His greed, taste for power and wealth, and the Germans' of what would be his after the war, pushed him to neglect the wants of the Italian people. Italy was his to dictate.

Mussolini had left his people to fend for themselves during this trying time.

A poor farmer and his family were riding in their mule-drawn cart toward their home in the village of Bisacquino. The village, located on the island of Sicily, was part of the Italian Commonwealth located south of the island's largest city, Palermo (the capital of the island).

Palermo was a thriving modern city before World War II, while Bisacquino was a quiet mountain village. Because of the poor country's communication, the farmer was unaware of an armistice that had been negotiated between the Italian Government and the Allied Mercantile Commander in Chief. While the Sicilian shores were overwhelmed by worldwide concern and hostile war conditions, the farmer traveled quietly, detached and unaware of life beyond his own.

The farmer and his family grew and harvested olives on land leased to them by Catholic nuns who ran the monastery, Muccune Di Povire Tarucco (Mouth of the Poverty Farm). The nuns cared for the old and the poor who had no one else to care for them. Their charitable work left them with little so they constantly asked the famer for donations.

It had been a long and tiring day of work in the cold and rain for the farmer and his family, but it was coming to a close. The daughters, twelve, nine, seven, four and one, were cranky after a long day of work.

The older daughters were unhappy because they wanted to be at school with their friends, and the baby was hungry and fussy. The farmer's wife opened her dress and gave her breast to the baby.

The farmer's mind wandered as the old work mule slowly pulled the family toward his village home. The farmer's wife was carrying their sixth child and he wondered whether their lives could get any harder. He was just as concerned for his wife as for the unborn child, and on top of that, the war and everyday concerns bothered him. He thought to himself, *Is it right to bring another child into this life?*

A strange sound in the distance, a low rumble, startled the farmer from his worries. He knew the sound couldn't have been thunder, for the clouds had already started to dissipate. He knew the sound couldn't be a herd of animals, for wild animals were rare on this island. It couldn't be Mt. Etna–the volcano that had erupted numerous times, leading to devastating earthquakes, destroying life and property in its path— because it was on the east coast side of the island.

The farmer stopped the cart and wondered, *What is this strange sound? If it isn't an earthquake…*

He listened closely, trying to determine where the sound was coming from. The farmer knew he was safe from the war because the shooting and bombing were on the outskirts of the island. He slowly turned around and looked up to see a mysterious silver spot in the sky.

At that moment, a German fighter pilot, bored and irritated with his day's run, loudly said to himself, "How could Headquarters give me this minimal assignment? Don't they know how many runs I have taken? How many enemy planes I have shot down? Don't they know how many enemies I have killed with my own gun? My loyalty has always been to the Fuehrer and the future of Germany. I will be part of history in the making! I will not put up with these silly tasks. There is fighting on this island and I should be fighting, not surveying this part of this island. I need to see action! I need to draw blood from our enemies. I need to be part of the glory of victory."

He hadn't yet gotten word that Mussolini had been overthrown by King Victor Emmanuel III and that the country had surrendered to the allies.

The fighter, in an effort to distract himself, flew angrily, diving close to the ground below. He approached and scanned the foliage but saw nothing of interest at first.

Still gazing at the silver spot in the sky, coming closer to the land and moving quickly, the farmer finally realized what it was. He pulled the reins on the mule fast and hard. The cart stopped quickly. He turned to his wife and shouted, "The children! Quick, get down."

The wife, stunned by her husband's unusually harsh command, quickly pulled her nipple from her baby's mouth. The child, interrupted so suddenly, started to wail. The wife watched as the farmer jumped down from the cart and grabbed the infant away from her.

"What is it?" she asked, alarmed.

The farmer, more urgently now, repeated himself, "Get down!"

This time the wife didn't hesitate; she got down from the cart and grabbed her youngest daughter back from her husband. The farmer helped his two smaller daughters from the cart and clutching their hands, turned to run. Quickly, the two older daughters leapt from the cart and soon the entire family was running together. The loud noise startled the mule and he ran, too.

Bewildered, the two younger daughters started to cry. In a panic, the farmer yelled to his family, instructing them to run toward a large, lone-standing olive tree standing about a hundred yards away.

After a short time flying low to the trees, the German pilot came upon a clearing and noticed movement below him. In the distance he saw what he thought was a small herd of animals running. Knowing that the island wasn't known for herds of animals, his curiosity got the better of him. As he got closer, he slowed his aircraft and wondered why animals would be running to a tree for protection, but then realized that the chaotic scene below him wasn't a herd of animals, but people. Intrigued by the sight, his adrenaline surges and he decided to dive closer, hoping to see who they were. After killing so many enemies, he thirsted for more blood.

The farmer ran to the tree, hoping it would be large enough, and the branches full enough to hide his family from their sky intruder. Although the family was very religious, in their frightened condition, they did not think to pray. The famer squeezed his younger daughters' hands so hard out of fear that they cried out in pain. He pulled them unyieldingly and made them run as fast as they could while his wife and older daughters followed close behind.

In the distance, the pilot noticed a mule running fast and pulling an empty cart. And then, disappointed, he realized that the commotion below was just a band of Italian peasants, his allies. He could make out what appeared to be two adults and four children running in fear toward a large, solitary tree. Amused by the situation, he said out loud, "Do they really think that tree would protect them from me?" He decided to season his monotonous flight by having some fun with these worthless, inept specimens.

The family was running. The youngest of the daughters, still holding the farmer's hand, slid on the slippery ground and he dragged her toward the tree. She screamed, more out of fright than pain, and her body was bruised from being dragged across the ground. During the last minute of their long run, the farmer noticed that beneath his feet was a low growth of autumn wet hay. These difficult, wet running conditions, in an open field, made them vulnerable to the sky predator. The figure in the sky now looked like a large silver bird approaching them quickly with an ear-piercing screech that got louder with its approach.

The family reached the tree where the farmer let go of his daughters' hands. With the help of the older daughters, who grabbed their younger sisters' hands, the farmer pushed his two smaller children up the tree as they cried in terror. He ordered them to climb to the highest branches they could reach. Then he helped his wife, still holding the baby in her arms, climb up the tree.

The farmer didn't have time to climb up the tree with his family because the silver bird was very close, so he put his arms around the tree, closed his eyes tightly, and dug his fingernails into the trunk. He prayed solemnly for the safety of his family and that instant, as the plane was flying in close, the farmer felt a warm wetness between his legs, and tears running down his face.

The German increased his speed as he approached the tree, flying as closely as possible. He wanted so badly to see fear in their eyes. What a glorious feeling of superiority, to have power and control over people's fate, even if only a small group of native farmers.

The farmer looked at the plane closing in and felt a throbbing in his chest. He tried to take a deep breath but was unable to do so. The farmer, out of desperation and anger, unable to protect his family, dug his fingernails deeper, harder into the trunk of the tree.

The roar and the vibration of the oncoming plane blotted out his pain. He didn't feel the blood running down from his broken fingernails to the palms of his hands and the tips of his fingers were numb. His head throbbing, his eardrums ready to burst, the farmer closed his eyes in terror.

The fighter zoomed toward his prey with an anticipation that aroused him sexually. Reaching his highest sexual point several seconds before impact, he climaxed. Amused, and pleased with himself after his sexual release, he quickly pulled the nose of the plane upward to avoid the inevitable crash.

The German flier expertly handled the controls. In a state of howling amusement, he lifted the plane's nose to the sky, flying up high and away, and out of his prey's sight.

The farmer courageously opened his eyes to watch the plane before the inevitable crash. He was almost sure that he'd seen the fair hair and pale face of the German pilot. He closed his eyes again, and swore to himself that he'd heard the pilot's satisfied, jovial laughter.

The plane never crashed into the tree or the farmer and his family, but the only indication that the threat was over was the pounding of the farmer's heart, louder and louder against the fading sound of the plane.

Still grasping the tree, he slowly loosened his grip. He opened his eyes and watched as the plane fly high into the sky. His chest throbbed harder and he tried again to take a deep breath. Within a few minutes the plane was gone and the farmer felt a chilly rush of wind between his legs, the wetness on his pants now evident. He looked to the sky and asked God to help him endure this humiliation and his weakness during this heinous situation.

When the plane was absolutely out of sight, the farmer's heart started to beat steadily back to normal. He indicated to his family that all was safe, and they could carefully climb down. In a stupor from their experience, confused and disoriented, they were unable to communicate for several minutes. After they assembled on the ground, the little ones started to quiet their crying. The older daughters stood next to their mother, their bodies shivering from the terror of what had just happened. They understood the danger that had just passed them by. The baby, on her mother's shoulder, cried softly for a while. Her mother rubbed her back until she fell into a sound and peaceful sleep.

The farmer eyed his family to be sure they were emotionally intact, and then looked at his wife and sighed. He touched her arm and together they turned away from the olive tree. The family walked slowly toward the mule and cart.

The sun was now high and its warmth was a relief after a chilly day and the intensity of running for their lives. The farmer held his second youngest daughter in his arms, and held her older sister's hand. The oldest daughter, walking next to her father, said, "Pappa, I don't understand. I thought the Germans were our allies!"

The farmer looked at her affectionately and guilelessly replied, "Yes, my daughter, I thought they were, too."

The children, understanding that their parents were near to protect them from the dangers of the world were exceptionally calm, considering what they had just endured. They walked quietly to their mule and then made their way back to the cart.

The farmer put his daughter on the ground and approached his mule, patted him gently on the head, and stroked his mane. The farmer looked into the frightened animal's eyes and calmed its fear. Then he went back to his family and helped everyone get into the card and settled into their places.

Once they were seated, the farmer picked up his second youngest daughter and held her gently in his arms. He kissed her cheek affectionately and then looked into her large, blue eyes and apologized for squeezing her so roughly earlier.

She responded with a dainty smile that showed the deep dimples in her cheeks. She followed with a hug, and then she sobbed.

The farmer held this daughter close, apologizing again, not with words but with his strong assuring hand. He gently rubbed her back to warm and calm his little daughter. Once she had settled down, the farmer placed her in the front of the cart between himself and her mother. Settled in the cart, unharmed and free from danger, the farmer and his family headed toward their home in the village.

The aged mule, now settling in a steady but slow pace, walked in the direction of the horizon. He seemed to know he was going to be okay now that he was going toward his home.

The farmer and his family approached their village just as the sun was setting. As they neared the safety of their home, the farmer could almost smell the aroma of dinner simmering. He could almost hear his daughters' laughter as they played inside the house. He turned to his wife, his intimate friend sitting next to him, and when he'd caught her eye, she slipped closer to him. Her arm draped around their second youngest daughter who rested her head on her mother's lap, sound asleep. In her arms, his wife held the baby. The man and wife, sitting so close to one another and with their family safe and nearby, each prayed silently.

The farmer's wife looked down at her husband's hands and shook her head. She looked at the drying blood, and he smiled to assure her that it was unimportant. She was proud of his physical and emotional stature. She looked ahead as the mule pulled them and pondered how she was blessed to have him next to her. While she reveled in her blessings, her husband turned to the back of the cart to check on his older daughters. The farmer saw his three oldest girls wrapped in a warm, handmade woolen blanket crocheted by his wife. They were fast asleep.

The farmer, feeling more like himself, gazed at the stars in the night sky and reveled in their still and shimmering beauty as they seemed to be winking back at him. The farmer knew that beyond the twinkling stars, today God had watched over him and his family. Grateful, the farmer took in deep breaths of chilly air. The scent of approaching winter was in the air and the farmer felt solace that his family was warm and safe together.

The farmer pondered his island and its landmarks. He thought of this rich, native land, filled with ancient Greek, French, Arabic and Norman history. The island, surrounded by the Tyrrhenian Sea and the Mediterranean Sea, was filled with history because of its strategic location. The northeastern tip of the island gave access to the Strait of Messina, a narrow body of water that separated the island from the main peninsula of Italy. Because the island narrowed to about two miles across, it provided easy access to and from the seas for historic conquistadors.

This island was mostly rugged terrain, but had low farmland near its shores. The main crop was wheat, but on the southern coast, smaller areas were devoted principally to growing grapes, almonds, olives, lemons and beans. Before World War I, this island was the richest and largest producer of sulfur in the world.

The language spoken on the island was a native dialect formed from a separate Romance language descended from Latin. Arabic, French and Spanish roots were also descends of the dialect, although, Italian was the official language. The farmer was proud of his heritage, and very proud to be part of the island's history during those stressful times. As the farmer and his sleepy family traveled closer to their village, which was nestled against a mountain, he couldn't help but notice an unusual sight a short distance ahead. There were lights coming from the windows of houses. Because of the war, his neighbors tried to remain hidden most of the time, especially at night. During this time, the use of indoor lighting and even candles was unheard of.

He shook his wife gently and said, "Look."

The farmer's wife looked around and acknowledged the sight in wonderment.

When they entered their village, the sound of the old mule's hooves made a familiar, homey sound as they clanked on the cobblestone street. Each old stone and concrete house had an ancient look and a history of its own. The houses were all attached and built upwards on the mountainside. Most of the stone roadways were narrow and hilly, and led to the outskirts of the village. Several steps led up to the wrought iron-adorned front door of each house. The balconies were also wrought iron, which gave the homes a Spanish look. Most of these houses were tall and narrow as he larger homes were owned by the more prominent families.

The farmer remembered that before the war each house had been sparkling clean. Some houses had many potted plants on their front steps, guiding the way to the front door. The upstairs balcony doors had been open to enjoy and welcome incoming sun and fresh air. The balconies had been filled with well-manicured potted plants and beautiful, robust flowers hung over the rails. Birds had made their homes and nested their babies in those fragrant hanging vines.

But these days, to the farmer's dismay, the village was dark and dismal during the day. The houses were unkempt and the flowers didn't bloom. Instead of the chirping of birds, the only sounds in the village were of the mule's steps echoing against the high-rising stone walls of the houses.

As the farmer and his family passed the houses on this day, however, there were no sounds of war in the distance to disrupt the moment. The windows glittered from the glow of the fireplaces and reminded the farmer and his wife of the way their village once was.

The rich scent of olive oil used for cooking wafted through the air and the farmer felt his stomach grumbling from hunger. He could smell and identify the different cheeses and spices and his mouth watered for the different flavors.

As the family traveled more toward the center of the village, the farmer saw a few people out on the streets. People were surrounding the fountain in front of the large and impressive Catholic Church, Matrice (Mother of the Church). The villagers and their animals drank from this fountain, but it had been a long time since so many had been seen out in public. Before the war, all businesses were located in the center of the village and all festivities were conducted freely, but since the war began this space had been silent and empty. Now people were milling about, chattering excitedly. Amazed at this sight, the farmer pulled the reins on the mule and the cart stopped with a jolt and woke the older daughters who were also amazed at the sounds around them. The farmer's oldest daughter asked, "Pappa, what's going on?"

There was no reply.

The farmer bent down to ask a man on the corner, "Why are the people not afraid to be outside?" The gentle man said, "God has answered our prayers. You must not have heard; we have surrendered to the allies. We're celebrating the fact that we are no longer in alliance with Germany." The farmer looked around his village and heard the sound of light cheering from the people of the village.

The man took a deep breath, looked at the farmer and said, "It's our King; he has overthrown Mussolini and has taken control of our country."

The farmer turned to hug his wife and they shared a joyous embrace. The farmer again turned to the man and asked, "Where are the Italian Communists? Aren't the village people afraid of them?"

The man replied, "Tonight we don't care. Tonight they should be afraid of us!"

The farmer thanked the man and as he and his family continued on their way, the sounds of cheering muffled the mule's steps. People waved happily as the family passed; they hugged and swung each other in their arms. Children, not fully understanding the occasion, jumped and danced around their parents.

Finally they arrived safe at their home.

— PART I —

Chapter One

After the farmer, Franco Gennusa, and his wife, Anna, settled into the safety of their village home, they closed the door behind them. They looked around at their warm but meager belongings and admired their vibrant family. Both took a deep breath and said another silent prayer.

The Gennusa home was large and warm, but humble. The concrete and stone foundation and walls helped keep the house warm in the winter and cool from the summer heat. The large kitchen with its double windows brought in light and warmth during the day, and the large fireplace at one end of the house kept the rooms comfortable and warm when needed. In the kitchen, the counters were made of tile processed from stone from the hills of the island. The cooking area consisted of large copper pots sunk down into the counter, which were fired from the bottom, and an open-hearth oven for baking. In the winter, the home was plenty warm from the ovens and fireplace.

There were two large bedrooms off the kitchen, one of which was shared by Franco and Anna, while the other was shared by the five daughters. The upstairs loft was a large empty room where odds and ends were stored. A door on the side of the house led to the attached barn. Before entering the barn, on the right side of the wall attached to the side of the house were steps that led to a mezzanine. This low-ceiling room was a cold storage area for food. On the back wall of the barn, a door led out to the back yard of the house.

The Gennusas were fortunate because, unlike some of the other homes in the village, their house had its own well to provide drinking, bathing and washing water for the family, as well as for their neighbors who gratefully shared the well. Even though the day was coming to an end, there was still plenty of work to do. Franco had to tend to unloading the cart and feeding his mule. Outside he took his time rubbing down his weary but dependable mule with a homemade brush. Although his fingers and fingernails ached, he wanted to let his long-time traveling companion know how much he was appreciated for enduring the long day and returning the farmer and his family home safely.

While Franco was out tending the mule, Anna fed their daughters, and then bathed them with water from the well, which she had heated over the fire. With the help of the older daughters, the younger ones were taken care of and put to bed.

After taking care of his mule, Franco sat outside in the crisp, fresh air to clear his thoughts. He rested for a few minutes on the low stone wall of the well, and lit a cigarette, inhaled its warm gray smoke, and contemplated the tense day.

A rustling sound came from the barn, but Franco didn't stir or look in the direction of the noise. Once the rustling had stopped, Franco picked up a pan sitting next to the well, filled it up with water, walked into the barn, and placed it on the floor. Next to the water he placed a basket of a few freshly picked prickly pears from a cactus plant at the farm. He then walked out toward the kitchen and up the stairs into the mezzanine where he grabbed a couple handfuls of raw wheat which he put in a small sack and quietly carried back down the stairs to the barn. From the barn wall, he took a torn and tattered blanket and placed it next to the food and water.

Franco turned and walked toward the kitchen. He entered the house thinking of the barn and said a soft prayer for the safety of its occupant. In the kitchen he said another soft prayer for the safety of his family. His heart weighed heavily when he thought of the ordeal from earlier that day.

The house was quiet now that his daughters were in their bedroom. Franco walked over to the kitchen table and sat down to a dinner left for him by his wife. He picked up a hunk of homemade cheese, broke off a piece of semi-stale bread, and picked up some prickly pears he had carried in from the barn. The pears' sweet juice dripped down his chin while he ate. When he finished, the rumbling sound from his stomach had stopped and his hunger had subsided. Franco walked into his bedroom and closed the door behind him. He found his wife sitting on their bed and sat down with her. Anna asked, "Did I hear you at the well?"

"Yes," he answered hesitantly, "I gave the mule a little extra water." Franco didn't look at Anna when he spoke to her for he hated misleading her. He turned to put his arms around her, and they held each other as both shook uncontrollably. Anna assured that her family would be okay, gently tended to Franco's broken fingernails and damaged hands. Franco winced from the pain as she cleaned his wounds.

"Since we have surrendered to the allies, what will happen to us now?" Anna asked.

"I don't know. Hopefully the war will end soon."

Anna finished tending Franco's hands, and then bandaged them. After a short time Franco's fingers stopped throbbing. Lovingly, he put one hand on Anna's stomach, feeling the unborn child moving comfortably, and then put his other arm around her shoulders. He reminded himself to remove all evidence of the person in the barn in the morning, before Anna or his daughters saw the leftovers. He buried his head on Anna's shoulder and, out of frustration, cried softly. Finally, they slid into their bed, covered themselves with their comfortable, old blankets and holding each other close, tried to sleep. They needed sleep badly—but, sleep did not easily come.

The following week, Franco sat on his empty bed in his farm house. Still in his wool pants, left on overnight for warmth, he put his foot on the cold stone floor. He looked around the room and felt empty, for his family was not with him. He had been at the farm with his poorly paid working helpers for a week. He couldn't risk repeating the frightening incident of the German flier from the week before even though Mussolini was overthrown. The loss of his family or one of his family members would be too much for him to bear. He not only missed his family's company, but missed the help from his older daughters and his wife. He felt overwhelmed without them, even though he had his employees.

It was early morning and looked like it would be another cold and rainy day. Franco got out of bed, stretched his lean but muscular body, and put on his only old wool coat. He walked over to the fireplace, sat in a chair, and rubbed his large calloused hands over the low-burning coal from the night before. He looked at his war-torn fingernails and noticed that they, with Anna's care, were healing well.

3

After putting his socks and shoes on his rough feet, he got up from the chair, lit a cigarette, and walked to the bath area. He looked into an old, worn mirror and put his cigarette in an ashtray. He poured water into his hands from a pitcher sitting on the sink, and ran it through his light blond hair looking into the mirror. Franco saw the resemblance to his father. Both he and his father were average size, but tall for their nationality. His face and hands were tanned but the skin on his face was youthful with few wrinkles, unlike the rough, worked skin of his hands. Under his clothes, his body was very light-skinned. With his strong, square Greek facial features and his light blue eyes, Franco looked more North European than South European. He was very handsome.

Thinking of his loving parents, both deceased, he thought about how much they would have loved his daughters. Franco had inherited his parents' strength and endurance. After wiping his face and hands, he picked up his cigarette, walked over to the window, and longed for his parents' loving touch. They were hard-working people, and their love for each other, and for Franco, was unforgettable.

Unfortunately, their lives had ended sadly. Franco's father was thrown from one of his horses and killed. Franco's beloved mother, as the story goes, died soon after from a broken heart.

Looking out the window at the dreary weather, and puffing on his cigarette, Franco's mind was now on the child that was yet to be born. He desperately needed a son to help work the farm, but sons had not, as of yet, been born to him. He dearly loved his wife and his daughters and was greatly fulfilled by their existence, but the physical burden of not having sons to work by his side was highly demanding on him.

During this week of isolation, Franco contemplated how he and his family were to survive this war and their future life. His older daughters already had great desires; they craved education, pretty clothes and freedom, like all young people their age. He was not in a financial position to grant this freedom. Gratefully for Franco, Anna wanted only to give their daughters a decent life.

Franco thought of his amazing wife and marveled wondered at how fortunate he was to have her. Anna had her pick of many suitors so when Franco heard of all the men that asked for her hand in marriage, he knew he had to act fast before she was committed to someone else. Franco was desperate to have her.

His parents and her parents arranged the marriage. Franco saw Anna one Sunday during High Mass at the village church and immediately knew he had to have her. Not knowing anything about her, Franco approached his father regarding his desire for her. His father said he knew of the family and their good reputation, but that he would have to look into the matter further before he approved or approached Franco's mother about the union.

A few days later, Franco's father approached his son with good news. He approved of the union and he would ask Franco's mother for her approval.

Franco's father told his wife, Teresa, about their son's desire. Before she knew anything at all about Anna's family, she said to Franco's father, "No, I will not allow my oldest son to marry just anyone. He is skilled, has money, and owns his own house. What does this girl have to offer us? Can she guarantee Franco a son to carry on our name? Why should he settle for just anyone? He could have his pick, for he is so handsome."

"Teresa," Franco's father said, "You know that no wife can guarantee us a grandson or even any grandchildren. He'll not be marrying just anyone, but a female who speaks two languages. She is very talented, I hear."

"What do you mean by talented?"

"Teresa," Franco's father answered, "not only is she bilingual, she also designs and sews beautifully. And she is an American citizen!"

Teresa eyes widened at the last comment from her husband. She looked at Franco and asked, "Are you sure?"

"Yes!" Franco said. "The two oldest daughters in the Rosato family are American citizens. Anna, her father, and her sister lived in America for several years where she learned the language."

"Is she a virgin?" Teresa asked. "I will not have my oldest son, or any of my sons, marry a woman who is not pure!"

Franco felt a cold chill run through his body and it brought him back to the present day, in his own home, smoking by the window. He went to the kitchen and prepared a light but substantial breakfast, and then packed a hearty lunch for he knew he had to work twice as hard to make up for his family's absence. There would be no time for a leisurely lunch in this house. He would sit in the center of his olive trees in the chilly mist, and take just enough time to eat and get back to work.

When he was finished eating his breakfast, he lit another cigarette and heard a knock at the door. He picked up his lunch, left the dishes from breakfast on the table, and walked to the door where his employees were waiting to start their day of harvest. He smiled to see them, the men who worked for him and who were also his friends. With a large blanket over his shoulder, Franco walked into the olive garden in the chill of the morning, chatting with his employees.

While working in the grove, Franco recalled an early morning several years ago when there was a soft tap at his door. He remembered the sorrowful eyes of this family standing before him, begging mercifully for work in the olive groves. The husband, standing outside that cold morning, was wrapped in a tattered blanket, surrounded by his family. The man's wife, also wrapped in a worn blanket, begged for help with tears in her eyes. Two prideful sons stood beside the wife, wrapped in warm woolen coats that were faded and worn. Anna came to the door to stand by her husband and seeing the sad faces at her door, waved the family inside their home to warm themselves by the fire. Franco pleaded to Anna with his eyes, "We cannot do this." Anna's own eyes responded, "With good conscience, we will somehow provide."

With the help of her older daughters, Anna served the family hot coffee and warm homemade bread spread with fresh olive oil and grated cheese. The family ate hungrily and then the father of the family offered his and his family's services for their breakfast. It was then, without an official agreement, and with Franco's deep appreciation, that the family began working for the Gennusas. Franco's new employees worked hard and their young sons never complained. They soon formed a friendship and Franco admired his loyalty of the family. He adored the sons and became their second father. And soon, the family moved in to the Gennusa's home, using the small upper loft as their sleeping area. Anna provided a blanket put down over hay for their bedding. The wives, together with Franco's oldest daughters, did the daily cooking. Franco knew that Anna was grateful for the help that she received around the house. The home was cramped but amenable for both families.

With the knowledge and experience of his new employees, Franco brought twice as many olives to market. Several years later, when the employees could afford their own place, they lived in an apartment next to the Gennusas where they stayed during the off-season months. When they weren't harvesting olives, Franco and his employees raised a few livestock and grew vegetables to sell at market. His employees were so grateful to Franco for saving them from destitution, that they worked harder and longer hours without stopping or making demands. The friendship, one of respect and gratitude, lasted for a lifetime.

Chapter Two

A t the end of the week, Franco was headed toward his village and home from his farm house to his family. He was eager to see his daughters' fresh faces and to hear their laughter. Away from the war that surrounded him, his wife and family would help him feel stronger.

Franco was greeted by his younger, vivacious daughters, jumping on him and giving him hugs. He missed this during the week. The daughters giggled and Franco said, "Settle down. Remember, I told you we must not have too much activity in the house. We must not carry any noises outside."

Now feeling stronger after the greetings from his family, Franco acknowledged a stranger around his age sitting at the kitchen table. Franco was surprised, but didn't think the man was dangerous, so he walked over to the man and held out his right hand. The small dark-haired man stood up and greeted Franco by introducing himself and holding out his right hand to meet Franco's. The stranger's hand trembled with fear but Franco's firm handshake and warm smile comforted the man, and he stopped shaking.

"Signore Gennusa," the stranger said, "I am Oscar Stein. My family and I are here asking for help from you and your family."

Franco said nothing, allowing the man to continue.

"We are Italian Jews hiding from the Germans. My wife and my two sons are in your attic. I have money, Sir. We can pay for our protection."

Franco nodded to Signore Stein and said softly, "Welcome to our home."

Signore Stein was relieved and replied, "Thank you."

Anna smiled, watching the two men, and went to Franco's side to explain. "Signore Stein and his family were in the center of town, looking for temporary housing until they could return to Palermo. Their home and neighborhood were bombed by the Americans several weeks ago. They've been living in the woods hiding and hoping to find a safe place to stay until it's safe for them to go back to their home."

Franco looked at the man and expressed his sorrow for their loss.

"Signore Gennusa—" Oscar Stein started to say.

"Please, call me Franco," he responded.

Oscar smiled and asked to be called by his first name also. He thanked Franco for accommodating his family and allowing them a place to stay. Sir," the man continued, "I have money. I can pay rent. I owned a jewelry store in Palermo and have cash and jewels. I hope that will be suitable. Of course, we'll be here only a short time. We're eager to get back to Palermo."

Franco looked at his generous wife and said, "Yes, it is fine." He turned to Oscar and asked where the rest of the Stein family was. Oscar responded that his family was in the upstairs loft. Franco insisted they all come to the kitchen and make themselves comfortable.

Oscar thanked him and called the family to the kitchen. Signora Stein and two small sons climbed down the ladder. Oscar introduced his family, and Franco walked over to Signora Stein and shook her hand. Franco looked at two boys, the same ages as his two youngest daughters, and gently ruffled their hair.

"It is imperative," Franco told Oscar, "that your sons stay quiet and do not attract any attention to their home."

Anna and the oldest daughters helped Franco carry the heavy baskets of olives from the cart, and put them in the back of their small yard for the night. When Franco and Anna were alone outside in the back yard, Franco put his arm around his wife to keep her warm and as he held her close, he asked, "Are you sure we should be taking on more responsibility?"

Anna hesitated and answered, "Yes, of course we can." She looked at her husband very seriously and replied, "We can use the money."

Early the next morning, Franco, Anna, and their oldest daughters, Teresa, Pina, and Vincenza, carried the clumsy baskets of olives to the cart, and then Franco, Teresa and Pina headed to the center of town. Oscar offered to help, but his hands were soft, and there was danger surrounding them. Franco thought it was best for him to stay close to his family. He was concerned that the Stein family would be caught and killed. He had become very close to them, and their survival was of great importance to him. He especially enjoyed the two sons. He did not want to be burdened with the Stein family if anything physically happened to them.

The clouds were gray that day on that cold and misty day. The daughters huddled together to keep warm in the cart as they traveled slowly because Franco did not want to alarm the mule and scare it into a run. He didn't want to alert the remaining Germans. Most of them had already left the island, but there were a few soldiers who had yet to go. Franco didn't want the soldiers to think that he and his daughters were running from them, or that they had something to hide; he didn't want to put his family in danger.

Safely and without any trouble, Franco and his daughters arrived at the town center. Several other growers arrived as well, most of them with their sons, to wait quietly and unsociably for their turn at the mill. Everyone worked fast to get out of town quickly to avoid confrontations with the German soldiers. As they waited, the temperature dropped and the stress of not knowing whether they were being watched by the Germans made for a very uncomfortable situation. The tension was heavy in the cool air. Franco kept an open eye on the German soldiers who were standing close to the building, keeping warm and dry. He also kept his eyes on his daughters.

When it was Franco's turn with the miller, he and his daughters proceeded to take the baskets out of the cart, working quickly. The miller took the basket of olives with shaking hands, nervous because of the weather and the Germans. He poured the basket of olives into his machine and the press crushed them, giving forth the liquid oil. The oil went through filters and was then put into large containers. After the oil ran into the containers, it would rest so that the impurities would settle at the bottom. A portion of the oil would be given to the miller for payment for the use of his mill, and Franco would take the rest of the containers of oil home.

This oil was a cash crop for Franco and allowed for household items such as cloth, food and shoes. During the war the oil made life easier because of its trading value. The oil was also given to Anna's parents for their use and survival. As he worked, Franco thought to himself, *There are so many people who depend on me. It is important that this liquid get home safely.*

Franco was finished with the miller, and stayed close to his daughters as they placed the last container of the oil in the cart. He gave his mule a tug and led the cart out of the way of the next cart in line. He nodded to the next farmer and recognized the farmer's son who had grown tall since last year's harvest, but didn't look well. He was around twelve years old, the same as Teresa, but he was thin and pale. The son appeared sickly as he helped his father take baskets from the cart. In peace-time, Franco and his daughters would have stopped to help the farmer and his son with their harvest, but now it was too dangerous to linger in town.

A German soldier standing by a building, out of the rain, close to a barrel of fire for warmth, noticed the son acting strangely. The soldier looked curiously at the son and held his rifle up in an aiming position and then began walking over to the sickly boy. The rain had started to dissipate but the clouds had gotten darker. The son and his father, working quickly, didn't see the approaching soldier until he was right in front of them.

They stopped working and looked up at the German in his dirty uniform. Both the son and the father stared as the soldier began asking questions in his native language. The farmer stiffened at the soldier's sharp voice as he waved his rifle at his son. Neither the farmer nor his son understood what the German was saying, but out of fright, he stepped in front of his son. The damp and cold made the situation all the more frightening and unbearable.

The farmer stood in front of his son to protect him and tried to communicate with the soldier in Italian and by trying to motion with his hands. The German reacted to the waving hands by pointing his gun at the father and telling him to stop. The father remained in front of his son and continued to try to communicate, now more gently, with the soldier.

The soldier, out of frustration, shot the farmer. All the farmers standing by their carts, the Germans standing by the building, and the olive miller standing by his mill all froze and turned to look where the shot was fired.

The Germans instantly drew their guns and ran toward the German shooter. The shocked spectators just stood staring at the farmer on the ground. They all watched as the young boy's dead father lay bleeding at his feet. The warmth of the blood was evident as it steamed in the cold air.

The sickly young son stood in shock for a second and then bent down to put his arms around his father. After a few minutes the son slowly stood up and looked at the blood on his hands, and then looked to the German and screamed with hate and vengeance in his eyes. He jumped upon the German soldier who fell backwards and hit his head on the hard stone ground. The other German soldiers and the rest of the spectators were stunned and looked on in shock.

The sick-hearted son was on top of the German, lashing out with bare fists on the German's face. The German wrestled with the young boy, and then there was another gunshot followed by silence. Both the soldier and the boy were still, but a few seconds, later the German rolled out from under the dead boy's body.

He stood up, gun in hand and slightly disoriented from the blow to the head. His body shook as he looked down at the dead boy. The soldier kicked the boy hard in his ribs several times with his heavy leather boot. Blood stained the front of the soldier's old, dirty uniform and his face was covered in cuts and blood from the fight. He pointed his gun at the other farmers as he backed away and rejoined the other German soldiers.

The soldiers, pointing their guns at the farmers, walked backwards together to the side of the street. The soldier standing next to the shooter asked him in German, "Hans, do you have any more ammunition?"

The nervous German soldier answered arrogantly, "No, but these stupid people don't know that."

"You're the one who is stupid," the other German replied, "I want to survive this war if I can."

The shooter asked, "Are you a coward?"

"No," said the other soldier, "I'm cold and hungry. If you cause unnecessary danger again, I'll kill you myself. Do you understand?"

Franco turned and commanded his frightened daughters who were crying hysterically to get into the cart and to stay down. Franco was breathing hard and his heart was pounding; all he wanted to do was get out of the center of town and back to the safety of his home. But he drove the cart as slowly as possible and prayed.

Chapter Three

Later that evening, Franco walked into his daughters' room, concerned for their well-being after the day's tragedy.

Oscar and his family, wanting to be alone, had retired early to their upstairs room. Frightened after the day's events, they longed for their home in Palermo. Oscar held his wife and sons and lay awake all night.

The younger daughters, Innocenza and Francesca, were asleep in the bed they shared. On one side of the room was the baby in her crib. Vincenza was on a small cot by herself. Pina and Teresa snuggled next to each other in the bed they shared, softly sobbing.

Franco walked to tuck them in and kiss their tear-streaked cheeks. He hugged them both and told them, "Today was a very bad day. There is killing going on around us, and there will be for some time here on our home island. The German soldiers are getting more desperate. They are cold and hungry like us. It is up to us to stay close together and be aware of the constant dangers around us. We have to be strong and accept what happened today as part of our lives. This war is horrible, and as I said before, death is everywhere." Franco continued, "Teresa, you are the oldest so you must stay strong for your sisters, but mostly for your mother. If you need to find strength, come to me and I will do my best to help you endure."

Teresa wiped the tears running down her face and said, "Thank you, Pappa," and reached out to hug her father once again. "Did you know the grower and his son?" she asked.

Franco responded softly, "Thank God, I didn't know them well. It will make it easier for me to forget."

Looking at Pina he said, "You, my daughter, are so young and so very tempting. I need you to stay close to your mother. I saw how those German boys looked at you today. It scares me to think what would happen if you were alone with them. Just promise to stay close." Franco

14

stopped and looked at both his daughters. "You must promise me that you will stay where you are supervised. Do not look directly at those German boys' eyes for they are dangerous. I have said this many times and I will say it again, always make sure I know where you are." Franco again looked at Pina and said, "I'll tell your mother to cut your hair tomorrow."

"Pappa, no, not my hair!" she cried.

Franco was heartsick. He ran his fingers through Pina's long blonde hair, looked at her big hazel eyes and said, "It should have been done at the beginning of this war. There will be no discussion on this. I also want both of you to cover your heads with scarves at all times. I'll tell to your mother to sew you both bigger clothes. I don't want the Germans looking at either one of you.

"Teresa, I thank God that your hair is short and dark. Men look at blondes first. I'll talk to your mother and make sure she keeps your hair short." Franco continued, seriously composed, "We must try to stay calm and live as close as possible to normal during this trying time, but I don't want you to forget what happened today. Remember the blood that you saw today. It will keep you both alert about the danger that is around at all times."

Franco looked sternly at his daughters and told them what he expected in the coming days. "Tomorrow," he said, "we will be going to the farm to finish the harvest. I know how hard the work is and how cold it can get, but I expect you girls to work diligently next to me with no complaints. Your mother isn't feeling well and is very tired because of this pregnancy. She doesn't need to feel any worse because you girls are tired and complaining. This work is serious and necessary. Do you understand? These times are hard for all of us, especially with the war going on around us. We need to eat, and to feed the others. The employees and your grandparents need help. I expect you to stay close to me and be aware that at all times the war is with us."

The girls instantly and together said, "Yes, Pappa."

"Pappa," Teresa asked, "how long do you think this war will last?"

Franco looked at his daughters and smiled proudly, "If we pray hard and are unselfish, hopefully soon. Now get to sleep and pray to God to forget today's massacre as you dream. We could all use a good night's rest. Goodnight, my dearest daughters. Remember, beauty can be a very dangerous curse, especially during war. Stay aware. Never forget how much I love you and what you both mean to your mother and me."

"Yes, Pappa," both girls replied in unison.

Franco walked into the kitchen and went straight to Anna's side. He looked at his wife and said, "Tomorrow before we leave for the farm I want you to cut Pina's hair short. Our older daughters are becoming women. I need you to sew larger clothes to make them as unattractive as possible."

"Franco—" Anna started to say.

Franco didn't give Anna a chance to finish. "I shouldn't have to tell you that I expect you to do your part in keeping our daughters as plain as possible during these times. Our daughters are beautiful. Are you that naive? Do you know what could happen to them if they should be in the hands of those crazy Germans?" Franco grabbed Anna firmly by her arms and then began to shake her, digging into her shoulders. "Do you understand? Our Vincenza, bind her breasts and make them flat. They are starting to show. She is already more endowed than the other two girls." Franco exclaimed, "I don't care if it hurts, bind her!"

Anna trembled as she looked into Franco's drawn, angry face. With tears in her eyes she replied, "Yes, Franco."

Franco walked out of the house, leaving Anna standing in the kitchen alone, feeling the pain in her arms. She rubbed them slowly, not feeling well, and exhausted from the baby she was carrying. She felt guilty for having to be reminded of the constant danger and what could happen if her daughters were captured. They would be raped, tortured, mutilated, and left with a lifetime of mental disturbance if they survived the horrendous treatments by their captors. She dropped her shoulders, longing for the reassurance that she needed. She felt older than her years. And for a few minutes she felt, for the first time in her life, absolutely alone.

Franco had gone through the barn and into the back yard. He sat on the wall of the well and shook his head, trying to take a deep breath. He wanted to scream, but instead he cried loudly. He knew there was nothing he could do to make the fear he felt for his daughters' safety go away. Sitting in the cold starless night on the cold wall, he imagined a stone wall building up around him, to protect him from his fears.

It was early the next day when the Gennusas filled their cart with supplies for the duration of their stay at the farm. They said good-bye to the Stein family and told them to make themselves comfortable in the house—they would be back soon.

"Remember not to light the oven or the fireplace after dark," Franco reminded Oscar. "Use what you need to stay warm, but make sure the house is dark at night." Franco turned to his sons and tousled their hair. "And you keep quiet and don't attract attention to yourselves."

The boys smiled back at him.

Through tired eyes, Franco looked at his daughters climbing into the cart. He was satisfied that Anna had done her best to make the girls look plain. Franco looked directly at Vincenza's breasts and she covered herself when she saw him inspecting her. Approving of her flat chest he climbed into the cart behind her. The Gennusa family headed out of the village.

While traveling with his family, Franco never forgot the ever-present danger that surrounded them. His eyes darted in all directions.

It was cold and damp. The children were dressed warmly, and Anna had put blankets on their laps for extra warmth. Even though it was cold, the sun was starting to rise and shine, which made the ride more comfortable, and made the family feel less afraid.

The trip was uneventful until Franco heard gunfire. He stopped the cart to assure his frightened family that they would get to the farm safely. Franco commanded his mule to continue toward their destination, praying for the safety of his family. The violence of the war had him worried and concerned. *Are Resistance members in the woods? Is that where the gunfire is coming from? Was it the Germans or the Italian Communists?* Franco's thoughts and anxieties were exacerbated by sleep deprivation and the violence he'd already seen. He prayed silently for the safety of his family and friends.

The family reached their land safely and everyone helped to unpack the cart. When Anna was out of earshot, Franco reminded his daughters, "Remember what I said last night."

The two girls looked at their father and then down at the ground, "Yes, Pappa."

"Remember to stay close to your mother and me at all times." And then more harshly, he repeated himself, "Remember!"

Anna breastfed and then put the baby on the bed to sleep while the rest of the family headed toward the olive trees to start working. She would join them when the baby was asleep.

The two younger daughters didn't want to work; they wanted to play, but they helped in their small way.

The older daughters, still upset from the outing to the mill, were quiet and filled with resentment. They were tired and too young to understand the war and its ramifications. They knew it was selfish, but they wanted their lives to be normal again, to be back in school with their friends. They wanted to forget the killing they'd seen the day before. They tried to understand the war, but they craved the life they once knew, especially Teresa, for she was the eldest and had fond memories of their pre-war lives.

The girls headed out to the olive grove in the cold and damp, not looking forward to the rest of harvest season, and wondering if life could be better somewhere else. They knew that school was geographically close, but that it wasn't in their immediate future.

After Anna's family left for the groves, she found their employees, the DiGorio's, standing in the doorway. The family was dressed in warm wool cloth that Anna had provided for them, and was ready to head out to the groves. The pants that Vincenzo and his sons wore were patched with extra material that Anna salvaged from their coats. The patching made the pants and jacket look liked a matching set. Anna made fine dresses for Signora DiGorio, always putting an extra button on the bust of the dress and layering a little extra lace. Anna knew that Lucia loved frilly clothes, and Lucia was so grateful and devoted to Anna that she worked harder with their chores than necessary.

Anna saved and reused any and all clothes that came her way. Her more fortunate neighbors asked her for repair services and paid her, not in money but in cast-off clothes. Her sewing provided a few extras for her family in the lean, long winter months. She was clever and talented in her sewing, taking apart older clothing and redesigning it into fashionable garments. She made warm coats for her daughters and lined woolen caps for the neighbor boys. What she could not do on her sewing machine, she did by hand.

Anna always picked out subdued fabric so patching looked natural on clothes. If the garment was bright, the patchwork was done in bright colors. If the colors of the clothes were dark or dull (and in wartime most cloths were dark), the patchwork was as closely matched as possible. The war didn't allow for many choices in fabric, but there was plenty of thread and yarn since the ladies who lived in the same village weaved them from their sheep and traded the yarn for other goods.

After the rest of her family had gone out to work in the grove, Lucia DiGorio stood in the doorway offering to take care of the baby. The smell of weak coffee wafted through the house and Anna offered a cup to Lucia who gratefully accepted.

"Thank you for watching the baby, Lucia," Anna said. "She has a cold so I don't want to take her out in the cold, damp air. Anna was reluctant to leave the child but knew she was needed at the grove. She wondered why Lucia wasn't out with the others, but then asked, "Lucia, when is the baby due?"

"I'm not sure, but I think in the spring. Anna, how can I bring a child into this world with so much death and destruction?"

"You will manage," Anna said. "Like all mothers, we manage."

"Anna, it's hard not to notice that Pina's hair has been cut," Lucia said.

"Yes, it's for the best. Her hair was unnecessary," Anna replied.

"How do you do it?" Lucia asked

Anna looked at Lucia, "How do I do what?"

"How do you handle raising five daughters, and another child on the way?" Lucia asked. "Your houses are always clean and the clothes you sew are magnificent, your spirit is always bright, even with death all around. You're always working hard to keep your daughters safe."

"Lucia, you give me too much credit. I have daughters who help a lot and a fine husband who works hard. Franco constantly reminds me of the dangers. There was a useless killing in the center of Bisacquino yesterday. One of the young German soldiers shot and killed two farmers. One was a male no older than Teresa. Franco was very distraught when he came home," Anna said.

"Then tell me, how do you keep your daughters satisfied?" Lucia asked.

"I don't. It's hard during this war time. There is no spoiling from Franco and me. We don't have the time, and there are no extras for them. This war limits us so much. The little ones are fine; they don't know the difference. But I feel badly for my older daughters, for they want to go to school and be with their friends. There are times I think my older daughters forget about the war. But reality is around them, and they do have to come to terms with reality." Anna put her arm around Lucia's shoulder and said, "Come and have a cup of coffee with me before I leave for the grove. Even I need a friend to chat with," Anna said with a smile.

The women were silent while Anna poured milk into their chipped cups. Milk was plentiful during this time of war because Franco had his own cow, but there was no sugar to be had. The milk was rich with cream floating in the cup of coffee.

"Anna, what I miss most in this war is not having sugar for my coffee. I pray every day and am grateful that my sons are too young to fight."

Anna took her first sip of coffee, "Mmmmm, this is so good." She looked into her weak cup of coffee and confided to her friend, "Franco always said we were lucky to have all daughters so we will never have to see them go to war. You know Lucia, I do have a secret that I can share with you."

Lucia said, "You do?"

Anna put her hand into her apron pocket and pulled out an object she held in her closed palm, squeezing it tight. "When I was a little girl," Anna revealed, "I fell in love with this. I love its shape. I love its smooth feel and I love how it makes me think of ways to use it." Anna held out her hand to Lucia and then revealed a spool of white thread.

"This little spool has been," Anna continued, "my best friend and my anchor. I keep it with me at all times. When times get tough I put my hand in my pocket, pull out my spool, and know I can handle anything.

"I even love the way the wooden spool smells. My grandmother, who taught me how to sew, gave it to me. I keep it with me at all times. I have had the spool rewound many times. My grandfather whittled the piece of wood and smoothed it with a stone."

Lucia's eyes were shining with the beginnings of tears.

"Do you know what I enjoy doing most and what my most private secret is?" Anna asked.

Lucia said, "What is it?"

Still looking at Lucia, Anna said, "The reason this spool of thread is always white is because my passion is designing and sewing wedding gowns. My favorite color is white because it is the color of purity. Someday after the war I would like to open a shop to make many wedding gowns from my own designs." Anna sighed shyly and said, "My shop will have to wait till my daughters are a little older. Okay, enough! I must go to the olive groves before Franco get cross with me." Anna put her spool back into her pocket and asked with concern, "Will you be alright with the little one?"

"Yes," Lucia said, "I'll have lunch ready for everyone. Go and help our families while I stay here with your daughter. Do you think fresh baked bread would be good for lunch?"

"Yes," Anna said, "that sounds good, and how about a large pot of hot soup to warm our weary bones." Anna laughed and continued, "You'll have to use your imagination because we're low on herbs. This war has really been hard on our pallets."

"Very well," Lucia replied. Anna was ready to leave when Lucia said, "Anna, I would love to have a daughter."

Anna, standing by the door in her worn, heavy coat, turned and replied with an enormous smile, "Yes." She gazed into the air and replied again with a gentle nod, "Yes, daughters are good."

As Anna opened the door, a gust of cold, damp wind blew into the kitchen. In front of her stood one of the nuns from the monastery, wrapped in an old, worn wool blanket. The nun wisely covered her head, trying to shield herself from the wind. Anna knew her and knew that she had come to beg for food. This small, worn woman who had dedicated her life to God had become a friend to Anna. The nun wasn't very old, but she had aged beyond her years from food deprivation and long, hard work caring for poor people. She always smiled around Anna, and never had to say a word; Anna knew she was in need.

21

Anna looked into the nun's eyes and affectionately and admiringly placed her warm hand on the younger woman's face. Anna wished her a good morning, saying, "Sister Maria, it is a cold morning. It would be nice if the sun would come to shine upon us."

"Yes," Sister Maria replied, "the sun would feel good."

Anna turned and went back into the house. She beckoned the nun to enter her warm home, but Sister Maria declined, as always. Anna shut the door behind her. Lucia turned and asked, "Is there a problem?"

"No," Anna said, walking to the cooler part of her kitchen. She picked up a small basket of dried figs and examined them.

Lucia knew then why Anna had come back into the house. She knew that the dried figs, always the largest and best, without mold, were to be given to the nuns at the monastery. Lucia watched as Anna also put several handfuls of fresh mixed nuts in the basket.

Anna walked back to the door and saw the smile on Lucia's face. Outside, she gave the basket to Sister Maria. "The DiGorio boys will come by the monastery later to chop firewood. And tomorrow I will send my oldest daughter over with some fresh milk."

"I am so grateful to you and your family. I will pray for all of you at Mass this morning."

"Sister," Anna said solemnly.

The sister, with loving, tearful eyes, replied, "Yes, my child?"

"Pray very hard and ask God to find in his heart an end to this terrible war," Anna said.

Anna put her arm around Sister Maria to warm her and the two women walked together in silence toward the olive grove. There, they said their goodbyes and went their separate ways.

Once Anna had gone, Lucia quietly got up from the table, put a log in the fireplace and checked to see if the baby was dreaming comfortably. She looked down at the resting child, noting how different she was from Franco and Anna's other daughters. The chubby, high-cheeked, round-faced child had a distinct deep cleft in her chin and a rare beauty. Her skin was dark and her long, thick eyelashes framed her near-black eyes. She was easy-going and mild mannered, a contented little person who asked only to be fed and changed.

Lucia looked at the baby and couldn't help but wonder where she came from. She definitely did not, at this early age, resemble her sisters. Staring at the sleeping baby in front of her, Lucia was entranced and wanted to pick her up, hold her and play with her. Knowing better than to disturb a sleeping child, she controlled herself. She walked back to the table, sat down, and drank her now cool coffee.

With the morning sickness from the baby she was carrying, Lucia tried to think of positive things. She thought of her two sons whom she dearly loved. Shaking her head, she tried to rid herself of thoughts of what might have happened to her and her family if it had not been for the generosity of the Gennusas. They had been saved them from a bitter cold winter and starvation.

Lucia felt a tiny stone in her shoe and took it off to shake out the pebble. She looked at the shoe and admired the carefully crafted sole that Vincenzo had sewn.

In his younger days, Vincenzo had worked in his father's well-known and successful shoe shop. Vincenzo's father made a good living from his craft and supported his family well. Although Vincenzo was not as artistic or as skilled as his father, he learned as an apprentice the basics of shoe repair.

Vincenzo had tried to get work as a shoemaker before working with Franco, but because of the war, people didn't have money to get their shoes repaired. Throughout the war there were no shoes to be bought because all the shoe factories were making footwear for the war effort. Vincenzo took apart old shoes, sewed several pieces of leather together, and cut the soles to the size of the shoe. He got his family through the war with decently repaired shoes.

Lucia remembered so well the first pair of shoes that her husband repaired for Franco. Soon after the DiGorio family started to work for him, Franco was sitting at the fireplace after a long, cold day of harvesting. He took off his tattered shoes and Vincenzo had noticed that Franco was looking at the top of his shoe where the sole was coming apart. Vincenzo asked if he could look at the shoe, and then went to his loft and brought back a box. Back at the fireplace, Vincenzo sat down and took out a thick needle and thick thread. He threaded the needle and sewed the top of the shoe to the sole, repairing Franco's only pair of shoes. Afterwards, Vincenzo was kept busy at night repairing shoes for the family and other farmers. His sons always watched their father, because they knew the value of the skill.

Lucia, still looking at her shoe, heard the child whimper and thought again how fortunate she and her family were for having the Gennusas. Together, they worked hard and they would weather the war easier than most.

Anna reached the groves and saw the clouds turning gray. A few sprinkles were starting to come down, and Anna shivered from the biting cold rain.

Franco was reaching up to the trees and stripping the olives from their branches, letting them fall to the ground onto a blanket. The younger daughters and one of the DiGorio boys, Peppe, were working with him. Teresa and Pina, Franco and Anna's oldest daughters, were working at another tree together, and Vincenzo was working at a tree with his older son, Dino.

The dismal rain fell harder. Anna reached for a blanket, heavy with rain, and dragged it to an unpicked tree where she stripped the branches until the blanket was filled with olives. The olives were then placed in baskets and brought back to the farmhouse to be culled.

Anna's lower back was stiff and sore from carrying the baby, but she always did her part in helping the family. She was only in her first months of pregnancy, but she was already showing and she knew this child was going to be bigger than her others. Even with the heaviness in her stomach, and the fatigue she was feeling, bending over and stretching to reach the tree branches, she spent as much time doing her share during harvesting time as the others.

When the day was over, Franco told his older daughters to head to the house with Anna and their bushels of olives. The younger children were sent home early because it had gotten colder.

Back at the house Anna had the little daughters separate the olives from twigs and clean out any other debris that had been collected. The little daughters were cold from the weather and didn't want to do the work, so Lucia and Anna sat down with the little ones and made the work into a game.

Later that afternoon, at early dusk, the oldest daughters entered the house carrying their heavy baskets. They were chilled through and when Anna asked the oldest daughter, Teresa, to hold the baby, she ignored her mother and walked instead to the fireplace. Anna needed help with the child so she and Lucia could finish making dinner.

"Teresa," Anna said, "take this child."

Teresa started to loudly protest, but when Franco walked into the house, she took the child from her mother and walked away bitterly.

Lucia looked at her husband as he walked into the house and asked, "Vincenzo, where are our sons?"

"Dino and Peppe went to the orphanage to help cut wood for the nuns."

Lucia smiled at her husband. She was so proud of her sons, for they never complained.

"Pina," called Anna, "come here and help me with dinner."

Pina started to whine to herself, but still went to help her mother.

After dinner the older daughters, tired from their day, helped with the dinner dishes and then joined the rest of the family to clean the bushels of olives. Normally this work was done outside, but because of the harsh weather, the olives were cleaned in the warmth of the kitchen.

A gust of wind entered the room as Dino and Peppe opened the front door to help the families work on the olives. Lucia went to greet them and then quickly shut the door. She took her sons' coats and caps and told them to sit at the table, for their dinner was ready.

When the olives were all cleaned, the families bathed and went to their beds. The DiGorios went to the loft to spend time together as a family before they went to sleep.

In the older daughter's bed, Pina was on her side, bundled up. Teresa sat on the side of the mattress, and bent over to soothe her lower back. Facing away from Pina she complained about how much her body ached and how she wanted to be in school with her friends. She waited for Pina to reply, but got no response. Teresa turned to find Pina sound asleep. Teresa, filled with frustration, punched at her pillow and softly cried herself to sleep.

Chapter Four

Several weeks later, the harvest was done, and the mule cart packed with the families' belongings. The cart was loaded with baskets of olives to take to the village so there was very little space for the family.

Franco was quiet most of the trip because he was worried about having enough olives to sell and olive oil enough for their own use until next year. Anna looked at her husband and saw his concern. Holding their youngest child, she clumsily slid close to him and touched his arm gently. Franco moved closer to her and looked into her face.

Anna's long, brown, wildly curly hair framed her lovely face, but like her daughters, her hair was always covered with a scarf. Franco gently pulled her scarf off her head and ran his fingers through her hair. Her thick eyebrows, hazel eyes, and deep black lashes were beautiful on her still youthful face. Franco never understood how his wife, after bearing five children, could still be so small. He wondered to himself whether she would still have her small waist after carrying this latest child. Still looking at her, he admired not only her great beauty, but also her strength and intelligence. Feeling her warmth, all his worries faded. He reached for the scarf on her shoulder and, with her help, put it back on her head.

Franco looked at his youngest daughter, a truly contented soul wrapped in a blanket with only her little red nose peeking out, swaddled in his wife's arms. Franco was concerned with the looks of this child for she had dark skin. Franco turned around to see his other daughters cuddled tightly together with blankets around them, sound asleep. He admired the mixture of his wife's satin skin and his fair coloring.

His daughters were all exceptionally attractive. The oldest, Teresa, resembled her mother with dark curly hair and light skin, but had her father's blue eyes. His second oldest daughter, Pina, showed the promise of a tall, long-legged, elegant creature with light blonde hair, hazel eyes, and thick eyelashes. The other two daughters, snuggled in each other's arms, were cherubic with their light skin, light curly hair, chubby rosy cheeks, and baby-plumped bodies.

After looking at his children in the back of the cart, he turned around and looked at his youngest daughter with some concern. This daughter had a mass of rich, dark curls that framed her round face. The tone of her skin was that of Anna's, but much darker, and the color of her eyes—almost black—was a mystery. He thought to himself, *Where did they come from?* He dearly loved this beautiful, rare-looking child, but there were times he wanted to hide her from the public because of her dark skin. He shamelessly hid her after her birth, for he was afraid of what his friends would think. He wondered if he was protecting her from criticism, or if he was truly ashamed of her.

Franco knew the history of Sicily, and that the island had been taken over by so many different nationalities. Those dark eyes could have come from anywhere. He was a mixture of many nationalities, but his eyes were so blue, and his skin and hair were very fair. Franco shook his head to get rid of the many ridiculous thoughts that haunted him. He smiled to himself recalling the teasing from his friends, *Franco, how could a man as ugly as you have such beautiful children?*

Franco was truly proud of his family. He thought to himself that he had to stop worrying so much and enjoy all of his children.

Another autumn passed and winter was soon coming to an end. In the middle of winter, the Steins left for their home in Palermo, anxious to be back to their city and store, hoping there was something left of their home. Knowing there would be no selling of jewelry during the war, they didn't worry much about sales. Fortunately, they had lots of cash and gold to sustain them now and for several years after the war.

These wealthy people left money for Franco and Anna for helping them. In private, Franco gratefully received an exquisite ring—a large ruby surrounded by smaller rubies and set in rose gold. The high prongs emphasized its beauty. Franco hid the ring in a safe place and never mentioned it to Anna. Franco decided to keep it for their future, wherever it took them.

Anna was in the kitchen holding and rocking her youngest child until finally the baby fell asleep. Quietly and slowly, she moved clumsily into the bedroom to put the child in her crib. The house was quiet because her daughters had been smuggled to her parents' home, and were being spoiled by her younger sisters for a few days. Anna was not worried about their safety in case of a raid because her parents had a hidden cellar. She was enjoying the quiet house and the quiet outside—there was no bombing in the distance.

On this cold winter day, the bedroom was dim from the clouds hiding the afternoon sun. Anna moved slowly, for her sixth child was soon to be born. After putting her youngest down to sleep, she decided to rest herself, when she noticed her closet door was slightly open. A small piece of lace was peeking out, tempting Anna to look closer. She opened the door to touch the hem of the garment—her wedding dress. She took the dress from her closet and admired it with love and pride. She inspected it carefully in the dim light from the window, at the sturdy stitching and lace which was still intact. She was so proud of the work she and her mother had done. She rubbed her stomach and wondered how she had ever fit into this tiny dress.

Anna sat on the bed, her wedding dress still in her hands. With a beaming smile on her face and a slight nod of her head, she remembered how angry she had been with her parents after they arranged her marriage. Anna wanted nothing to do with the pre-arranged wedding, for her plans were to escape this weary life. She had hoped to move to the mainland and work as a wedding dress seamstress.

Anna could still hear the stern voice of her mother saying, "Anna, come here to the kitchen because your father and I want to talk to you."

"Yes, Mamma," Anna had said," I'll be there in just a minute."

As Anna was putting on her nightgown, Giuseppa, her second oldest sister, said "I know what Mamma and Pappa want to talk to you about."

"What is it?"

"I can't tell. They'd be very angry with me," Giuseppa said.

"Giuseppa, tell me…am I in trouble?"

Anna thought to herself, *Have they found out about my secret boyfriend?* Whenever she or one of her sisters was called in that stern manner by her parents, it was serious. Anna heard her mother call her again. She looked at her sister Giuseppa with concern and walked into the kitchen where her mother and father were sitting at the table.

"Anna, sit here with us," her mother said. "Your father and I want to talk to you."

Anna sat at the table, her hands trembling in wonderment of what was to come. Her mother sat next to her and her father across from her.

"Anna," her mother continued, "you are going to be married."

Anna looked at her mother with such shock on her face. "What did you say?"

This time her father spoke, "Anna, your mother and I have decided it is time for you to take a husband. We have chosen one for you. He and his parents will be here for dinner Sunday afternoon, for you to meet him."

Anna looked at her father as if he'd just told her she was dying from a terminal illness. She thought of her secret love, and was fearful to tell her parents about him. Tears welled up in her eyes and her face flushed with anger. She composed herself, looked at her father and exclaimed, "Pappa, I will not marry this stranger."

She started to get up when her mother firmly squeezed her knew, telling Anna without words that she wasn't to get up.

"You have no choice. The decision has been made," her father said.

Anna tried to control her anger, "Who made this decision?"

Anna's father replied sternly, "It is of no concern to you. You will do as I say, and I say who and when you are to marry!"

Anna knew her father's power over her. She calmed down to reason with him. "Pappa," Anna whispered in a gentle voice, "I was hoping that I could go to Palermo or the mainland and work in a bridal shop because I want to have a shop of my own someday."

"What?" Anna's father exclaimed. "The mainland! Where did you get the notion that you would go to work in a large city away from your family? You? Own a shop? You will stay here and get married. You will bear children and work next to your husband. Women are not smart enough to get along without a husband to take care of them. What are you thinking of? Since you will be married soon, there will be no reason for you to continue such talk."

"But, Pappa—"

"That is enough. I will hear no more," said her father. "I expect you to handle yourself properly on Sunday when your expected husband and his parents visit about the marriage."

"Father," Anna cried, big tears running down her face, "may I go to my bedroom now?"

Anna's father waved his hand in the air in frustration. Anna instantly jumped up from her chair, sending it crashing to the floor. She held on to the kitchen table for a second until she had steadied herself. With wobbly legs, she ran to her room and slammed the door.

After Anna left the kitchen, her mother questioned her father, "Giuseppe, should we have told her a little about this man she will wed?"

With a scowl on his face, Giuseppe said to his wife, "What for? The choice has already been made. This is the man she will marry."

Anna ran to her bed, buried her head in her pillow and cried. Giuseppa went to her sister and placed her head on Anna's shoulder. She cried along with Anna, feeling her sister's sadness. "It will be alright. I'll help you get through this. We'll get through it together."

Anna turned to look at Giuseppa and asked, "How did you know?"

"Anna, I am so sorry for not telling you. I overhead Mamma and Pappa discussing a marriage arrangement. I know that I won't get married until you do, so I figured it was you they were talking about." Giuseppa was still for a few minutes while Anna looked at her. Giuseppa said shaking, "I am so sorry, Anna, I was too nervous to tell you. Oh, Anna, I'm sorry. I know about the boy you're seeing."

Anna cried, "How do you know?"

Giuseppa replied, "I saw you in the square the other day. I looked to see if Mamma or Pappa were around. I was so afraid for you."

"You did?" Anna asked.

Giuseppa continued, "I saw the way you were looking at each

other."

Anna, with a tear in her eye, threw her arms around her sister and said, "Oh, Giuseppa, I think I love him!"

"Who is he, Anna?"

"Just a boy I met at the market a while ago. He's a farmer. He and his father sell fruit from his cart. They're from Chiusa Sclafani," Anna said.

"It doesn't matter what you feel, you will marry whomever Mamma and Pappa choose for you. Someday I will do the same. That's why I try not to like any boy I meet. I know love is foolish for us for we can never have it," Giuseppa said.

Anna, sobbing in Giuseppa's arms, cried, "I can't...I can't marry a stranger. How will I ever be able to share his bed? I am so scared. What can I do?"

Giuseppa rubbed Anna's back and told her older sister, "You have no choice. We will get through this together, somehow. And someday when it's my turn, please help me."

The daughters got into bed, pulled up their covers, and in each other's arms cried themselves to sleep.

The next day Anna woke up from a frightful night's sleep with red, puffy eyes. She sat up in bed and shook Giuseppa's shoulder to wake her up.

Giuseppa rubbed her eyes and looked at Anna's weary face. She asked, "Are you alright? What are you going to do?"

"Giuseppa, I will not marry this man," Anna said weakly. "I can't."

"Anna, what choice do you have?" Giuseppa asked.

"Giuseppa, I will not marry him!" Anna cried.

Giuseppa sat up in bed, put her arms around Anna, and held her close. They cried again.

Anna went to the kitchen and waited patiently for her father to leave the house before approaching her mother and whispering softly, "Mamma, I will not marry this man."

"Anna, the decision has been made. I've talked it over with your father, and we agreed that this is best for the whole family. Her mother continued, "He is hardworking, he comes from a good family, and he owns his own house."

At the last comment, Anna sat down at the kitchen table.

Her mother, now upset, exclaimed, "You know someday you'll have to marry, so why are you objecting to this union? He's a good man and he will take good care of you. Now stop your crying."

"Mamma," Anna said with tears in her eyes, "I am not objecting to marriage. I'm objecting to getting married *now*. Mamma, I want to go to work and I want to design clothes. I want to be something other than a wife and mother."

"Anna, stop all this foolishness," Anna's mother said. "You have to think about the whole family. The combining of our two families will be best for all of us. You'll marry this man, and you will marry now. Do you understand? You will marry this man."

"No, Mamma, I don't understand," Anna cried.

"It doesn't matter whether you understand or not, you will take your vows and commit yourself to this man," Anna's mother said sternly.

Anna got up from the table and looked at her mother. "I will not marry this man." She walked angrily to her room.

"Anna," Giuseppa said, "I heard what you and Mamma were talking about. You have no choice."

Anna got dressed for the day, with no reply to Giuseppa's comment.

The week was stressful for Anna. She dreaded the thought that she was expected, for the rest of her life, to live with a man she did not know or love. She had known that someday her parents would seek and choose a husband for her but she had hoped, in those modern times, to speak to her parents about choosing her own partner.

Anna knew she was just dreaming when she thought of falling in love some day and marrying a man she had chosen. She thought of running away, but would miss her five younger sisters; life without them would be unbearable. She would miss her youngest sister Santina the most, because of the care Anna had given her since her birth. She cried a lot that week, with her sister Giuseppa right by her side. Giuseppa did what she could to make Anna's life bearable but there was little she could do.

Sunday arrived and the house was filled with anxiety, exhilaration, and exhaustion. The house was spotless and dinner was cooking. Anna's father had hunted and skinned a rabbit to be cooked in tomato sauce. There was plenty of homemade wine to drink and different kinds of fruit, delicate cheeses and roasted nuts. For dessert, a wonderful cassata would be served. The aroma of homemade bread filled the house.

Anna's sisters wore fine-looking dresses sewn by their mother, with help from Anna. They had scrubbed their faces and their curly hair had been wrapped with matching ribbons. All the family was prepared to meet and welcome these new people into their lives—except for Anna, who was crying in her bedroom.

When Franco and his parents arrived, Anna's parents and sisters were ready to greet them. Anna was still in her bedroom but after everyone had been introduced her mother came to get her.

Sternly and impatiently, Anna's mother said, "That will be enough. Come to the kitchen now."

Anna walked out of the bedroom ahead of her mother, her eyes red from crying looking down at the floor.

Franco's father couldn't take his eyes from beautiful Anna and understood why his son's heart ached for her. She was far more beautiful than other women.

Anna's mother pushed her right in front of Franco. Shaking slightly, Anna finally lifted her eyes to meet his. She was shocked, and then in awe of the tall, light-haired, blued-eyed man standing in front of her. She was mesmerized by his handsomeness. She stepped back and blushed, and when Franco smiled at her, she looked to the floor.

At dinner Anna tried not to be nervous as she picked at her dinner. She ate only a small portion of the meal and at various times during dinner, she could feel Franco staring at her, which made her feel very uncomfortable and, for some reason, unworthy. After the dessert was served and the table had been cleared, Giuseppa was instructed to take the children to their bedroom where they were ordered to be very quiet. The children abided, but the older daughters stayed close to the door and listened to every word.

The conversation was light as the men talked about their wine-making expertise and the women talked about sewing and their children. Meanwhile Anna, with her eyes downcast, sat quietly listening to the table-talk. She only spoke when spoken to, but secretly admired Franco's strong hands.

Franco's mother looked at Anna and said, "Anna, I hear you sew quite well."

Anna looked up and replied, "Yes."

"I also heard you worked in America a few years back?"

"Yes," Anna replied.

Anna's mother tried to get her daughter to converse more, but this only made the situation awkward for all of them. As night fell it became evident that Franco and his parents had to leave for the evening. The adults got up from the kitchen table and said their goodbyes.

Franco approached Anna and Anna's father immediately walked over to his daughter to make sure there was no bodily contact. Franco knew that he was not to touch Anna in any way, so he stopped just in front of her. He held out a small pouch tied with a ribbon, "I hope you take my gift with my genuine love for you," Franco said.

Anna looked to her father for permission to take the gift. After he nodded in approval, she looked into Franco's blue eyes and saw security. As Franco put the pouch in her hand, careful not to touch her, Anna looked down at the floor. He stepped back, not wanting her to be afraid of him, but knowing she felt awkward.

After their last goodbyes, Franco and his parents left the house. Anna's mother closed the door behind them, turned to her daughter and said, "I can't believe that one of my daughters could be so rude. You didn't say anything to Franco's parents when they asked you a question. I expected you to talk about America since one of our bargaining agreements with Franco's parents is the fact that you speak English. I expected you to impress them. What were you thinking? You are going to marry him. Do you understand me?"

Before Anna's mother could say another word of criticism, Anna walked over to the window to see Franco and his parents depart from her view. She watched as the three of them left her house, got into their horse-drawn cart and rode away, fading into the moonlit night. When the guests were out sight, Anna stood for a few minutes and looked at the moon and the bright twinkling stars. She turned away from the window and walked straight to her bedroom and shut the door.

Anna's mother angrily followed her daughter, but Anna's father gently stopped her. He said to his wife, "She will come to terms."

Anna's mother, irritated, said, "Yes, she will."

Anna leaned up against her bedroom door to catch her breath, trying to make sense of what had just happened. She looked at the pouch in her hand and stared at it for a few minutes, before sitting down on her bed. She looked at her sisters, but they said nothing and went back to their beds.

Giuseppa knew Anna was confused so she crawled into bed with her sisters Vincenza and Francesca, her back to Anna.

Anna was in a daze as she held the pouch in her hand and wondered about this handsome blue-eyed man to whom she was promised to marry. Franco's blue eyes fascinated her, not just for their color but also for their calmness.

She thought back to the conversation at the table. His honesty and kindness made her feel safe and assured her that he would treat her well. She knew so little of him, but what she did know, she admired. She liked feeling that he would protect her. The way she had felt so at ease around him surprised her; she hadn't expected to feel a thing for the man.

Anna looked around the room and saw that her sisters were not watching her, which she was happy about; she wanted privacy. She placed the lace-covered satin pouch on her lap, looked at it for a few minutes and then untied the ribbon. The pouch fell open and she separated it from the cotton. There, in the center of the cotton, was a gold necklace. She lifted the gold chain from her lap and it sparkled in the lamplight. At the end of the chain was a small, delicate gold charm in the shape of a disc embedded with a purple and yellow pansy.

For the first time since learning about her arranged marriage, Anna smiled as she looked at the stunning piece of jewelry. She lifted the charm upward and twirled it. The gold in her hands shimmered even more while it danced in the moonlight coming through the windows. Mesmerized by its shine and glitter, she was still smiling when she lay her head down on her pillow and placed the gold charm on her heart. As she held the charm she closed her eyes. She didn't want to share this private moment—not even with her sister, Giuseppa.

Chapter Five

During their courtship, Franco and Anna were never left alone. Their conversations were always monitored by one of their parents, so the topics were light. Anna's sexual emotions stirred, but because there was no physical contact, she was left confused by feelings she'd never experienced. Anna wanted so much to talk with someone about her feelings, so one night in bed with Giuseppa, she asked, "Giuseppa, do you every wonder what it is like to be, you know, with a man?"

Giuseppa looked at Anna in surprise, "Do you mean have a man touch me?"

Anna blushed slightly. "Yes," she answered. "I've never talked to anyone about what to think about these feelings."

Out of concern, Giuseppa asked her sister and best friend, "Anna, are you afraid of your wedding night?"

Anna looked at Giuseppa and said, "No, I'm not afraid." Anna looked out into the air and continued, "But I have such feelings and I do wonder what it's all about."

"Anna, has mother talked to you about that night?" Giuseppa propped up her head with her hands and looked at Anna.

Anna lay back on her pillow. "Yes," Anna said, "and I'm even more confused."

"How is that?" Giuseppa asked.

"Mother told me that I had to do my duty and that I was to do whatever Franco asks of me. She said that she didn't want to be humiliated and that if I didn't comply with his wishes he could give me back." Anna had been surprised and frightened by her mother's advice. She understood that if she didn't satisfy Franco, he could leave her. If that happened, she knew she wouldn't be welcome back with her family. "Giuseppa, something else that Mamma said really scared me."

"What was it?" Giuseppa asked with deep concern.

Anna took a deep breath and said, "Mamma, told me that after I've been with my husband on my wedding night, there should be blood on the sheets."

Giuseppa looked puzzled and asked, "But why?"

"Mamma said something about not being pure and that the blood would be proof to Franco and his parents that I had never been with another man," Anna said

"Anna, where does the blood come from and what happens if there is no blood? Did you ask Mamma where the blood comes from?" Giuseppa asked.

"I was too afraid to ask. I don't know where the blood comes from, Giuseppa; and I guess my husband can give me back to Mamma and Pappa," Anna said.

Giuseppa looked in horror at her sister. She started to cry, and Anna put her arms around her, "Giuseppa, I was frightened at first, after Mamma talked to be about my wedding night, but for some reason, I know I have nothing to be afraid of. I feel in my heart that this man I'm about to marry won't harm me or give me back. I know he is honorable. I don't know where this marriage will lead, but I'll make the best of it. Even though I have no choice, I want it to be good."

The sisters lay together in each other's arms that night, sharing their strength for what lay ahead for both of them—a new husband and the loss of a best friend.

Anna looked exquisite on her wedding day. She was dressed in a long white gown with a long train she had designed. With the help of her mother, Anna had spent countless hours stitching her dress and securing each stitch by hand. The fabric was Italian lace, chosen carefully for its quality. The soft long sleeves were scalloped at the ends, and tiny buttons were sewn at the wrist to fit the sleeve snugly. The front was fitted to the waist, hugged the hips, and fell to a soft flared bottom, hemmed in scallops. The back was snug, with tiny buttons running down the center to the waist. Handmade light pink roses were scattered around the back of the waist and down the four-foot train.

Pieces of lace were cut at the opposite end of the scalloped hem. The lace was gathered together at the straight end to make the flower shape. The lace was dyed in a light, red-berry juice to give the roses a hint of a pink color. Part of the lace was also dyed green from grass taken from the fields to make green leaves, which were a medium shade to enhance the pale pink roses that were scattered and along the back of her dress. The color of the leaves gave the pink roses a more delicate look. Anna's dark, curly hair was piled up on top of her head with long spiral curls surrounding her face and in back of her neck. The handmade pink roses were tucked just above the nape of her neck in a half-moon shape under her hair.

A long matching lace veil was attached to her hair and extended to the bottom of the dress and another four feet past the train. The lace of the veil matched the dress, and the entire veil was scalloped from end to end. On top of Anna's head, a spray of small, fresh, light yellow flowers were sprinkled among her curls. She carried a bouquet of the same pink lace roses and the wildflowers that had been scattered in her hair. She wrapped the bouquet with pink, light yellow, and green ribbon tied into a large, floppy bow. Her sister's handpicked both the fresh wildflowers for her hair and the bouquet that morning.

Around her neck, she wore the gold charm that Franco had given her the first night they'd met. The neck of the dress was high and round with a scalloped edge and fitted lace. As Anna looked at herself in the mirror, Giuseppa was put the last of the wild flowers in her hair.

"Giuseppa," Anna said sadly, "I will miss you, my sister. You've been my best friend."

Giuseppa bent over and kissed her sister on the cheek.

Anna turned to her and put her arms around Giuseppa. "I will always be your best friend."

"Anna," Giuseppa said, "Franco is a very nice man. I think he'll make you very happy. Are you happy?"

"Yes," Anna said, looking at her beloved sister. And the looking down at the floor, she repeated softly to herself, "Yes."

The marriage took place in the center of the village at Santa Maria Maggiore, a Roman Catholic Church. It was the last Saturday of the month in September, 1930. A sweet Indian Summer breeze blew in for their special day.

The sacred union between Anna and Franco was holy event for

Anna's parents who walked beside her and escorted her through the village. Anna's sister was behind her, holding her veil and train as they walked the quarter of a mile procession through the village to the church. Anna felt proud and pleased as she walked through her neighborhood, feeling the warm breeze and warm sun on her face, knowing that God was watching.

Franco was joined by his parents and their guests as they walked behind the Anna's immediate family. They did so to observe the tradition that the groom was not to see his bride or make contact until they were in front of the altar.

At the church Anna's younger sisters threw pink wild rose petals in front of her as she walked down the aisle. The ancient church was filled with Franco and Anna's families and guests, embracing them in prayer. The couple would soon take their vows to stay together for eternity before the statue of Mary watching with her approval.

The priest, along with God, waited at the altar to say Mass. He was proud to have the privilege and honor of performing the ceremony. He stood in front of the altar knowing both families, and he felt blessed to officiate this union. The guests were filled with much happiness.

Franco watched Anna as she floated toward him like an angel out of heaven. It was hard for him to believe that the moment had come for her to belong to him. He prayed and thanked God for answering his prayers and giving him the woman he had longed for.

Anna's family and guests were in awe of Anna's unusual gown. As she passed them in their pews, they admired the long train and the lace roses on the back of her formal dress. Anna's mother heard praises from the guests and felt such pride as she watched her oldest daughter pass by.

When Anna had reached the front of the church to join Franco, the two stood side by side as they walked up three marble steps to the altar. Before the priest, who was for them a representation of God, Anna and Franco proceeded to exchange their marriage vows. And after being pronounced man and wife, they walked together from the altar down the long aisle outside the church. The newlyweds stood at the entrance of the church and were greeted with applause and pink rose petals thrown by their younger guests.

After the ceremony the bride and groom walked through the

town toward Franco's house, followed by their party guests. While Anna's younger sisters held the train of her dress and Giuseppa held the veil, several of Franco's friends played their fiddles while walking with the wedding party. Along the way, people looking out their windows and standing in their doorways greeted the newly married couple as they passed. Farmers driving their mules to market waved at the couple, children playing "kick the stone" stopped to watch the parade, and people in the street cheered them and congratulated them on their special blessed union. They still didn't touch or hold hands for Anna felt uncomfortable.

When the wedding party and guests reached Franco's house, he instructed them to help themselves to food and wine. With the help of Anna's mother, Anna's sister undid her veil but left the lace roses in her hair.

"We did well my daughter, for there have been so many compliments and whispers echoing through the church, praising your wedding gown," Anna's mother said.

"Mamma," said Anna, "I feel so beautiful in the dress. Thank you for all your help."

"Anna," her mother said sternly, "you don't give yourself enough credit for this heavenly creation. I only did what you instructed me to do. I wasn't sure at first what your thoughts were but I'm glad I followed your directions. You are a true marvel when it comes to your sewing. I am so proud of you. You look beautiful."

Anna's mother helped with tucking and pinning the lace material under each rose to shorten the train and make the dress floor length for dancing. She and Anna's sister pinned each rose with a spray of wild yellow flowers that were cut short so that the dress turned into a bustle of layered lace roses and wild yellow flowers.

The band started to play a waltz and for the first time, Franco walked to his bride and took her into his arms. He tried to hold her close but she resisted from embarrassment, so they danced at arm's length. After the dance, Anna stepped away from her new husband, looked down to the ground, and bravely walked over to Franco's mother just a short distance away. Taking a deep breath and still looking down at the ground, sheepishly and very unsure of herself, Anna whispered, "I will work very hard to be a good wife to your son. I hope to give him many sons. I also want to be a good daughter to you."

Franco's mother, bewildered, looked at this innocent breath-taking creature, her new daughter-in-law. Overwhelmed and overjoyed with unexpected emotion at this child's words, she placed her hand under Anna's chin and gently raised it so their eyes could meet. "You are already a wonderful daughter to me. I will enjoy you and will be a good mother to you." She kissed Anna on the cheek with tears in her eyes and realized what a magnificent person her oldest son had chosen for his wife. "Come with me, my new daughter. Let us go find my son so we can both dance with him and celebrate this union."

They smiled at each other and, arm in arm, went to Franco. Together, the three of them danced with their arms around one another. With the union of his bride and his mother, Franco was happier than he could have imagined. On this most festive occasion, with an instant impulse, he picked up his mother and his new bride and danced the polka. All three laughed with every happy step.

The wine, food, music, and singers made for a very merry festivity as everyone danced and danced. Anna's family was happy, but Giuseppa felt lost, for she would miss her older sister very much. During the reception, Anna chose a quiet time to take Giuseppa into her arms, hug her, and tell her how much she loved her.

"Our lives together won't change," she told Giuseppa.

The girls started to dance together and Giuseppa whispered into Anna's ear, "You have to promise me that you'll tell me about your honeymoon night."

Anna blushed, looked at Giuseppa and exclaimed, "Giiiiiiiii, no!"

Giuseppa looked at her big sister seriously, "Oh, yes you will, Anna!"

There was a quiet moment between them and then they laughed as Anna put her arms around her sister, swung her toward the music, thinking to herself that it was time for Giuseppa to stop being pensive and enjoy the wedding. They started to dance a polka, flailing widely around and around, laughing to the music when they were stopped by Franco, who asked, "Am I allowed to celebrate in this dance with the two of you?"

Giuseppa looked at her new brother-in-law and, with her arm still around Anna, said, "Franco, you must promise that you will never take my sister away from me. Promise on your life that you will always let me be a part of her life and yours. I love her so much."

Franco looked at Giuseppa, laughed and replied sincerely, "Yes, little sister and best friend of my new bride. I promise never to separate you. I also promise that you will be the first to be called on when your older sister needs you to help take care of our many male children."

Anna shyly stepped back, taking in Franco's comment. When her baby sister Santina ran up and wanted to dance, Giuseppa took her hands and started to swirl her around, and Franco took the opportunity to step toward his new bride.

Anna looked into her new husband's blue eyes and smiled gently as she let him get closer to her for the first time. Anna could feel his strong muscular body. She could smell his body's poignant odor, warm from dancing. His smell was intoxicating and she tried to hide her sexual desire.

Anna placed her head on his shoulder as the music slowed. Dancing intimately to a romantic song, their bodies touching, she blushed. She was embarrassed and didn't want her wedding guests to see her like this. Her nipples had grown hard and the most private parts of her femininity ached for him. It was exhilarating and exhausting for her to look at the face of this handsome man she had just married. She had no experience with men, and was confused at her body's reactions. She wanted to stop dancing, to stop feeling like that. She wanted to run away and hide her shame. And yet, she never wanted him to let her go and she never wanted to stop dancing. She was so confused.

Franco let her go after the dance and held her hand as they walked over to their guests. She yearned for his touch and wondered, *Why am I so confused? Why do I feel this way? What is wrong with me? Am I supposed to feel this way?*

Walking toward their guests, they were distracted by Anna's sisters who all wanted to dance with Franco. He let go of Anna's hand and started to dance with the little ones. Anna had noticed how much Franco enjoyed her sisters, which pleased her. Her youngest sister, Santina, seemed to have stolen his heart.

Anna's parents were blissful with the new family union. They were satisfied with their choice for their oldest daughter, and happy that Anna, in the last months while planning the wedding, seemed to come to terms with their choice for her husband. They knew the marriage would last, for Franco was a good man and would work at the marriage. Their daughter would obey her husband. Never did it occur to them that this union would end in real love.

Worn out from the celebration, one by one the guests started to leave at dusk. When Anna's parents were ready to leave with their lethargic, tired daughters, they kissed Anna goodbye. Anna's mother took Anna aside and reminded her of her duty to her husband. "Just remember daughter that you have an obligation to do what your husband wants. Do not disappoint him."

After her mother's warning, for just a second, Anna became frightened at what was ahead of her. She looked at her mother, lowered her head and answered in a shallow voice, "Yes, Mamma."

When the all guests had gone, Anna found herself alone with Franco in his home for the first time. She had never been in the house before, and she also had never been alone with Franco anywhere until that moment. It was a large house with sparse but simple decorations, but immaculately organized and clean, which pleased her very much. Her artistic mind was already at work, planning colors and fabrics she would use for the kitchen curtain.

Franco, being considerate of their new life, gently told Anna to make herself at ease in their home. "I am going to pour myself a glass of wine. Would you like a glass?"

She looked at him shyly and nodded.

He walked to the sink, picked up two glasses and poured the wine, and then handed one to her. Franco looked at his adorable new wife in disbelief and pride as they drank their glasses of wine in silence. Franco finished his glass first and said he was going outside to smoke a cigarette. After he left the kitchen, Anna carried her glass of wine as she looked around her new home and sipped slowly. . The rich red liquid felt good going down her throat and calmed her nerves. She was both scared and physically excited, for she didn't know what to expect in the unity of this marriage. She thought back to the other night, when she had asked her mother what she was to do. Her mother, unconcerned, replied, "Anna, do as your husband tells you." Her mother had said that it was her duty to be there for her husband, and to do as he said. She had been scared at the thought of what was to come, but now she wasn't frightened. Eagerly, she prepared for her new husband.

Anna bathed for some time, trying to prolong the inevitable. She felt warm from lying in a tub of hot water and finishing her glass of wine. She felt the hot soothing water on her breast and secretly wished that Franco would join her. She stayed in the tub for a while, trying to get the tightness out of her muscles. After a while, she felt she was ready to join her new husband, but when she got out of the tub, she felt awkward. She stood and gazed at her wet body in a long mirror on the back of the bathroom door. Looking at her own nakedness, she shook slightly from the chill in the air.

Experiencing the deep sexual desire that she'd felt every time she thought of these next moments, Anna blushed. She felt an overwhelming desire for this stranger who now was her husband; she lowered her head and feeling ashamed, reached for a towel to wipe down her chilled, wet body. Still standing by the mirror, slipped her silk nightgown over her bare skin. She shivered again from the silk and her desire returning even stronger. A soft knock on the bathroom door interrupted her thought; she hesitated before answering.

Anna took a deep breath, feeling awkward and uncertain of her young shy self, but slowly opened the door. She stood in the doorway, feeling embarrassed to be seen in her thin, off-white nightgown, and then stepped into the kitchen where Franco had started a warm and inviting fire.

Franco could smell the fresh fragrance of Anna's bath on her skin. He looked at her and had to catch his breath as his young wife stood in front of him in her sheer nightgown. Her firm breasts showed through her sheer nightgown and he ached for her. Franco stepped close to Anna, who was still looking at the floor, and he could feel the heat from her body. He put his hand under her chin and gently eased her eyes up to meet his. He took another step toward her, looked into her large, young hazel eyes, and bent his head slowly to kiss her for the first time.

As Anna slowly drew one step back from his warm kiss, she looked at his strong muscular body. She felt wetness between her legs and tightened them together as Franco approached her. He slipped off one of the straps from her nightgown and gently bent down to kiss her shoulder. Anna shuttered at his moist, tender kiss. She stood for a few seconds and then, bravely, she slipped off the other strap.

Franco knew now that she was unafraid as her nightgown fell to the floor. He took one step back from his wife, looked at her beautiful body, and a tear welled in his eye.

Although naked, Anna was not embarrassed and her desire was very strong. She looked deep into her husband's entrancing blue eyes and fell immediately, and intensely, in love.

That night lovemaking came easily for Anna and she felt more fulfilled than her young years ever promised.

Although still shy, she felt much more confident. She wanted so much to please her new husband. Franco, knowing his wife's desire to please him, giggled at her. He looked at her in the midst of their lovemaking and said, "All I have to do is look at you and I am pleased."

Anna looked down, embarrassed and blushing, but Franco lifted her chin and kissed her again. He kept looking at his wife, happier than he had ever been and said, "I will do everything to be a good husband to you, and I'll spend the rest of my life showing my love for you." Anna smiled at him and they again made passionate love.

Anna's desire for Franco had not changed in all the years that they'd been together, even when Anna felt her sixth child moving within her. Feeling her unborn baby moving inside of her brought her back to reality, to the present, as she picked up her wedding gown from her lap and gazed at it once again. She remembered the first year with her husband, their excitement for each other, and the testing of their sexual ecstasy. Anna had a shy smile on her face when she remembered, after their wedding night, Franco explaining about the blood on their sheet. Anna shyly asked Franco if he was going to show the sheet to his parents and he smiled and assured her, "I don't think that will be necessary."

Looking at her new husband, Anna asked, "Does that mean you won't be giving me back to my parents?"

Franco looked at Anna and laughed. He picked her up and held her in his strong arms, swirled her around the bedroom and said, "No!"

Franco stopped whirling her and put her down. Anna was still puzzled, "Why does the blood mean that you won't give me back?" Franco, enjoying the tender moment, looked at his child bride and said,

"In time, my love, I will explain it to you."

Anna still remembered how embarrassed she had been and how relieved when her new husband told her that the blood-stained sheet wouldn't be shown to his parents. She remembered how naive she'd been and how much she loved learning all about sex from Franco. She got up from the bed and walked over to the closet to hang up her wedding dress.

After all the years she had been married to Franco, Anna still loved him. Her breath was still taken away by his handsomeness and she was grateful to have him and her memories of life with him from before the war. It was good for Anna to remember the more wonderful parts of her life with Franco, if only for a few moments. It gave her strength to believe that someday her world would be peaceful again. One day it would be like it used to be. Getting away from the war and all the tragedy around her to reminisce about her quiet past helped her to endure.

Anna crept quietly out of the bedroom to let her baby sleep. She stood in the kitchen for a short quiet moment, enjoying the silence. A noise came from the mezzanine and she smiled, because she knew it was Franco.

Chapter Six

 ❧

All throughout Europe, battles were being fought and people were dying in the throes of an ugly war. Winters were exceptionally long and cold for the people of Sicily. Information about the death camps was drifting throughout the island as people talked of Jews being marched by the thousands from their homeland to other countries in the bitter cold, to work camps or death camps for extermination. Rumors about the gas chambers in Auschwitz ran rampant on the island. The world didn't know, and would never know, how many of the Jewish population perished. At best, the count after the war was six million—a difficult fact to accept.

As these horrendous events were happening, Anna grew larger, and was tired most of the time from carrying her heavy unborn baby. Much of the house responsibility and caring for the younger children fell to the older daughters. She knew her older daughters were unhappy, but she was helpless to do anything to change the situation.

Finally, at the end of March Anna felt herself go into labor. At first the pain wasn't too difficult, but it got worse and the labor pains lasted longer with this baby than with her other births. Anna never complained about the labor because there was still so much work to be done in the home and in caring for her other children. Her youngest daughter wasn't feeling well and seemed to be coming down with a cold, which worried Anna.

Anna stayed close to her youngest daughter, but on the second day of labor, she began to worry about herself and the labor she was experiencing. These birth pains confused her because they were inconsistent.

In the early evening on that second day, she was in the kitchen preparing dinner with her older daughters when suddenly, her pain increased. As she looked out the window she saw the trees blowing in the merciless wind. The sight gave her a chill through her body.

Anna walked over to the stove and, as she reached for a pot, a sharp violent pain hit her, sending her tumbling to the floor. She screamed out in pain and Franco and the older daughters ran to her. As she lay on the floor, the pain stopped and she started to get up. Franco helped her into their bedroom as another pain, although not as strong as the first. A trail of warm water mixed with bright red blood streamed down her legs and followed her. Franco helped her to bed and as Anna started to lie back, she screamed from the third pain.

"Teresa!" Franco called to his oldest daughter, "Hurry and get your grandmother!" Franco then came out of the bedroom and instructed his second eldest daughter Pina to go and get the midwife, for the baby was coming.

"Pappa," Teresa said, "the baby is sick, too."

Franco stopped Teresa, grabbed her by the shoulders and shook her. He pushed her toward the door and yelled to her to immediately fetch her grandmother. Pina started to cry and ran out the door to get the midwife without questioning her father.

When the midwife came to the house, Anna's mother and her sister Giuseppa were already there. Giuseppa was dressed in a black dress, black stockings, and black shoes. She was mourning the death of her husband who had died two years earlier. To honor him and respect tradition, she would wear black for the rest of her life. Giuseppa and her mother were sitting on one side of the bed holding Anna's hand while Anna tried hard not to show her suffering.

The midwife entered into the bedroom and instructed Anna's sister to boil water and keep it coming. As the midwife examined Anna, she looked worried and asked Anna's mother and Franco to step outside the bedroom. Giuseppa saw the look on the midwife's face and knew something was wrong. She quickly went back into the bedroom and stayed close to her sister's side.

Just the two sisters alone in the bedroom, Giuseppa bent down and whispered whimsically to Anna, "I told you that you and Franco were having too much sex. Didn't I tell you to stop?" Anna started to laugh and Giuseppa continued, "Did you listen to me? No!"

Anna responded wearily to her younger sister, "Gi, you just wait."

Giuseppa, trying not to laugh too hard, but she was only trying to lighten the conversation for her sister's sake. "I can't wait. Being a widow, bringing up two sons alone, and not having any sex, is no fun. Mother sneaks around me all the time. She lets me know she's watching me and it's driving me crazy. I swear she's protecting my virginity all over again. Of course, having a little sex would help me endure my loneliness. I keep telling you, Anna, it's hard being a mother of males, always telling them to keep it in their pants. I worry that some woman is going to claim one of my sons as the father of her unborn child. My sons are so handsome; I know it's hard for women to stay away from them. You know how much I loved my husband, but no sex until I remarry? It's just not right. Do you know of any man who can indulge me without a commitment and not have mother find out? Sex will be every night. That I can promise. I might even consider remarrying."

"No," Anna replied, "you can never have sex unless you remarry. Besides, if I did know of someone, do you think I would introduce him to you? That poor soul, whoever he was, wouldn't be able to keep up with you." More seriously, Anna continued, "Be careful with whom and how you talk about sex. You know how you'd be scorned from our relatives if they ever heard talk like that. You know even after marriage, you can only hint about sex but not be explicit."

"Don't worry big sister; you know what a coward I am," Giuseppa replied.

Giuseppa felt Anna's hand squeeze hers, and she held on tight. Anna felt the contraction, and she held her sister's hand firmly. After the contraction had stopped, both girls started to giggle. A second later Anna felt another strong pain, a sharp pain that made her wince.

Giuseppa sadly whispered, "I love you, my sister. I'll help you get through this."

"Thank you. I've always been able to count on you," Anna said. Then, trying to return Giuseppa's light joking, said, "It is a comfort to me that you're here even though you'd rather be someplace else having sex." She smiled through the pains that had started again.

Franco came from the bedroom into the kitchen, concerned about how pale his wife was becoming. The midwife approached him and told him and his mother-in-law that there was a serious problem—the child's head was not in the right position. She thought she felt the child's feet but was unsure.

Franco questioned, "What does that mean?"

"The child is coming feet first so all I can do is wait for it to right itself in the birth canal," the midwife said.

"How long will that take?" Franco asked.

The midwife shook her head and said, "I don't know."

Then, she and Anna's mother went into the bedroom to take care of Anna.

Franco started to demand that his oldest daughter put the two small children to bed but was interrupted by Teresa.

"Pappa," she cried, "it's Innocenza. She–"

Franco hushed her again and demanded she do as she was told.

Teresa picked up her youngest sister and took her to her bedroom. She heard her mother screaming in pain and closed the door to the bedroom. Teresa placed the child on her bed. "Pina?" she called. "Will you bring me a blanket to wrap the baby?"

Pina walked out of their bedroom and returned shortly with a blanket.

"What's wrong?" Pina asked.

"I don't know, but the baby is too warm," Teresa said.

The smaller daughters came in then, crying from the confusion of what was happening in their parents' bedroom.

Pina whispered to the girls, "You have to be very quiet and stay away from Pappa and Grandmother."

The older of the small girls, Vincenza, asked if their mother was having the baby and Pina lovingly replied, "Yes."

The night was unending, with little sleep for the girls because of the horrible screams coming from their mother's room. Franco could hardly stand, hating to see his wife in such agony and nearly feeling her pain himself. His heart pounded fast wishing the whole thing would be over and praying his wife would be alright.

Finally, by dawn, the screaming had subsided and the quiet of the morning was almost eerie. The sun shined warmly in the kitchen, but the warmth and comfort of the kitchen went unnoticed by anyone in the home.

The midwife, Anna's mother, and Franco came out of the bedroom. Giuseppa trailed behind, wanting to know what was happening.

The midwife told Franco that Anna had lost too much blood and that there was no change in the child's position. The pain had stopped for a while but she wasn't hopeful for either the mother or the child. Franco stood stunned.

"I am sorry, Franco…I don't know if Anna can stand any more suffering," said the midwife.

Giuseppa looked at the midwife and said, "My sister is strong. She will do what she has to do."

"Your sister can only endure so much," the midwife said. "She's lost a lot of blood and she's very weak."

Giuseppa went over to Franco and put her arms around him, trying hard to control her emotions. The midwife continued speaking with hesitation before saying that she would have to kill the child to save Anna's life. She chose her words carefully, but the message was all the same.

Anna's mother was startled by the midwife's words. She looked at her and said, "No!"

Franco sat down at the kitchen table, put his hands up to his face and cried. Anna's mother went to him, put her arms around him and cried along with him. Giuseppa, still standing with her head high and strong, looked at the midwife and asked if there was an alternative.

"Franco," Anna's mother said, now standing next to him, "you cannot kill that child. Anna would never forgive you. God will never forgive you."

Franco looked at his mother-in-law and asked, "What should I do?"

Giuseppa looked at Franco vengefully, "You will not kill my sister."

Anna's mother's arms were still around Franco. She cried, "Pray, my son, pray."

As the morning proceeded fairly calmly, the unborn child stayed in the same position and Anna didn't feel much discomfort. This gave Anna time to rest, and to regain some of her strength. As the day went on, Teresa and Pina stayed close to their baby sister, and because the house was quiet now that their mother had stopped screaming, the sisters fell asleep next to the baby for a short time.

By noon the sun was still shining through the window, and Teresa and Pina kept the children quiet while eating lunch. But when the screaming started again, Teresa said to the girls, "Let's go back into the bedroom. Pina and I will tell stories."

Pina had Innocenza in her arms while Teresa escorted the girls back to their bedroom. The children were frightened by the sound and started to cry, only this time all of the girls cried together. Vincenza looked at her older sister, shaking, and asked, "Teresa, is Momma going to die?"

Teresa was shocked by the question and for the first time thought of that possibility. She looked at her sister and said, "No." Teresa, shaken by the question, took Vincenza's hand and sat her down beside her on the bed.

"Teresa," Pina said, "I think the baby is getting worse. What should we do?"

Teresa, with tears in her eyes, said to Pina, "I don't know, but I need to talk with Father."

Teresa walked into the kitchen and saw her father with his head down on the table, and her grandmother standing by the kitchen door, staring in a daze out the window. Giuseppa and the midwife had gone into the bedroom to be with Anna. Teresa walked over to him and calmly said, "Father, I need to talk to you."

Her father, ashamed that his oldest daughter had caught him in a weak state, lifted his head and asked sternly, "What is it?"

"Pappa," Teresa said, "it's Innocenza. She is sick and needs help."

Franco got up from the table and again the horrid screams came from the bedroom. "What's the matter with you? Aren't you capable of taking care of her? Are you good for nothing? Always complaining that you want this and you want that." Franco roughly grabbed Teresa's shoulders and started to shake her. "Just once in your life, stop complaining." In a rage he slapped her hard across the face.

Teresa fell back on to the floor.

With his fist in the air, Franco said, "Take care of the baby or you'll get more of what you just got."

Anna's mother turned from the window in horror.

Franco walked away from his daughter and over to the cupboard to pour himself a large glass of wine. After gulping the wine, he left the empty glass on the sink and walked to the bedroom where the screaming had resumed.

Anna's mother put her hands to her face and cried violently until she could stop for long enough to go in the bedroom and be with her daughter.

Teresa stood alone in the kitchen, shocked at what her father had done. With no tears in her eyes and her hand on her face, she slowly got up from the floor and walked into her bedroom. Inside, Pina came to her and put her arms around Teresa, but the older sister pushed her away and walked instead to baby Innocenza. "I hate you," she said to the sick child. Teresa looked around the room with her hand still on the cheek where her father had struck her, and said to all her sisters, "I hate all of you."

They were scared and confused—they didn't know what to do or say to their sister.

Evening was falling, and the birthing progress was the same. Everyone was drained, especially Anna, who had lost more blood and had less energy. The midwife knew that Anna couldn't handle much more. Franco and Anna's mother were in the bedroom with Anna, and the midwife asked them to please go out to the kitchen. Giuseppa was asked to stay with Anna. Franco looked at his drained, frail wife, praying desperately for her life. He reluctantly left her side, but as he got up to go, his heart ached as he walked into the kitchen.

Evening was approaching and the house was getting darker when the midwife disclosed, "I'm afraid for Anna and the baby, for neither can endure much more—we're losing both of them. I'm going make a suggestion and, before you say no, hear me out." Both Franco and Anna's mother were frightened.

The midwife secretly prayed and hoped that Franco would disagree with her suggestion and dreaded that she was even about to suggest such a thing. "Years ago, before becoming a midwife, I worked with my father on our farm and helped him with his animals. I saw a foal being born to one of the mares." The midwife took a long, deep breath and continued. "The foal was coming out feet first just like this baby. My father wasn't sure what he was doing, but in desperation to save the mare and the foal, my father went into the mare's birth canal. The mare was held firmly by several of his workers while my father entered the animal up to his elbows. With all his strength, and making sure not to strangle the foal with the umbilical cord, he turned the foal around to its proper position for birth. When the head was in the position, the birth took place naturally and the foal was born with no harm to the mother. I'm not sure what the outcome will be with Anna and this baby, but I do know we need to do something, or they both will surely die."

Franco jumped up from his chair said, "Are you telling me we should treat my wife and child like a horse and a foal?"

The midwife said, "No, Franco, I'm saying we need to do whatever is necessary to save your wife and child. We must take care of your wife and child the best we can, before it's too late."

Anna's mother said, "Franco, I've heard of this practice being done before, with success." Anna's mother looked at him with tears in her eyes and continued, "Franco, please don't let my oldest child die. Her children need their mother; I need my daughter. We must to do whatever it takes."

Anna's mother put her arms around him, and her body shook violently as she sobbed. Franco held his mother-in-law fixed in his arms for several seconds, let her go, and gave the midwife his consent.

"You, Franco, must prepare yourself for what we are about to do." The midwife explained the procedure plainly and said, "It is very painful. What we have to do is tie Anna's hands and feet to the bed. They need to be held firmly. It's important that she stays as still as possible, so there is no damage to the child when I move it. We'll have to explain what we will be doing to Anna, so that she'll cooperate with us. Franco, I need you to get me the sharpest knife and a bottle of brandy. I'll have to cut her in order to get my hands inside of her. I also need you to get me a piece of rawhide for her to bite down on. With her concentrating on the rawhide, you'll have to talk her through it. I'll need plenty of hot water and clean towels." The midwife took another deep breath and said, "We must pray. I want you to know, Franco, I will do my best to get all of us through this."

Teresa, lying asleep next to Innocenza, was suddenly awakened, not from the child crying, but because she was so quiet. Teresa jumped up from her pillow and looked at the baby. The baby wasn't moving. Teresa touched her and realized that the child wasn't breathing either, and on closer inspection, she was blue. Teresa ran to where Pina was sleeping in a chair in the corner of their bedroom and woke her, "Innocenza isn't breathing!"

Teresa ran back over to the child and with her motherly instinct, put her mouth to Innocenza's and blew. Teresa picked up the child and placed her onto the bed where she breathed more air into her mouth until Innocenza gasped for air and started to breathe on her own. Innocenza was breathing on her own for a few seconds when Teresa said to Pina, "Get my coat." Then she wrapped the child in a large warm blanket and when Pina had returned with the coat, grabbed it from her and started toward for the door.

Pina followed her. "Teresa, where are you going?"

Teresa stopped for just a second and said to Pina, "To get help for Inncenza before she dies."

Teresa directed Pina to watch the other girls and make sure they stayed out of the way until she returned.

Preparation for the operation was complete. The midwife made sure everyone had their instructions and knew exactly what they were to do, and then put the rawhide into Anna's mouth and secured it on top of her tongue. She took the knife in her hands and dipped it into a bowl of hot soapy water to wash it thoroughly. She skillfully cut into Anna's flesh, making sure not to touch the baby inside.

Anna bit down hard on the rawhide and Franco whispered in her ear to distract her. As the midwife cut, she saw some of the baby's foot slightly descending. Placing pressure to restrain the blood as she cut, she instructed Anna's mother to take over holding the clean soft cloth on her daughter. After she was sure she had cut enough to get her hand inside of Anna and around the unborn child, she looked at Franco and said, "Let's get ready."

Franco moved closer to Anna and started to talk in his wife's ear. He told her how much he loved her and their daughters. He explained what the midwife was about to do, because he needed her to cooperate. But he didn't tell her the risks; he only explained that when the midwife was finished the child would soon be born. Franco rubbed a cool cloth on Anna's face and kissed her gently. Looking at his tired wife, he started to reminisce about the first time he had seen her at Mass, and how he had fallen deeply in love.

She smiled back at him, knowing she and the baby were in great danger, and that she must obey him and do as he said.

Franco whispered to Anna that his life had only begun at the moment he saw her and that it was because of her that his life was fulfilled. As he spoke, Anna dug her nails into his arms and screamed. The midwife pushed inside her and she screamed again, but tried not to move.

Franco got closer to her ear and started to ramble about everything—and nothing—trying to keep Anna from focusing on the pain.

Anna couldn't help but feel this bulky, uncomfortable thing turn inside her. She looked into Franco's eyes, trying to concentrate on what he was saying. The sound of his voice and the smell of his familiar breath brought her some solace. At the last thrust, she felt the child being moved inside of her and screamed while biting down as hard as she could into the rawhide.

Once the child was in the proper position, it began to move into the birth canal.

"Anna, you're doing a good job," The midwife said. Your child will be born within the next few minutes. Keep yourself together for your child. Take deep breaths and listen to Franco, for he will keep you calm. We'll get you through this."

Ten minutes later a baby girl was born, perfect and screaming from hunger. Anna couldn't produce any milk to feed the baby so the midwife told Giuseppa to go down the street and ask Signora Scarpa to come and breastfeed the child.

After her wet bedclothes were changed and she was given plenty of water, Anna finally fell asleep. The midwife suggested the rest of them get some sleep as well, and said she'd stay with Anna until morning. Anna's mother and Giuseppa left to rest and promised to return.

Franco sat alone in the kitchen, physically and emotionally drained. In the quiet, drinking a large glass of wine, he promised himself that this would be the last child that his wife would bring into this world, no matter the cost. He thought about the new baby, his sixth daughter, Maria, and thanked God for her, and for sparing Anna's life. He got up from the table to get some bread and a piece of cheese and then sat back at the kitchen table to eat. The house was finally quiet and he was grateful for the peace. Finally able to relax, Franco poured himself another tall glass of wine and remembered what the midwife had told him. *Franco, you must be very careful, for Anna should not have any more children. Another birth like this would surely kill her and the child.*

Franco began shaking at the table so he reached for another glass of wine to calm his nerves. Relaxed once again, he felt tired enough to put his head on the table and there he fell sound asleep.

Chapter Seven

$\sim$

The next morning, Franco woke up at the kitchen table, restless but anxious to check on his wife and his new baby daughter.

He walked into the stuffy bedroom, stale from the smells of last night and needing fresh air. Franco found the midwife sound asleep in a chair next to Anna, who was very pale, but otherwise sleeping comfortably.

In the crib, the new baby slept soundly and would sleep for some time, Franco was sure, because Signora Scarpa had breastfed her well. He looked at the child proudly and filled with so much love. She was truly lovely for a newborn; fair-skinned with his light hair. There was little physical evidence that she'd had a difficult journey into this world.

Franco shut his bedroom door quietly behind him and went into the kitchen to make coffee in peace before the household was up for the day. The coffee filled the house with its comforting smell and Franco gratefully took his fresh-poured cup over to the window, surprised to see winter snow on the ground. Franco couldn't believe that it had been cold enough last night for snow. This Mediterranean island saw little snow, and it amazed him that his daughters didn't tell him about it. He hadn't noticed either, of course, but he was much too preoccupied with Anna and the baby's delivery to take notice of what was going on outside his house. He smiled at the bright early sun reflecting on the fresh snow and making it sparkle all around the house. Though cold outside, the sun shined through the window and warmed his face.

A second later, Franco's trance was broken by a slight knock on the door. He stretched his aching body and then went to the door where he found his next-door neighbor and long-time companion, Saverino Marconi. Franco greeted Saverino by rubbing one eye with his fist and holding a coffee cup in his other hand.

The strong wind blew cold air into the kitchen while Saverino stood in the doorway, waiting to be invited in. Saverino, a short stocky man with a dark complexion and dark curly hair, was around Franco's age. This man who was almost considered ulgy, gave his friend a hug. Franco proudly declared that he now had another daughter and asked Saverino to come in for coffee.

Saverino entered the house, looking around him to make sure he wasn't being watched by the enemy. Saverino congratulated his friend and before he had a chance to comment further, Franco raised his hand to his heart and said, "My daughter is beautiful. Of course, she looks like me!"

Together, they laughed and Saverino sat at the kitchen table while Franco poured coffee. After taking his first sip of coffee, Saverino said to Franco, "Coffee is always good in the morning even if it is old and diluted." Because coffee was scarce during the war, grounds were used several times. Saverino continued, "Your oldest daughter told me what was going on last night. I wanted to know if there was anything I could do. Are Anna and the new child okay?"

Franco answered in a low and concerned voice, his hands trembling, "I almost lost both of them last night. God was with them through all the pain they endured. They will be fine. Anna will have to rest for some time." Franco explained to his friend about the delivery. "She can never have another baby. The midwife told me how unsafe it would be for her to deliver another child."

"Well, my friend," Saverino said, "I don't want you to worry about Innocenza. She's fine and she'll stay with my wife and me until she is well. We'll bring her home when Anna is well and can take care of her."

"Saverino, what are you talking about?"

"Franco," Saverino said, "Teresa brought Innocenza to my house last night. Teresa was pounding on our door. We had no idea who it was, but the pounding wouldn't stop so I finally got the courage to open up the door. I figured if it was the Germans, they wouldn't be knocking; they'd just smash the door down.

"So when I finally opened the door, Teresa was there, with Innocenza in her arms. Teresa told us that the little one had turned blue and stopped breathing, but that she'd brought her back to life. My wife took Innocenza from Teresa and realized the baby had stopped breathing again. Deanna began rubbing her back but she couldn't get the child to breath, so out of desperation she put the baby down on the floor and put her finger down Innocenza's throat to clear her windpipe. The child gasped for air and started to breathe. Still, she had a high fever so Deanna gave her a cold bath, and after, Innocenza's temperature had gone down a bit. We wiped the baby down, put her in dry clothes, and wrapped her as warmly as possible.

"My wife told Teresa to get the baby to the doctor for care. Teresa went to Dr. Capetti in the center of town for help. We prayed that Teresa would make it safely. There was no choice but to send them to the doctor; the baby surely would have died there with us. Teresa left Innocenza at the doctor's house after she'd been assured that the child was out of danger. The child was sound asleep when Teresa came home to us, safely thank God. Teresa is still at my house, asleep."

Franco was completely taken aback.

"Your daughter Innocenza has pneumonia," Saverino said. "She almost died last night. Teresa saved her life."

"Oh, my God," Franco said putting his hands up to the sides of his face. "Last night I yelled at Teresa harshly. I was so angry with her. She kept mumbling something to me about Innocenza, and I lost my temper. Oh my God, I hit her. She told me that Innocenza was sick, and I told her to take care of her. I had no idea."

Franco's eyes welled up with tears as he sat alone at the kitchen table comprehending what his best friend had just told him. After crying for some time, Franco eventually controlled his tears.

He walked over to the cabinet and took out a large jug of wine. He poured himself a large glass and drank it quickly. His face was pale and his hands were shaking.

Franco walked over to the kitchen table with the jug and two glasses in his hands. He sat down with his friend and asked Saverino if he'd like a glass of wine.

"Yes, of course," Severino said.

Saverino took the glass and sipped the wine. After placing his glass on the table, he got up from his chair and went over to put his arms around Franco; the two men cried together.

Franco cried as he asked Saverino, "What have I done? I've

never raised my hand to any of my children. Will my daughter ever forgive me?"

"Deanna and I will go to the doctor's and bring the child back home with us," Saverino said.

"No," Franco exclaimed, "I'll take care of her myself. There's too much danger outside. The Germans are dangerous in the village and I'd never forgive myself if anything happened to you or your wife."

Later that morning, Anna's mother and Giuseppa arrived to help care for Anna and the new infant. Franco headed to the doctor's house but stopped at Saverino's on the way, taking several deep breaths as he walked to help clear his head. The cold air felt good on his warm face.

As he waited patiently for Saverino to come to the door, he was grateful that his oldest daughter had the intelligence to save her baby sister's life and knew that he needed to tell her how much he loved her.

Saverino's wife, Deanna Marconi answered the door and seeing that it was Franco on her door step, took him into her arms and held him close. Deanna and Anna were close friends and the same age. Deanna still had a nice figure even after having two children. She had high, firm breasts, long, dark hair that fell in shiny waves and dark eyes that lusted for Franco. Even under the circumstances of his visit—coming to collect Teresa after a night when Innocenza was saved from death by her older sister, and his wife and unborn child risked death—he could feel her yearning for him. Deanna made the most of every opportunity to get close to Franco, and she didn't hide her intentions, taking advantage of any chance she had to get him alone. Franco stiffly released himself from Deanna's embrace and waited for her to move away. She invited him into the house and offered him coffee, but Franco politely refused and asked to see his daughter.

Deanna led Franco into the living room where Teresa was lying down, but not asleep. Franco went to the couch to sit next to her. The room was dim as the shades on the windows were drawn. Franco looked at his eldest daughter with such pride. He put his large strong arms around her and brought her close to him to tell her how much he loved her. Without a reply from Teresa, he told her how grateful he was that she took control and saved Innocenza. Franco let Teresa fall back onto her pillow, kissed her cheek, and told her to stay there and rest as long as she needed. He would go to the doctor to see about Innocenza.

Teresa lay on the couch without saying a word to her father.

As Franco walked to the door, he stopped, turned and looked at his quiet daughter and said, "I am sorry for last night. I hope you can forgive me for striking you. There's no excuse for what I've done. Thank you for taking care of Innocenza. I love you." Franco walked out of the room, leaving Teresa in tears.

Franco, with a heavy heart, thanked Deanna for all her help. He stood away from her, hoping to avoid any physical contact, but she rushed to him and put her arms around him. Franco stood stiffly, not reciprocating the hug. He simply thanked her again.

"I'm going to see if Innocenza is well enough to come home," Franco said. "Thank you again for helping my daughters, Deanna. Is it alright if Teresa stays here a while longer, until she is rested up and ready to come home?"

Deanna agreed and Franco nodded in thanks. He put his head down, not wanting to make eye contact, and left the house.

After leaving Saverino's house, Franco got into his wagon feeling quite uncomfortable. He felt guilty about Deanna, and even guiltier about his daughter Teresa. The cold fresh air felt good on his face though, and relieved him a little.

Traveling slowly through town, and trying hard to concentrate, Franco paid careful attention to the young, war-torn German boys that were standing in the street, still waiting for their orders to go back to Germany. They were tired, underfed, cold, and armed. For these German boys, the alliance that Italy had with Germany meant nothing. War-torn between their youth and their loyalty, they continued to serve as dedicated German soldiers. With very little communication from their commanders, these young Germans were not aware of what was happening in the war, or where they stood.

Franco traveled nervously, trying not to go unnoticed, for he didn't know if he had the strength to be interrogated by them this morning. He noticed that the few people who were out on the narrow incline streets were having trouble dealing with the snow on the narrow inclined streets. There were a few children playing quietly in the snow, with their brave parents close by, protecting them from any unwanted visitors. The parents knew that their children might never again experience snow, and they refused to let war deprive their children of this spectacular event.

The night before, Franco had thought of nothing but the safety of his wife and new child, forgetting that war was still all around them. This morning, while riding in his wagon, he was reminded again that war was there, and it was evident at every turn. Everywhere there were small groups of soldiers trying to stay warm by handmade fireplaces. Even though the wind had died down, the day was still cold, and the sun wasn't warm enough to melt the snow. Franco hoped that he'd make it home soon enough to enjoy the snow with his daughters, if only for a few moments.

He approached a small stone townhouse and sighed in relief that he had arrived safely. A shingle hanging from the door said "Dr. Capetti." Franco hitched his wagon in front of the house, walked up the stairs, and knocked on the door. Signora Capetti smiled when she greeted Franco, and it was like being greeted by the sunshine. The war that surrounded their village did not change the Capettis' home. Both the Capettis were small people around fifty years old with graying hair and wonderful, vibrant personalities. They were kind-hearted, love people who should have had children, but children never came to them.

"Come in, Franco," Signora Capetti said. "Your daughter is doing fine. She has slept peacefully. Her temperature is down and she took milk and a little bread this morning. She even has color in her cheeks. The doctor is in the examining room with her now. Let's go and see them."

Signora Capetti opened up the door to the doctor's examining room. There in the sunny room, Franco was greeted by the smiling doctor, "Come, Franco," he said, "look at that sweet child of yours." The adoring doctor continued, "She's doing well. She's strong, just like her Pappa."

Franco approached the table where his daughter was lying and stood over her, overwhelmed with guilt. He looked at Innocenza, who didn't resemble his other children, and gently touched her dark hand. She turned her face to see her father standing there beside her. Although Innocenza was quiet, and didn't normally smile very much, when she saw her father she smiled. Franco picked her up, wanting just to feel her little body and hold her close to him. The baby clung to him and he gently kissed her small forehead. She smiled again and he put her back down on the table, but she wouldn't let go of her father's hand and he didn't take his eyes off of her.

Franco finally looked at the doctor, still holding his daughter's hand, and asked, "Dr. Capetti, will she be alright?"

Dr. Capetti smiled as he said, "She is so strong."

"I need to take her home," Franco said. "I need to hold her. I need to let her know how much she means to me."

Dr. Capetti replied, "Franco, you shouldn't feel that you have done wrong by your daughter. Last night was a trying time for you. Teresa told us that Anna was having problems with delivering."

Franco put his head down, never taking his eyes away from Innocenza, and said, "Yes, it was difficult. I almost lost both of them." Franco wiped a tear from his eye and asked again if he could take his daughter home.

Signora Capetti started to object but Dr. Capetti replied, "Of course." Looking at his wife with his reassuring eyes, he said, "My wife doesn't want to part with your daughter. You know she gets attached to all children. We have grown to love this child overnight, but she'll get better more quickly in her own home with her family. She needs her sisters' energy to get better."

Franco was grateful for the doctor's help to save his daughter. "Dr. Capetti, I will pay you."

The doctor stopped him and said, "Franco, don't you worry about payment. My wife and I loved your last crop of olive oil. The flavor of the last supply was wonderful. Your oil is the best we've ever had! If it's all right with you, we would like payment in oil, when the oil is ready."

Franco smiled.

The doctor returned his smile and instructed that Innocenza needed to be kept warm. "Fresh air would be good for her. I only have a little medicine, but if you follow a strict diet for her, with lots of liquids and lots of rest, she'll be fine. In a few days she'll feel stronger and will want to run around with the rest of her sisters; however, make sure she doesn't go outside for a few weeks. Signora Capetti will wrap her up for you. When riding home, make sure her face is covered from the wind but not the sun. Sun is a natural medicine ..." looking down at the child, the gentle doctor continued, "...just like love."

Franco left the Capetti's carrying Innocenza in his arms. She felt comfortably warm and, although she smelled like medicine, she smelled sweet to him. He climbed into the wagon and placed her next to him where he could look at her. When he was sure she was resting and safe in the wagon, he started for home. Riding through the village slowly, listening to the familiar and comforting sound of the clicking of his mules' hooves on the cobblestone road, again he was aware of his surroundings.

The atmosphere hadn't changed much, except that the young German soldiers looked a little warmer, although they were still standing near their fire. It was noontime, but Franco hadn't eaten breakfast and felt hungry. As he traveled slowly past the soldiers, he noticed that two of them were watching him. They were talking and giving hand signals. Franco felt nauseated and then he heard in German, "STOP!"

Franco looked at the soldiers and stopped his wagon. By now it was evident that the Germans were talking to him, for they were walking quickly toward him. Franco froze as the smaller of the Germans walked nervously toward him with his rifle pointed directly at him.

Franco stayed very still and straight. He looked at their dirty uniforms, and into the young, thin, dirty faces of the boys, and they were only boys, just a few years older than his daughter Teresa. Franco recognized one of them as one of the German soldiers who stood by the building when the grower and his son were shot that day in the center of the village, when they were getting their olives pressed. His stomach felt queasy. Franco felt as if he was going to vomit from fright. He placed his hand on Innocenza's blanket.

The small soldier standing in front of Franco took his rifle and viciously shoved it into Franco's ribs. Franco stiffened at the touch of the hard steel barrel. The soldier moved the rifle away from Franco and pointed it at the bundle on the seat beside Franco. He waved the barrel, indicating that he wanted to see was wrapped in the blankets. With his hands shaking, Franco carefully picked up the child, trying not to wake her and hoping she wouldn't cry. He opened up the blanket to uncover her face and showed it to the soldier. Franco was afraid that the soldiers would notice her dark skin and react badly because she didn't resemble him. The Germans looked at the sleeping child and the soldier lowered the barrel of his rifle and stepped away from the wagon. The other soldier waved his hand for Franco to go on.

As the soldiers walked away from the wagon, Franco heard them speaking:

"I told you there was nothing hidden under the blanket. I don't think there is a bomb in this peaceful farm village, especially carried out in the open. These people are too poor. What would you have done if he tried to get away? We don't have any ammunition." The German soldiers approached the fire, and the boy continued talking, "The Americans aren't far away. I'm tired; and when they come to take this village, I'll give up easily. I'm too hungry and cold to fight. I want to go home."

The other soldier, still with the rifle in his hands, stopped shaking from the cold and put his rifle down on the ground. He put his hands out over what was left of the fire. Wanting to impress his partner, he said, "I want to kill more of the enemy before I'm done here, just like Hans."

"Hans is dead, and I'm glad," the other soldier said. "He got what he asked for. If he had just left these people alone and not threatened them, he'd still be alive. If these people don't kill you like they killed Hans, I will." The young, hungry German soldier looked at his comrade closely and into his ear again said with vengeance, "I will."

Franco's body was stiff with fright, but he tried to move a little more hastily. He could feel the sweat running down his armpits and his forehead. He wondered, remembering those baby-faced boys that stood in front of him threatening his daughter, what he could have done. He only had a knife under the seat of the wagon but knew it would be useless. Nevertheless, he would have tried to protect his daughter.

Chapter Eight

It was March 27, 1944, and Franco and Anna's youngest daughter, Maria, was only one day old, well fed, and sleeping comfortably in a crib next to her mother.

It was early morning and Franco was in the kitchen making coffee while Anna and his daughters slept.

The kitchen was bright as he looked out of the window to see the snow was still on the ground. Franco heard the squeaking of the kitchen door and turned to see his eldest daughter standing in the doorway looking at him. Franco admired the fashionable coat that Anna had made for Teresa, a knee-length design made from old fabric and tailored with big shoulders that made Teresa look taller. He wasn't sure about the men's pants that Anna had fashioned for Teresa, but then what did he know about fashion? Besides, it made Teresa look boyish and Franco liked that. He didn't want the Germans looking at her.

His daughter stood in the doorway with her short black curly hair, looking so much older this morning. He admired her blue eyes that she'd gotten from him. She was very wise for her thirteen years and her intelligence astonished Franco, for she would surely be a brilliant woman. She had been named after his mother, a strong and magnificent woman, and she carried the name with pride and dignity.

Franco smiled and walked to Teresa, but she moved away and went to the other side of the kitchen to Innocenza. The little girl was sleeping soundly on soft blankets on the floor. Franco let Teresa have a few moments with her younger sister, and then he approached them both. He put his arm around Teresa, but she was stiff to his touch. With tears in her eyes and a little bitterness in her voice, she said, "Pappa, she almost died."

"You, my daughter, did what you had to do in spite of my insensitivity. I am so indebted to you for your quick and intelligent decision. Thank you for being dependable and always doing what is right."

She moved away from her father, feeling that a large load had been taken off her shoulders.

Franco said, "I am so sorry for striking you."

Teresa said, "Pappa, Innocenza and I needed you so much. I was afraid to stand on my own."

Franco hugged her and Teresa let go of some of her rigidity; she needed her father to hug her. Together, father and daughter, arm in arm, walked to the kitchen table and let the warm sun shine on them through the window. Franco asked Teresa if she'd like a cup of coffee and she nodded yes. He brought the coffee to the table and then sat down across for her. The coffee, though it was weak, tasted good, and the warmth going down Teresa's throat was soothing. With a choking sound coming from her tight throat, Teresa said, "Pappa, Signora Marconi told me that Mamma and the baby are fine. I need to hear it from you. Are they fine?"

"Yes, your mother is fine and so is the newborn. Your mother will need rest, for she lost a lot of blood," Franco said.

"Pappa, what is the baby's name?" Teresa asked.

Smiling, Franco answered, "We named her after my sister, Maria."

"She must be an angel from heaven, to be honored with that name," Teresa said

Just as Franco was about to reply, he heard Innocenza stir. Teresa started to get up from the table to get her sister when Franco stopped her by placing his hand lightly on her shoulder. He got up and lifted the little girl up from the floor. Innocenza smiled when her dark eyes focused on her father's face. Franco kissed her forehead and, with the child in his arms, walked back to the table. He looked at Teresa and said, "I won't let Innocenza out of my sight until she is completely well. We'll wait until your mother is well to tell her about Innocenza's battle with death."

Franco turned at the sound behind him and saw his other filing out of their bedroom, ready to start another active day. Franco looked at Teresa and without either of them exchanging a word, she got up from the table to start breakfast for her sisters.

☙

On June 6, 1944, Maria, two-and-a-half-months old, was sleeping in her crib with no cares regarding the outside world. She was warm, fed, and secure. Little did she know that her parents and older sisters were huddled in the kitchen waiting for news of the attack on the beaches at Normandy called Operation Overlord. Maria stirred for just a second, opened one eye, put her thumb in her mouth, and closed her eye to finish her morning nap, unaware that the British had invaded and captured Rome.

Teresa was walking through the countryside as she did every morning. She went to fetch fresh milk for baby Maria. Because they had no refrigeration, milk had to be gotten daily. Unlike their home in the country, Franco didn't have room for his cow in the village. Franco was afraid the Germans would seize his cow for food if he kept it in town. It was warmer than usual that morning and Teresa was already tired from her daily walk.

Teresa hadn't gotten much sleep or rest over the last few months. She had to accept the fact that she had taken on more responsibility in the care of her younger sisters since the birth of the new baby. The birth had taken a toll on her mother, and it had taken her a longer time to recuperate. Aunt Giuseppa came often to help with the children, but her time was limited.

Teresa's first responsibility was to help with her younger sisters, and then take over Anna's duties at the farm.

There was so much tension in the house and in the neighborhood because of the war. Teresa was so tired of getting up early for her daily run to a farm for fresh milk. If she could, she would find a soft, cool spot during her walk and indulge herself in some leisurely time to bask in the day. It wasn't so long ago that she had been able to do just that.

All of a sudden Teresa realized that she hadn't laughed in a long time, and there was no laughter from her family or other people. She thought to herself, *This war has had a hard effect on everyone. I feel so old. Why is it always me who has to take care of the family? All I want to do is go to school. I want to attend a university and become something other than just a wife to a man I won't know, whom my father will someday choose for me. Am I asking for so much, to be more than just a wife to a farmer? Why do I always feel so confused and angry? Will I ever grow out of this feeling? Stop,* she said to herself. *This war has been hard on everyone. Stop being so selfish and always thinking about want you want.*

Teresa, of course, knew why she had all the responsibility. She was the oldest and therefore, she was expected to take care of all her sisters. Walking and feeling sorry for herself in the open field a mile from her home, she was aware of danger and watched cautiously. In the direction that she was walking, she was fairly safe, for most of the war activities were in the village and she was heading in the opposite direction. Still, she was well aware of the danger and walked briskly.

Teresa had traveled for about half a mile toward the farm when she heard a noise in the low brush behind her, several feet away. She stopped and listened to the rustling. She stood frozen in her path and slowly turned around. The heat of the sun beat down on her and mixed with fear to make her sweat profusely. She stood stiff, not knowing where to run or what to expect, and watched as a bush separated. A large but thin wild rabbit ran across her path and made her jump.

Teresa took a deep breath as she watched the rabbit run out of sight. Because of the war, rabbits were hunted for food almost to extinction, so it came as a surprise to see one. Teresa continued to walk, almost run, toward the safety of the farm.

When she got home with the fresh milk from the farm, she didn't tell her parents about the rabbit scare; there was so much apprehension in the house already.

The house was abnormally quiet when Teresa got there. Teresa's father had controlled most loud activity since the start of the war but today it was even quieter.

In the kitchen, as Anna came to Teresa for the baby's milk. The Marconis and their good-looking, dark-eyed sons, ages thirteen and fifteen, were gathered around a radio at the table. The Marconi boys looked very much like their mother with their dark, curly hair.

Anna placed the milk in the sink, and walked over to the table to listen to the radio with the others. Franco had Innocenza, half asleep and back to health, on his lap, while the other younger children sat quietly on the floor. Everyone was listening closely to the news on the radio that the Americans had hit the beaches of Normandy. Although the Italians were supposed to support Mussolini and work against the Americans, most Italians—and the rest of the world—were tired of war, and wanted the

Germans defeated.

The feeling of hope rose in the kitchen when the radio spoke of the invasion on the French sandy beaches.

The voice on the radio reported:

Although, the weather conditions are not favorable for the attack on the French beaches due to heavy rains, the attack has started. Heavy casualties are on all the beaches of Omaha, Gold, Juno, Sword and Utah. The shooting is so fierce that a large number of soldiers are being killed while leaving their transport, and before reaching the beaches. The shooting is heavy from both parties. The allies need to progress toward higher ground in order to get to the Germans. With determination and strength, the allies, are pushing their way off the beach and toward enemy fire. It looks like there will be no letting up by the allies. This operation will be going on for some time.

As the reporter recounted the historical event, the reception was interrupted with static that got louder as the report continued. Seconds later, the reporter's voice disappeared completely and the radio went dead. The look of disappointment was evident on the adult faces, for they wanted to stay abreast of the invasion, but the tension lessened in the kitchen when there was no sound from the radio.

"Franco," Saverino said, "I'm going to walk to the center of the village to see if I can get any more information."

Franco looked at his friend and said, "I'll go with you."

Anna's face filled with concern and she pleaded, "Franco, please be careful. There might be animosity among the Germans today. They look as tired of the war as we are, and losing this war might make them more dangerous than usual."

"Don't worry," Franco said. "We'll go the back way, out of sight, to avoid them."

Anna looked deeply into Franco's eyes. Deanna watched the very moving scene, turned to her husband, and said, "Saverino, please be careful, you know how I worry."

Franco bent down and kissed Anna's forehead and walked with Saverino to the door. Saverino turned to his sons and said, "Make sure your mother gets home safely."

Deanna walked over to her son Mario and looked at him with loving eyes while she stroked his dark curly hair and ignored her younger son. Mario returned his mother's love and then turned to his father, looked strongly into his eyes, and answered, "Yes, Pappa."

– *PART II* –

Chapter Nine

Franco and Saverino headed toward the village through backyards and small alleyways, avoiding contact with the enemy, or even other civilians.

Along an ancient low wall, seldom traveled, they crunched down, hiding from view as they approached an abandoned building. This building was the oldest building known to the village. This empty building of Greek architectural style, with its worn look, appeared unsafe, which made the Germans stay away. It was located in the center of the village, directly across the square from the Catholic Church. In secret rooms beneath the floor of the building, constant anti-Germany meetings were being conducted and had been going on for the duration of the war.

The men that gathered there were against Mussolini's regime and were working toward a free Sicilian democracy. They wanted to be free, not only from the mainland, but also from Communism. Among these men were known, active members of the Mafia. Although Mussolini's Fascist government had succeeded in suppressing the Mafia, there were several small groups still active who gathered together against the war. During the war any person who was willing to give their life for the cause of freedom, even a Mafia member, was welcomed and treated with respect.

All members of the Resistance group depended on one another for safety, and pledged their undying loyalty to each other. Particular members of the Mafia were a great asset to the group, for they had many contacts on the island and could deliver messages almost anywhere with little or no acknowledgement from the enemy.

Franco had, on many occasions, helped deliver messages to Resistance Party members. The messages would be given to Saverino at the meetings when it wasn't safe for Franco to attend. Saverino would give the message to Franco the night before he left for the farm. When a quiet moment occurred, he would go into the woods and put the message in a hole of a trunk of an old tree. Franco was asked not to read these messages; it wasn't safe for him to know what was contained in the message. He surmised that the messages he carried to Party members had to do with the German movement. On some occasions, Franco would hear of German troops killed nearby after he had placed a message in the tree trunk. He never asked the head of the Resistance group if the killings were related to his delivery.

Although this was just a handful of people, they were active and loyal members of the group throughout the war. The Sicilians' Resistance Party from Franco's village consisted of the mayor of the town, several prominent merchants, unsuspected, mild-mannered Dr. Capetti, and a few farmers like Franco. The citizens were aware of the group's existence; however they didn't know the identities of the individual members. Franco had been a member of this party from the beginning, when the group formed even before the war began, but when it was obvious that trouble was ahead.

Another of Franco's duties was to hide in his stable any member of the Resistance Party who was en route to the next village. Franco would sneak out food and water to the occupant in his stable at night. Anna and his daughters were unaware of his activities. These Party members Franco was hiding and housing were simple residents, doing their regular, daily work until they got word that the Resistance Party needed movement.

The soft-spoken Party members were the unacknowledged, unsung heroes of their village. After the war these heroes faded back into to their daily routines, not wanting to remember the unimaginable duties they had performed, but haunted at times by their consciences. They had carried out murders, torture, and even rape when required, if only to save one Sicilian's life.

Most memories of these heinous duties were buried along with fallen Party members after the war. In order to emotionally survive after the war, this group of people never spoke again of their activities to each other, or to anyone. In most cases they never spoke to each other again at all. It was the only way they could go back to their simple lives after the war had ended. Franco had a perfect cover-up for the Resistance Party, taking advantage of his position as a quiet, disinterested farmer. Across the street from Franco's house, located at the edge of the village, was another house, the perfect spot for the Resistance to watch for unwanted visitors. The people in that house kept an eye on the traveling members that rested in Franco's barn. It was important for these travelers to have a safe hiding place before heading to their next destination.

Franco was unaware of the Resistance Party watching him and his family, although the party was only there for his protection. The Party kept an eye out because of the importance of Franco's job, allowing the travelers to stay and rest in his barn.

Franco's family made him look harmless to the enemy, but Franco knew the danger in which he put his family by being involved in this activity. He was very aware and concerned about being found out. He knew the potential consequences of his actions, but he had to do his part to protect his fellow Sicilians.

Franco prayed for the safety of his family, and he prayed diligently for himself that the enemy wouldn't capture him. If captured, his family would be tortured horrendously. The Resistance Party had agreed that if any member was caught and, if his family could not be hidden before being apprehended by the enemy, the family would meet their deaths. The deaths of these people, by the Resistance, would be undertaken as painlessly as possible. Franco's family was included. The price was great, but the Resistance Party thrived, working secretly and efficiently. The hope was that the outcome of this war would give their families a free and economically better life.

Wealthy family members and Mafia members who had hidden from the enemies during and before the First World War, built homes throughout the island with secret stairwells and hidden underground rooms. At every turn Franco and Saverino's eyes darted in all directions as they entered one of the buildings known to certain villagers.

The outside of the building was intentionally uncared for and unattended to distract any dangerous on-lookers. Beneath ground-level was a strong and structurally secure space. It was here that countrymen who owned the buildings shared secrets with the resistance party—the occupants. In these desperate times, the building was given to the Mafia to be used appropriately. If discovered, it would be destroyed to protect surviving Party members.

Franco separated a low brush that covered the entrance to the building and then he and Saverino waited a minute before entering to look around and make sure it was safe before they slipped in. They slowly stepped down into the depth of the stone stairwell and waited for their eyes to adjust to the dim light, proceeding with caution. The strong odor of mold and mildew hit their nostrils and turned their stomachs. At the bottom of the stairwell, they turned right into a narrow passageway and carefully opened another door that led into a second dark, long, narrow stairwell. Franco shut the door behind them.

Franco felt the cold wall and pressed his thumb against a stone by his knee. The stone released a small hidden trap door that went through to the other side of the wall. Franco and Saverino listened for sounds of footsteps but heard none. They crouched down on the stairwell landing and entered crawled into the secret space and then Saverino shut the door with his feet, leaving its entrance undetected.

They crawled several feet in this cramped space, came to another trap door, knocked three times and then waited for a return knock. If it didn't come, they knew they could survive in this hole, if needed, for a long time. It held plenty of fresh air; and if this secret room behind the trapped hole was discovered, they could return to the stairwell fairly safely. The knock was returned and the trapdoor opened. Franco and Saverino entered a large lit room. The trapdoor was then securely closed and locked by one of the occupants.

In the room were tables, several chairs, and two sleeping cots against the wall. Ashtrays filled with stale cigarette butts were on every table along with guns, bullets, and grenades. Radio and communication equipment was sitting on a small table by one of the walls. A high-tech radio was on, and the radio announcer was talking about the happenings at the Normandy beaches. The reporter was stated that the progress the Americans were making was slow, but they were indeed making progress.

The people in the room were listening intently to the radio and no one turned to greet Franco and Saverino as they entered the room. Franco walked over to the table in the center of the cool room and sat down. The smell of mildew and mold that had been so strong in the stairwell was almost entirely gone in the secret room. Even with the ashtrays full of cigarette butts, the stale nicotine smell was minimal. The room was so architecturally well-built that no one knew how fresh air was ventilated into the building. Franco admired how the old building was so well insulated and comfortable. He was fascinated by its twists and turns and hoped that someday, when it was safe, he would return to this building and explore all its secret rooms.

While Franco sat comfortably at the table, Saverino walked over to take a seat on one of the cots. One of the men sitting at the radio table turned to nod at both of them

The room remained quiet for a few minutes until the man who had acknowledged them reached his hand out to the radio and lowered the sound. This small, thin, muscular man with a balding forehead and graying was about the same age as Franco. He turned again to Franco and smiled. "It's good to see you my dear friends." He got up to go and sit across from Franco at his table. "This is a good day for the war. The Americans and all the allies are starting to reach beyond the beaches of Normandy."

The man was known to Franco and Saverino only as Marco. He was a member of the Resistance and had been the leader of the Mafia in his earlier days before the war. Marco handed Franco an American cigarette, and Franco greedily took it. He put the cigarette to his mouth and Marco lit it for him. Franco took a deep drag, enjoying its flavor and the strong smoke as it touched his lungs. It had been some time since he had a good cigarette, let alone an American one. There were other men in the room, including Dr. Capetti and several village merchants, but Marco controlled the conversation and made all the commands.

"I see that you, my brothers, are well," said Marco, looking at Saverino and Franco. "I have news from the High Command." The High Command was known only by Marco and remained anonymous to the rest of the immediate Party members. Many dangerous missions had been performed by the present members in the hidden room, including Saverino, but because Franco and Saverino had so much to lose, their duties in the Party were typically minimal and less dangerous.

Marco looked seriously into Franco's eyes and said, "Franco, I have been told to ask you to step down from the Party. The High Command feels it is getting close to the end of the war and the few enemies left on our island are more hostile than before. There is deep concern that you'll be found out and our constituents don't want any harm to come to you or your family. If you had sons it would be easier— but daughters, and so many daughters—that's different." Franco's eyes widened with surprise and he looked at Marco with disappointment.

"Franco, the night that your oldest daughter took your baby to Dr. Capetti, we got the signal. We watched to make sure she got to the doctor's office safely," said Marco.

Franco asked, "Was the German soldier who shot the farmer and his son in the center of the village during harvest time–was he the one that was killed that night?"

"Yes," Marco replied. "He was a foolish, dangerous, nervous kid. He got what he deserved. He had to be dealt with."

"Who in the Party killed him and those other German soldiers that night?" Franco asked.

Marco tilted his head, shrugged his shoulders and asked, "Does it matter, Franco?"

Franco took a deep breath and responded, "No, it doesn't matter. Thank you for ensuring the safety of my daughters."

Marco knew that watching over the safety of Franco's daughters was a small commitment to a Party member that needed to be fulfilled. He couldn't afford to have his men lose a family member during this war. Marco knew that the safety of one family member meant the safety of all the members of the Resistance Party. "We will still protect your family in case of an emergency. We'll be around all the time. If your services are needed, we will contact you," Marco advised.

Franco had known it was only a matter of time before he'd be asked to leave the Resistance Party because he had only daughters. He flicked the ashes from his cigarette into a tray in the center of the table and asked, "Am I not needed to help in any way?"

"Oh yes," Marco replied, "you'll be needed, but not so openly. We still need you to take our people in, hide them, and feed them while they are en route. You'll receive fewer visitors, but on occasion they will rest in your barn. Franco, it's important that you do not attend any more of these meetings. It's too dangerous for you and your family. You know what we have to do if you should get captured."

Dr. Capetti was one of the members of the Resistance Party who knew about most of the involvements, and he helped to carry out those dangerous missions. He said, "Franco, I know how you feel and how you want to be involved. At this point in the war, if you're found out, it will be hard for us to live with the death of you and your family. But we still need your help to get our people safely to other towns. Your house is the safest path for them to rest and eat a little. If we keep up our transport of important messages, we have a good chance of defeating the Germans here on our island. It is imperative that our people get safely to where they are needed."

Franco looked at all the men in the room and said that he understood and would do his best to help when they needed him.

The decision had been made and all was said and done. Once Franco was out of earshot, Marco turned to Dr. Capetti and said, "It's best that Franco doesn't know how close his daughters were to falling victim to brutality. For them and even the baby, rape and murder were inevitable. We did to those German soldiers what needed to be done. Now that the war is at this stage, and the Germans are starting to lose their individual self-control, we must keep Franco calm for he is desperately needed for our travelers; we have to assure him that his family is safe. He doesn't realize how much we need him in that area of our work. His home is a safe haven for our people and we still have our hidden view of his house from the house across the street. The house gives us a great advantage for keeping our Party safe and for keeping peace in the village."

"Marco, is it fair to use Franco and his family this way?" asked Dr. Capetti.

Marco took a cigarette from his pocket and offered one to the doctor, who politely refused. Marco lit his cigarette and said, "Franco and his family have been the lucky ones in this war, to have constant protection. His daughters have especially benefitted from us watching their house."

"But," Dr. Capetti replied, "he's been an excellent Party member with more to lose than the rest of us. Is it fair not to tell him about the protection and let him rest a bit?"

"No, my friend," Marco said, "it's more dangerous for him and his family. We need him to be alert and aware of his surrounding at all times. We cannot afford any suspicion aimed at him. If he looks less stressed than the other village people, it might draw the Germans' attention to him. This way is the best. No one will rest until this war is over."

That evening, in the secret room in the dilapidated building,

Marco sat alone and thought about his day. He thought about how much Dr. Capetti didn't know–all the secret operations in which he was involved on this island. Marco had direct involvement with a high-level Mafia member, Don Calogero Vizzini, a Sicilian Mafia member who kept in constant communication with an imprisoned Mafia leader, Lucky Luciano, in America.

Lucky Luciano had been in an undesirable prison but after cooperating with the U.S. Military, they sent him to a better prison in Albany, New York. While serving his prison time, Lucky Luciano was visited regularly by military officers. With his influence in Sicily, and with the help of Don Calogero Vizzini, Lucky Luciano provided the Americans with the layout of the land in Sicily. The information he offered enabled the Americans to take Sicily from Germany, and to capture the Italian Communists with little resistance. The Mafia protected the roads, and the Mafia snipers protected the advancing troops. They provided guides through the confusing mountain terrain.

It was documented, at that time in the history of Sicily and World War II that Don Calogero Vizzini, aboard an American tank, spent six days traveling through western Sicily with the American troops. He traveled through Bisacquino with the Americans, and Marco was aware of his movement before he reached the village. He directed spies who were housed across from Franco's home, and other contacts around the village to prepare for the Americans' safe journey. These spies travelled safely and without any disturbances. Safely traveling through the territory, the Americans conquered the next village with no resistance from the Germans or the Italian Communists.

During this time it was never noted how extremely important the Mafia was on the island, nor the large impact they had on the Americans obtaining control of Sicily. In the future, this part of the war would never be acknowledged, only briefly mentioned in history books.

Chapter Ten

F ranco bent over to get a bucket of water for his mule. He took a long drag on the cigarette he had hanging out of his mouth and thought of the war, as always. Franco's body was tired, his head ached, and he was sleep deprived and in a state of constant worry. It was August of 1944, and Franco felt like it had been years since Maria was born, rather than only a few months.

The night was hot and sticky, and Franco's clothes stuck to his skin. He worried about providing enough food during the war and enough warmth during the cold, upcoming winter. These concerns weighed heavily on him.

In one respect, he was glad that he was asked to step down from the Resistance Party; there would be less pressure on him. As Franco sat on the edge of the well, taking in the night's muggy air and smoking his cigarette, he thought of Anna. He hadn't been intimate with her since Maria was born. He craved her smell and longed to hold her and feel her warmth. His longing, emotional thoughts for his wife were interrupted by a noise coming from the barn.

Franco automatically looked to see if his daughters were in the yard. He knew they weren't, because it was dark and past their bedtime, but out of parental instinct and fear for their safety at this dangerous time, he looked around before walking to the barn. Franco snuffed out his half-smoked cigarette and saved it for later. He picked up his bucket of water and headed to the barn. Once inside, he shut the door behind him and walked over to a pile of hay. He set the bucket of water down and began to walk away to find what little food he could offer a visitor when he heard a moan. He stopped to listen and heard the soft, controlled moan again.

Franco's heart raced as he stood very still. A voice called out to him. Franco went to a pile of hay, knelt down, and pulled some of the hay back. There on the mound was Saverino's oldest son Mario. Franco was shocked to see him there, and then noticed that Mario was holding his shoulder, trying to stop the bleeding of a large wound. Blood ran through his fingers and down his chest.

"What is this?" Franco asked. "Who did this to you? Let me get you up and take you home."

Mario, trying not to show his pain, whispered, "Signore Gennusa, you must not tell my father. He thinks I'm in Chiusa Sclafani working. He doesn't know that I am a member of the Resistance Party."

"You're a part of what?" asked Franco. But before Mario had a chance to answer, Franco said, "I'll go to the house and get some clean towels."

Mario nodded his head and Franco rushed into the kitchen. No one around and he was grateful that his family was asleep, for he did not need any confrontations. He went to the kitchen sink and picked up some dry cloths and cleansing soap. He returned to the barn and hastily opened the door, then closed it quietly behind him and went to Mario. He dipped the cloths in the bucket of water and lathered them with soap.

"Mario," said Franco, "you must be very still as I clean your wound. It's imperative that you don't wake my family." Franco started to wash the blood from Mario's shoulder and Mario made a terrible face, biting down hard and trying not to yell out in pain. The cleansing of the wound took only a few minutes; and when the process was finished Franco said, "I don't have any medicine to put on this but if it's kept clean you should be alright. I'll wrap the wound the best I can."

"Thank you, Signore Gennusa," Mario said.

"Mario, you must get home quickly so this wound can be looked after," said Franco.

"I'm so sorry for you and your family, for my being here; but I had nowhere else to go. I knew that you worked with the Resistance Party and that you would help me." Mario said.

Franco looked puzzled, "How do you know that?"

Mario, holding back the pain, grunted to Franco, "I've been part of the Party for several months. I knew the Resistance asked you not to attend any more meetings because of the danger to your family. They were very concerned for your daughters."

Franco looked at Mario and exclaimed, "I don't understand."

The members were willing to let me be more active because you were asked to step down to take me because they needed to replace you. I asked that my father not be told because I'm only fifteen and knew he would strongly object. We, the Party, did this in secrecy."

"Mario, you must tell your father that you're a part of the Party. If anything happens to you, your father has the right to know," Franco said.

"It's too dangerous for my parents to know. You must keep this to yourself, Signore Gennusa, for you owe it to the Party. Remember that the safety of the Party comes first, before the safety of a Party member. My brother is young and so affected by this war. He is innocent and watched closely by my father. I wouldn't want him to know, if anything should happen to me, that I'm a Party member. We are very close. I don't want him to have to live with my decision to be part of the Party, thinking he could have protected me for the rest of his life if I don't live to the end of this war," Mario said.

Franco knew that Mario was right. "What else can I do for you?" he asked. Mario said in a low voice, "Go back into your house and forget that I was here. Let me do my job and please, if anything happens to me, stay close to my parents. My father honors your friendship. Goodnight, Signore Gennusa. I'll see you soon," Mario said.

Troubled and weary, Franco got up from his knees, turned to the door and walked out of the barn without looking back at Mario. Once in the house, Franco walked over to the kitchen sink and reached in the cupboard for a bottle of wine. He got a glass and poured wine into it. He took large gulps of wine to calm his nerves, and carried the jug of wine with his glass to the table where he drank two more glasses, the second quickly and the third slower.

Franco couldn't feel the warmth of the wine sliding down his throat the way he had only a few months before. He was numb. He sat in the quiet of his kitchen for a long time before going to his bedroom and when he did, he lie down on the bed and restlessly fell to sleep.

Franco woke with a start at the crack of dawn. He jumped out of bed, awakening Anna who beckoned him back to bed.

Franco sat at the edge of the bed holding his head in pain from the wine he'd drunk the night before.

When he got his thoughts together, he headed straight to the kitchen, not taking any time to enjoy the sun shining through the windows, and out the door. He went to the barn, to his mule to pat the animal's head. He needed a few minutes to collect his thoughts from the night before.

Franco looked at the hay and a saw some of the cloths he'd used to clean Mario lying on the ground. He picked up the blood-stained material, rolled it in a ball, and headed out to the back yard. His head was pounding when he bent down to the ground and, with his bare hands, dug a hole in the corner of his property. After burying the bloody cloth, he went to his well, and then soaked his hands in the water until all the evidence on his hands and fingernails of digging in the dirt was gone.

ᔕ

Back in the house, Franco was greeted by his wife. "Franco," Anna said, "is there something wrong? You were so abrupt this morning getting out of bed. Is there anything I can do for you? Let me help when I can."

"Why are you always so perfect and why do you always think you can fix everything? No, I don't need your help. I can handle it myself," Franco said angrily.

Anna was quite surprised at Franco's harsh manner. She didn't answer, but just walked over to the stove and started to make coffee.

Franco watched his wife and said in a loud voice, "I hate weak coffee, I hate secrets, I hate this war," and then stormed out the door to the barn.

Anna turned to watch her husband and saw her older daughters standing in the doorway of their bedroom. "Mamma," Teresa said, "what's wrong with Pappa? He's been so hard to talk to since Maria was born."

Anna looked at her daughters, knowing well that Franco hadn't been himself for a long time, and replied, "It's this war. It's been hard on all of us. There are so many dangers that your father hides from all of us." Anna put her hand in the pocket of her apron, feeling around for her spool of thread and held it tight. "I think it has taken its toll. We must be patient with your father, for he carries so many burdens."

Teresa moved over to her mother and started to take the coffee pot from her hands. The strain on Anna's face was evident. Teresa hoped that her mother knew that she and Pina would help in any way possible. All three turned at once to the crying coming from the bedroom. Pina said, "Mamma, I'll get the baby and feed her."

Anna smiled at her second oldest daughter, still holding her spool of thread, and said, "Thank you, my daughter."

Franco headed to the center of town, desperate to hear the latest news of the war. He needed to forget the burden he carried from last night, needed peace in his life and to breathe calm air again.

At the center of the village, there was not activity. He stayed close to an open doorway and looked around, but seeing nothing, decided to head back to his house. He stayed close to the houses as he walked up the street and looked in all directions to make sure it was safe.

He was approaching Saverino's house when he heard someone call his name. He looked around but didn't see anyone. Still anxious from the night before, he walked carefully and knocked on Saverino's door. The door opened slightly at the sound of his knock and he stepped inside. Deanna was standing behind the door and pushed it closed behind Franco.

"Deanna, is everything alright here?" He continued, "Oh, I know that Saverino isn't home. He told me he was going to Palermo for some trading."

"Yes," Deanna answered, "he thinks he's so sly."

Franco looked surprised and, thinking that Deanna suspected that her husband was in the Resistance Party, asked hesitantly, "What do you mean that Saverino is so sly?"

"I know that he has received food from someone who got the food from the Americans after they arrived at the Capitol. I know he's been handing out food to the Sicilians. I know who he's giving to. I just don't know who he's getting the food from. I heard people talk at the village center. They didn't know I was listening," Deanna said.

Franco, a little frightened, asked "Did these people say anything more?"

Deanna stepped closer to Franco and said, "No."

Franco took one step back toward the door. With his back up against the door, he was trapped as Deanna took another step toward him. He closed his eyes for a second and smelled Deanna's scented hair.

"Franco," Deanna whispered, and she got closer. She rested her head on his chest, put her arm around his neck, and started to rub her breasts against him. "My Mario is up in bed asleep. He isn't feeling well today."

Franco was surprised, and sweat started dripping from his armpits. "Mario is home safe?"

"Yes, Franco, my beloved Mario is home. Why do you sound so surprised?" Before Deanna gave Franco a chance to answer her question, she said that Mario had asked to stay in bed. "I heard him moaning this morning, but he assured me he only had a stomach ache. I just checked on him, and my angel is asleep."

Franco wondered when and how Mario had gotten home. How did he get into his bedroom without his mother noticing? How could Deanna not see his wound? He wondered if Mario had somehow made it to Dr. Capetti for help.

Deanna put her hand on Franco's leg and started to move it up toward his groin area, looking straight into his eyes. Franco moaned as Deanna touched his penis and Deanna continued to stroke him. "He would never hear us."

Franco felt Deanna's warm body next to his and it excited him, but he pushed her away and said, "I have to go." Franco stepped aside and turned his back to Deanna. She grabbed his arm and pressed herself against his back.

"Please don't go," Deanna said, as he opened the door.

Franco moved away from her and quickly left the house. Ashamed and flushed at what had just happened, he hurried over to his back yard, wanting desperately to be alone. He couldn't get her out of his mind; her smell made Franco feel guilty as he thought of what a good friend he had in Saverino, Deanna's husband.

He spent the remainder of the day in the barn cleaning and tending to his mule. He didn't want to be near his family. He needed some space; and cleaning his barn, for some reason, gave him a sense of peace.

The day fell into night and Franco sat on the wall of his well in the backyard in solitude. Gazing into the night sky, thinking about Deanna, he put his hands into the well, soaked them and washed them thoroughly. He splashed cool water on his face and started to relax.

Franco heard Anna walk into the yard. She walked over to the well and sat beside him. "It's such a hot night," she said.

He looked at his wife, put his arm around her and brought her close to him. He felt extremely safe when she was near.

"Anna," Franco said, "you know how much I love you. I'm sorry for being so difficult this morning."

Anna touched his arm and said, "Shhhhhh, there's no need to apologize. This war is hard on all of us. Was there trouble in the center of the town?"

Franco shook his head and responded, "No, it's very quiet there. Sometimes when there is no shooting, I forget there is a war going on."

"I know. Sometimes when the war is quiet, I feel normal; I forget," Anna said.

Franco asked, "Where are our daughters?"

"They're safe inside the house, trying very hard to be quiet. Our lives were so simple when there was no war. I'm so sick of this war, Franco. I'm sick of what war does to people."

Franco, thinking of Deanna and Mario, and what had occurred earlier that day, took a deep breath.

"Come to the house and I'll make some delicious, weak," Anna started to giggle while talking, "very weak coffee."

Smiling at his wife, Franco said "That sounds good, even on a hot night." They walked into the house casually, arm in arm. It was good to hear his wife giggle, Franco thought, as he and Anna walked into their house. Somehow Anna always made life lighter and better for him, even during war time. Somehow, he always felt stronger when she was near.

Chapter Eleven

Olive harvest time was again upon the island and the islanders scurried in the cold, damp months to harvest their crops. On one cold September night in 1944, when the day's work was done, Dino, the older son of the DiGorios, had come into the farmhouse. He had returned from the monastery to tell Franco, Anna, and his parents the latest news about the war. He was anxious as he spoke of a traveler at the monastery who was resting for the evening. The traveler had news that Hitler had lost both Sicily and North Africa due to the incompetence of Field Marshall Erwin Rommel, and that the Marshall was being sent back to Germany.

Franco listened to Dino and wondered how the traveler could have obtained such news. News like this was only privy to inside military personnel or the highest ranks of the Resistance Party.

Anna asked Franco, "What you think this means?" Puzzled, Franco turned and asked, "Vincenzo, tell us what you think this means."

Vincenzo answered, "It sounds like the Germans are losing the island, and they might be leaving soon. It could be a big defeat for the Germans."

"Franco," Anna questioned, "does that mean the Germans will be leaving Sicily?"

"It means that we must be even more careful. Danger is imminent, even if the Americans are here. Instead of one of us staying up at night watching, there will be two of us at all times. Vincenzo, you and Lucia take the first shift. Now let the rest of us get some sleep," Franco directed.

The families had started to get ready for bed and Franco lingered over by the fire, smoking his last cigarette of the night. Dino took the opportunity to speak to him in private. "Signore Gennusa, the traveler at the monastery asked me to convey a message to you."

Surprised, Franco asked, "To me?"

"Yes," Dino replied in a low and nervous voice.

Confused, Franco asked, "What did he want you to tell me?"

"This person is seriously injured from several bullets, and he's dying. He wants you to make sure you see him," said Dino.

"What does this person look like?" asked Franco.

Dino, with concern, replied, "I don't know. I didn't see him, but he asked one of the nuns to relate that to me. He's spreading the news of Hitler's loss of Sicily and North Africa. He said he knew you and your family well. He also asked me to relate this message in private so as not to put your family in danger. The nun said for you to come as soon as possible, for he will not live long."

Franco looked at Dino with concern, trying hard to figure out who the dying man could be. Franco said to Dino, "When the family is asleep I will go to the monastery. If I'm not back by daylight, tell your father where I've gone. Make sure the families don't leave the house unless your father knows for sure that there is no danger outside. Do you understand, Dino?"

"Yes, Signore Gennusa," Dino replied.

A short time later, everyone was sleeping except Vincenzo and Lucia who were still on lookout when Franco snuck out the back door into the cold and damp night. He looked behind him as he left to make sure the DiGorios hadn't seen him leave and then headed toward the olive grove in the dark.

Franco pulled the collar to his jacket up high, holding it over his ears. He followed a narrow path through small brush that headed up into a high rocky hill. It was hard to see on this concealed path and there were no stars in the sky, but Franco knew his way well. He reached the top of the hill and walked to the monastery's front door. He approached an old, large, thick wooden door and tapped on the heavy iron handle that hung in the middle. Knowing that a nun was expecting him, he waited until finally, the nun opened up a small hatch door and inspected him. After recognizing Franco, she opened the door quickly and quietly.

With no communication, Franco was let through and once the door was closed, the nun led the way and Franco followed.

They walked in silence through an open courtyard that was the center of the monastery. They approached another heavy wooden door and entered, the nun leading the way through a dim hallway lit only by candles. They came to a doorway that led to stairs which they descended down to a small kitchen.

The kitchen had a small wooden table in the center of the room, a small fireplace for cooking against a wall, and many iron and clay pots on the floor. The nun walked over to a large floor-to-ceiling shelf that was built into the wall. The nun removed a heavy pot and placed it on a small table, revealing a lever hidden inside the center of the shelf. The nun pulled the lever, and the shelf started to move forward, opening to a hidden room. The nun made a sign for Franco to enter.

The nun stayed in the kitchen as Franco entered through the door and was greeted by Sister Maria wearing an old blanket draped over her shoulders. After the heavy door shut behind him, Franco saw in the room a single bed next to an end table with a single lit candle sitting on top.

The room was damp and cold and Franco shivered from its frigid temperature. The man in the single bed was wrapped it several old blankets. Sister said to Franco, "This man insists on speaking to you. The only reason I allowed Dino to come for you was because the traveler knows so much about you and your family. I've been frightened for you and your family's safety ever since he came through the monastery door. I didn't know what to do. He wouldn't tell me who he is, or how he got hurt."

Sister Maria stayed by the door as Franco slowly approached the bed, smelling death with each step. He moved toward the injured man and stopped at the side of the bed, his heart racing from fear at who—or what—he might find. Franco looked at the dying man's face and had to catch his breath when he focused his eyes on his dear friend and neighbor, Saverino. Franco moved closer to his friend and whispered into his ear, "Saverino." A little louder, Franco repeated, "Saverino, it's me, Franco. You sent for me. I'm here my friend."

Saverino opened his eyes and said weakly, "Franco, thank God you have come." He stopped talking, took a breath, and continued, "I need help. Come closer to me...I need to speak to you privately."

Slowly, Franco approached him, "What is it, Saverino, how can I help you?"

Saverino, in his dying words, said, "Franco, I need you to take me home. I cannot be found here in the monastery. They're everywhere. They're looking for me." Saverino stopped to rest for a moment and then continued, "If I'm found they'll know I'm part of the Resistance Party. That will endanger the Party. The members will be hunted and murdered. We must do what it takes to protect the Party."

"Who is looking for you?" Franco asked urgently.

Saverino replied weakly, "The Germans."

Franco, shaken by what Saverino said, replied, "You're too sick. You need medical care. Your wounds are deep and you have lost so much blood. These nuns can nurse you back to good health. You can't be moved."

Saverino whispered to Franco, "There isn't much time. I have to leave here before the Germans come. If I'm found here, the nuns will be killed. It's safer for the nuns and the Party if I'm found dead in my own backyard. You have an obligation to the Party to get me home. Whether I live or die doesn't matter."

"I no longer have obligation to the Party," Franco exclaimed, "but I do to you."

"Yes, my friend, you do have obligations to the Party, and their success in helping to defeat the Germans. It is everyone's obligation. Hitler cannot win this war. What matters now is that I leave quickly and get home without being detected. Please, think of your family. The Germans are very near."

"Are you the traveler who has been telling the people of Hitler's defeat?" Franco asked.

"Yes," Saverino replied.

Franco shook his head and insisted, "No, I need more from you. I need you to tell me who did this to you."

Saverino, very weakly, pleaded, "I was a member of the Italian Communist Party. This person somehow found out about my being in the Resistance Party and came after me. I can't tell you his name—there can be no connection to you. You're still valuable to the Party. Please Franco, hurry and get me home," Saverino cried urgently.

"No, I won't move you," Franco said. "I have no involvement in the Party. You, my friend, come first."

Saverino, barely able to speak, started to beg, "Please, Franco, as your friend, take me home where I can die in my own backyard." Barely able to speak, Saverino whispered, "Please, Franco, I want to go home."

Franco, with tears in his eyes and a heavy heart, straightened up from the bed and walked over to Sister Maria. "Sister, it is imperative that I take this man out of the monastery immediately. He is being hunted by the Germans and the Italian Communists. If he is caught, many people will die at the hands of the Germans, including your people. I'm going to go to the farmhouse to hitch up my mule and come back for him."

"No," Sister Maria exclaimed, "there is no time, for I have gotten word that the Germans are close. Do what has to be done, but it has to be done now."

"Sister Maria," cried a nun, "we have unwelcome visitors at the main entrance. They sound like German soldiers."

Sister Maria said to the nun, "Go to the main door and open the porthole. Talk slowly to the soldiers and stall them. I need a few minutes to get these men through the escape door. Take your time, and Sister, do not let them see that you are alarmed. Let them search the whole monastery if needed. Just do it calmly, and I'll catch up with you as soon as these men are safe. Do you understand me?"

The nun bowed her head and headed up the stairs slowly, as ordered.

Sister Maria turned to Franco and whispered, "The Germans are here."

Franco walked over to Saverino, wrapped him in a warm blanket. Saverino moaned from the pain as Franco secured him. "Sister, is there another way out besides the front door?"

"Yes," Sister whispered, "stay behind me."

Sister Maria and Franco started walking quickly. Sister turned to Franco and said "Stay close to me, my son, for these many tunnels will surely absorb you into oblivion. Only a few of us know the way."

Franco carried Saverino through several dark hallways, through many doors, and down many narrow stairwells, following Sister Maria who lit their way, carrying only one candle. They went deeper into the caves of the monastery, and the deeper and darker the area became, the heavier the smell of mold and mildew. After many turns they ended up in front of a small, thick door that opened to the outside. It was located on a stony hill close to his house. After the small door was opened, and some dense heavy bushes pushed aside, they stood in the dark on the outside of the monastery. "Thank you, Sister," Franco said.

Sister said to Franco, "Be careful, go slowly, and try not to make any sounds. I'll take care of the German soldiers and—"

Franco interrupted, "Sister, my family?"

Sister finished, "I'll direct the soldiers away from the farmhouse. May God be with you."

Franco carried Saverino to his farmhouse. It wasn't far, but the weight of Saverino's body was exhausting to Franco.

He approached the house and went to the stable where the mule and cart stood, and then placed Saverino on the ground in the corner of the stable and told him he would be right back.

Franco walked quickly and quietly across the yard, and went undetected into the house. He walked directly to Vincenzo, who was seated on the hard stone floor by the door, drinking weak coffee. Franco asked where Lucia was, and Vincenzo responded that she was at the outhouse. Franco brought his finger to his mouth and whispered, "Shhhhhh, there are German soldiers around the monastery. We must be very quiet."

Vincenzo was frightened. He started to question but Franco interrupted, "Go to the outhouse and bring Lucia back quickly. Bring her to the house and then come to the stable. You must hurry."

Vincenzo went quickly to the outhouse and then hurried back with Lucia into the kitchen.

"Vincenzo, what is it?" she asked, "I see such fear in your eyes."

"I am not sure," Vincenzo said, "but I'll find out. Stay in the house."

Vincenzo headed out to the stable to find Franco hitching up his cart and a man on the ground next to the mule. "Franco, what's going on?"

Franco looked at Vincenzo, "I need your help. I need to go to the village right away. You must trust me and not ask any questions. The Germans are all around us and I need you to stay in the house and keep everyone quiet. If the Germans come around the house, keep our families still. I'll be back before morning. There are lives at stake, and that is all I can say. Don't worry; I'll be back safe. Now go into the house and do not watch me leave."

Vincenzo headed into the house as directed.

Franco finished hitching up his mule, picked up his dying friend, and slowly and gently put him in the back of the cart. Then he walked around to the front of the mule, took his reins and led him slowly away from the farmhouse. When Franco felt he was a safe enough distance away from the house, he climbed into the cart and headed toward the village. He stopped several times to check on Saverino and found him still alive. Halfway to their destination, Franco thought he heard shots in the distance, and the mule heard them too because he stopped abruptly. Franco climbed down from the cart and walked to the mule. He patted his head and tried to calm the animal.

Franco's touch and hand movements always calmed the mule. Listening, he heard nothing in the distance and the mule seemed to be calmed down so Franco got back into the cart. After several miles he entered the village and all was frightfully quiet aside from the sound of the mule's hooves echoing through the narrow streets.

When Franco approached his home safely, he tied up the mule by the barn and quickly got a bucket of water which the mule drank thirstily. Franco knew that while the mule drank, it would stay quiet. He went to the side of the cart and took Saverino into his arms. He could see that Saverino was barely breathing as he carried his friend into the barn and placed him on the ground. Franco bent down to Saverino and whispered into his ear. "Saverino, you are home."

Saverino, with difficultly, said to Franco, "You must take me into my yard and leave me there."

Franco said, "I can't leave you to die alone."

Saverino insisted, "You know you must!" He coughed several times, hesitated and continued, "There cannot be any link between us. It's too dangerous. The Party must come first."

"What about your family?" Franco asked.

"Deanna and my boys will bury me in the backyard when they find me dead in the morning. They'll know not to have an open funeral. There will be no questions. No one will miss me until the war is over. Our families need not to be questioned by the Germans for any reason. Saverino hesitated again and gasped for another breath. "Franco, you've been such a good friend. I can't ask you to watch over my family, for already you have so many to watch. Just remind my sons during their growing years how much I loved them."

Saverino closed his eyes for a few seconds, having difficulty breathing. Regaining a little strength, Saverino opened his eyes and, with his last breath, whispered, "Goodbye, my good friend. Thank you for bringing me home." Saverino closed his eyes for the last time, and Franco knew his friend was gone.

Franco couldn't believe that his long-time friend was dead. He picked up Saverino in his arms and held him tightly, trying in vain to control his crying. He carefully carried him through bushes that separated their two properties In Saverino's backyard, Franco heard a soft noise coming from the house. Franco stopped; he quickly bent down and placed Saverino on the cold ground and then waited for a few minutes. The back yard was dark and it was hard to see if there was anyone else there. After a few seconds of silence, Franco bent over Saverino's dead body and kissed his beloved friend on the cheek. He said a silent prayer and wished him farewell before walking out of the yard, his legs heavy like stones.

Franco walked to his barn, not feeling the cold wind that blew through his hair. He did not hear the night sounds as the world spun on its axis. He could not feel his heart beating, for he felt numb. Franco approached his cart and didn't pat his mule on its head as usual, but got into his cart and silently started back to his farmhouse.

Early the next morning Franco reached his farm with no interferences from the war going on around him. He walked into the kitchen while the whole family was still asleep, except Vincenzo and Lucia, who got up from the kitchen table to greet him. Vincenzo couldn't help but see that Franco was very tired. He looked into Franco's face and, for the first time, Franco looked old and haggard. Not only did Franco's face look old, but his posture was slightly bent.

Vincenzo asked Lucia to leave them alone. Lucia, obeying her husband, watched as Franco approached the table. She had also noticed the evident change in Franco in the last twenty-four hours. Vincenzo poured Franco a hot cup of coffee and Franco drank it down fast. There were no words spoken, for words could not explain the pain Franco showed on his face.

A few minutes after Franco drank his coffee, the first of his youngest daughters woke up. They ran to their father and hugged him and he returned the hug, lovingly and gratefully.

That morning, as everyone worked in the grove, Anna had noticed that Franco looked more tired and was quiet and withdrawn. She was concerned, for Franco had acted differently at breakfast. She wasn't sure what caused the change, but it worried her.

Anna was working with her daughter, Teresa, when she decided to go and work with Franco. She walked through several rows of olive trees, heading toward her husband. She tightened her coat around her, blocking the damp, cold, blowing wind, and light rain.

"Pina," she called, "go and work with Teresa, please."

Anna walked to Franco and stood close to him. She didn't say a word, but worked diligently by his side for the remainder of the day.

Chapter Twelve

A lthough the island was steadily quieting down during October 1944, the Red Army was moving west in Europe and the Nazis were being pushed back to Berlin. Meanwhile, in the Gennusa house, Anna watched as her two youngest children played together late on a chilly afternoon. Maria, now seven months old, sat up with a blanket supporting her back. Innocenza, a little over two years old, was walking and rolling as she played with her baby sister.

Innocenza had recovered perfectly from her episode of pneumonia during the birth of Maria. She was a good older sister and didn't mind her hair being pulled and sucked on by baby Maria, who was her entertainment and her best friend. Anna watched with delight as the daughters cuddled and giggled on the floor.

Anna looked at these two children and acknowledged the difference in her two daughters' complexions; Maria with her fair skin, light-blonde curly hair, and bright, blue eyes; and Innocenza, who was darker skinned, had dark curly hair, and very deep dark eyes with thick eyelashes. They were equally beautiful, but dramatically opposite.

Anna recalled Franco's look of surprise when he first saw Innocenza as a newborn baby, a reaction that even after a few years, hurt Anna. She knew that Franco loved the child—it was hard not to love Innocenza, for she had an easy-going personality that garnered her more attention than Maria from the older sisters. But Franco's unusual behavior at Innocenza's birth shocked and hurt Anna, and she had carried that feeling with her.

In the late afternoon, the older daughters were in the kitchen preparing dinner when Franco came into the house. It was obvious that he'd been indulging in his wine. Franco walked over to the cupboard and took his jug of wine and poured himself a large glass. Lately, his drinking was more frequent and Anna was becoming concerned. "Franco, dinner will be ready soon," she said.

"I'm not hungry." He carried the wine into his bedroom and shut the door.

Anna watched helplessly as he disappeared. She then turned to her daughters and directed them to put plates on the table. Anna went to the stove to stir the pot with one hand, and with the other, reached into her pocket and rubbed her spool of thread, finding solace in its familiar touch.

As the afternoon fell into night, Anna instructed her older daughters to clean the kitchen after they had finished dinner, and then get ready for bed. Anna went to her bedroom where she found Franco sitting in the rocking chair by the window, staring out at the night. His empty glass was on the floor beside him. Anna went to the nightstand and lit a candle, creating a gentle glow in the room. Without saying a word, she walked over to Franco and put her arm around his shoulders. Franco didn't move at first, but then, responding to Anna's warmth, he reached out and touched her soft hand, rubbing it and momentarily enjoying the bonding between them.

Franco was distracted and lost in thought about his friend Saverino, and burdened by questions and uncertainties. *Why did I take him home and not to Dr. Capetti on the night of his death? How could his life have endangered the Resistance Party? What was going on around the farm that caused the Germans to be after him? Did I do the right thing by letting him die? Now his sons will have no father to watch them grow into men.* All these thoughts and questions swirled in his mind, and Franco knew he would never have the answers.

"Franco," Anna said, "I know you've been troubled since the death of Saverino. Is there anything I can do to help you endure your loss?"

Anna's question brought him back to reality. He gently rubbed her hand again and said, "I don't know. It's this war. It has taken away so much of the life we used to know."

Franco got up from the chair and put his arms around Anna, but then let her go and lay down on their bed. Anna left the bedroom to help get the girls to bed. The kitchen table was cleared. Anna walked into the bedroom to find her younger daughters in bed, while the older ones were undressing. Anna went to all the little ones and kissed them each goodnight. Pina was already under her covers when Anna walked to her bedside. She bent down, hugged her, and said, "Goodnight, my daughter."

Pina sleepily replied, "Goodnight, Mamma."

Anna stood in front of Teresa and admired how wonderfully she was growing up. She ran her fingers through Teresa's short, boyish haircut and said with such pride, "Goodnight, my daughter."

Teresa hugged Anna tightly and asked "Mamma, is Pappa all right?"

"Yes, he is fine. He's just tired," Anna said. "Now go to bed."

Teresa got into her bed and turned on her side as she watched her mother blow out the short candle by the door. With concern, she watched as her mother walked out of the bedroom and quietly shut the door. Teresa lay quietly, trying to make sense of her father's changed personality. Lately, he seemed so tense and irritated. She knew that the death of Signore Marconi was difficult for her father because they had been such good friends. There were others that Pappa knew in the village who had died at the hands of the Germans. Teresa wondered if it was the Germans who killed Signore Marconi and if so, why? No one talked about how Signore Marconi had died.

Anna returned to her bedroom and, standing at the door, saw that Franco was not asleep but staring at the ceiling. The candle was still lit and flickered a shadow against the wall. Outside the window, there were no stars in the soft, deep blue sky. The room was comfortable and inviting.

It had been a long time since they'd made love. Anna couldn't get Franco to respond to her advances since Maria's birth. She didn't worry about being rejected, for she knew that he had so much on his mind. But now, as she looked at her handsome husband, her body stirred sexually in longing for his touch.

She walked over to Franco and slowly took off her clothes. She stood naked by the side of the bed, looking at her husband, her whole body aching for him. Franco turned to see Anna standing by his side. He reached between her legs and found that she was moist. He inserted two of his fingers inside her. She moaned at his touch as he started to move deeper into her. She cried softly with pleasure until Franco released her and put the moisture from his hands to his lips and kissed it. He stroked her long, curly hair and gently brought her lips to his. He kissed her and

Anna shivered from their long, deep kiss. The warm poignant smell of his breath, a blend of fresh tobacco and wine, was exciting. After devouring her kisses, he released her. He looked at her still slim and desirable body, touched her breast, and brought her to him. He put her breast into his mouth. Her warm nipple rose to Franco's touch as she responded to his lust.

Before Franco had touched her, Anna wished that her breasts were as firm as they were when she was younger, but breastfeeding her babies had taken a toll on them.

Franco let go of Anna's breast and, with his strong muscular arms, lifted and placed her on top off him. They kissed more eagerly, and then pulled away from each other. Anna helped Franco take off his pants. She moaned with satisfaction as he entered her. Feeling rapture with him inside of her, she slowly removed his shirt. Anna lay down on Franco's chest and stroked his hairless, pure, white skin. She kissed his nipples intensely and, with each other's rhythm, they started to make deep, passionate love. Franco, enjoying his hard manhood inside of Anna, started to breathe heavily as he plunged deeper within her. The deeper that Franco went into Anna, the more satisfaction she felt.

"It's been too long," she said.

The lovemaking was at its highest point, approaching climax point for both of them, when Franco abruptly pulled Anna off of him. He threw her onto the other side of the bed and screamed out in pain, "Noooooooooo!"

The morning came early as Franco woke up to find he was in an empty bed. He was ashamed of himself for how he treated his wife the previous night. He hadn't climaxed with Anna because he was afraid of conceiving another child. In his head he'd heard the words of the midwife saying to him after the birth of Maria, "Franco, Anna barely survived this birth. She couldn't survive another birth like this one. It is up to you to be in control of the situation." He knew he could have explained to Anna why he had been rejecting her at a crucial point of their lovemaking last night, but would she listen? Would she accept his reasoning?

The sun was bright on this cold early morning when Franco put on his pants and shirt and walked into the kitchen. Anna was there alone. Franco approached her and put his hand on her waist but she abruptly pushed him away. She walked away from the stove, walked out of the kitchen, and to the barn.

Franco was angry he hadn't gotten a chance to explain. He stood in front of the cupboard and took out his wine. Instead of pouring it into a glass, he guzzled it straight from the jug. As the strong red wine dribbled down his chin and onto his shirt, he wiped his mouth, and angrily said to himself, "I'm the man of this house. I don't have to explain myself to her or anyone else." Franco lifted the jug and again gulped the wine.

— *PART III* —

Chapter Thirteen

The winter of 1944-45 was long and dreary, and in March the island was wintery, but the future started to shine brightly because there were more Americans and a few French soldiers arriving. These troops would be used, if needed, as backup for a land strike that was planned on the island of Sardinia. The land strike, secretly scheduled to take place at the end of March, would attack Corsica.

The Sicilians graciously and enthusiastically welcomed the American and French soldiers to their country and tended to all their needs. The soldiers were given the best accommodations and some fathers offered their un-objecting daughters to the American soldiers.

On every corner of every street, in all the large cities and small villages, the Sicilians cheered with glee. All the churches rang their bells and blessings and prayers were said to Americans as they passed. The islanders shook hands the Americans' hands, "Welcome!"

The village of Bisacquino was a minute dot on the Island of Sicily. The village was fairly quiet and a little safer than at the start of the war as most German soldiers had been captured, imprisoned, or killed.

The villagers cautiously proceeded with their everyday activities, since the war continued with heavy battles in Europe and other parts of the world. Never knowing what was lurking in the bushes, the villagers' eyes darted in all directions, at all times, wherever they went.

Franco and Anna waited patiently for spring to bring its warmth and sunshine so they could get to the farm and start planting their summer vegetable garden. Food was getting scarce, and the varieties were limited. Anna did her best to keep flavor in her meals.

Her daughters were getting restless for sun and fresh, warm air. It was difficult for Anna to watch her younger daughters so confined inside the walls of their house. She knew that in order for her children to grow and develop normally, they required lots of sun, fresh air and exercise.

"Anna," Giuseppa, called as she opened the front door. "Hi, big sister. I brought some herbs that survived the winter by the side of my house. I figured you could use them; and if you could, please spare me a couple of potatoes for my family? If we can make a trade for a few potatoes, that would be great."

Anna looked at her sister as she walked toward her and asked, "Why do I feel that your needing herbs is just an excuse for you to come here? You don't need an excuse to see me. You already brought me herbs the other day. I know that Franco has supplied you with plenty of potatoes for you and your sons for another month."

Giuseppa stood next to her sister as Anna picked up a knife and started to peel a sad-looking carrot. "I've been worried about you and Franco."

"The war will be over soon," Anna said, "and all our lives will get back to normal."

"Franco is drinking so much. I'm just worried," Giuseppa said.

Anna stopped peeling her carrot. She picked up her apron to wipe her hands, and her spool of white thread fell out of her pocket, rolled across the floor, and landed near the kitchen table. Anna walked over and bent down to pick up her precious spool of thread and then turned to her sister and gave her a hug. "Stop worrying about me. See, Giuseppa, I have my spool of thread and you know what that means."

Giuseppa rolled her eyes and said, "Yes, I know what that silly spool of thread means to you! I love you, Anna, my big sister."

Anna hugged Giuseppa and said, "Sit at the table. I'll make us some fresh, strong coffee."

Giuseppa said, "What? Really ground, whole coffee?"

"Yes." Anna said.

"Where did you get it?"

"Franco traded with one of the Americans for some of his olive oil. He also got some American cigarettes. So sit, my little sister, for I also have fresh cream and I can spare a teaspoon of sugar."

"Sugar! Start up the oven, I'm ready," exclaimed Giuseppa.

Spring of 1945 finally arrived on the island. Plants sprouted from the earth and erased the harshness of winter, replacing it with warmer sun and warm colors on the hilly countryside. The birds sang their songs of happiness for the coming months, flying on the soft breeze and rustling through the new greening grass. The earth was awakening ever so quietly.

The people of Sicily watched the birds and wondered if they knew there was danger in the midst. Nature awakened and delivered its natural changes, as in every spring, unaware of human concerns. The colors of spring changed unnoticed by the people engulfed in the war and its new developments.

Franco and Anna, with their daughters, were at the farm plowing the earth to plant seeds for their fall and winter food. The days were long and hard, but comfortably warm as the family worked hard to get their land ready for planting. Franco loved this time of year. He loved breathing in all the sweet spring scents. He worked hard with Anna next to him, helping to produce the food for their family's need.

Franco loved the smell of fresh dirt and the promise of life that would come from it. The baby was asleep on a blanket, close to her working family, while the other little ones, not realizing that they were helping in the planting, happily played in the dirt.

Anna watched her little daughters with pride as their hair and hands filled with soil. Franco saw that Anna was taking a moment to watch and enjoy her daughters, and Franco enjoyed the scene as well. He went to Anna's side and said, "I see our daughter Francesca is playing and not crying for a change. That little one of ours seems to love to cry."

"Franco," Anna said, "I think she's too busy playing to think about crying right now. Besides, I think she cries to get more attention from her grandmother and her aunts."

Franco looked at Francesca and said, "I love her deep dimples when she smiles."

Anna answered, "I love her beautiful blue eyes and her turned-up nose. Those big tears she produces seem to come from nowhere, but are always there."

"Our daughters don't seem to be too affected by this war," Franco observed.

"Franco," Anna said with confidence, "if we watch over them closely they'll have few scars left when this war is over."

Franco didn't comment, but put his arms around Anna. Together they watched the little ones at play, and then let go of each other and went back to their plowing.

Working diligently, as perspiration streamed down his face, Franco heard a noise coming from the distance and stopped his planting to look over at Anna in fear. Anna instantly ran to the younger daughters and picked them both up. She was starting to run and yelled to her older daughters to follow her when she heard Franco shout, "Anna, the Americans are coming!" Anna stopped and turned to look down the road where she saw the Americans were coming toward the farm in large tanks with American flags. She put her hand up to her forehead to shade her eyes from the sun and saw a small parade of vehicles and soldiers slowly marching down the road. Surprised but relieved, she put her small daughters back on the ground.

Franco yelled to Teresa and Pina to get the DiGorios who were working in the next field, further away from the road. "Tell them to come and bring buckets of water. Tell Dino and Peppe to get more water from the house. We'll welcome the Americans with our hospitality."

Anna turned to Franco and said, "It would be nice if we had fresh fruit to give to them in thanks for fighting for us."

Franco smiled at Anna and her thoughtfulness and he wished they had fruit to share, too.

The families stood close to the side of the road as the American troops approached them. The convoy slowed down. The children all cheered and waved as the parade marched past them. One of the trucks stopped near the families and several soldiers got out of the truck. Franco put out his hand to shake the soldier's hand and the DiGorio boys offered water to the soldiers who took it and drank it politely. Anna, speaking in clear English, thanked the soldiers for being there. The soldiers were delighted to speak to a person in English.

"We love the island and its people," one soldier said to Anna.

"We are so grateful to the American soldiers for their coming" Anna replied.

"Your English is very good," another soldier said. "Where did you study the language?"

"I was born in New York. Later, as a young woman, I lived in New York City for several years with my sister and father where I learned the language. I'm an American citizen and my daughters are citizens too."

"Why don't you take your family and live there?" one of the soldiers asked.

"Oh, my parents and other sisters are here on the island. It would be hard for me and my daughters to be away from them."

The second soldier was staring at Pina, in awe at her beauty. Franco saw the young man staring at her, walked over to his daughter, and stood close to her. Dino also noticed the soldier looking at Pina, and immediately went and stood by her other side. The soldier appeared to be embarrassed after the two men stood on either side of the young woman, protecting her. He hadn't meant any harm but was just overwhelmed at the most wonderful creature he had ever seen.

"My husband and I are sorry that we don't have any fresh fruit to share with you," Anna said, "but thank you for being here to protect us."

The soldiers smiled and thanked them, and said that the water that they were given was plenty. The soldiers said that they had been given a warm welcome in all the villages and cities and were grateful for the warm hospitality they had received.

The soldier talking with Anna turned to tell another soldier sitting in the bed of the truck to bring him several boxes from the truck. The young soldier who was staring at Pina wanted an excuse to move from his spot so nervously and quickly, he moved to the truck to help with the boxes. The boxes were filled with American cigarettes, wheat, cornmeal, dried milk, rice, and cans of peaches and pears. The most needed supply in the box was a First-Aid kit. The sergeant opened another box and pulled out a small box wrapped in paper. He unwrapped it, handed it to Anna, and then said, "I wish I had ice cream for your daughters, but maybe this will do."

Inside there were individually wrapped chocolate bars.

The little ones, standing quietly by Anna, started to jump and giggle as the candy bars were handed to them. The older daughters waited until they received the candy, and thanked the soldiers, who handed the rest of the chocolate bars to Anna. She smiled at the soldiers, delighted to hear her daughters giggle while eating their candy.

The sergeant dug down into the second box again and pulled out a roll wrapped in paper which he handed to Anna, stating that it was from her American people. Franco watched Anna as she unwrapped the package. She stared at it in shock to find a large roll of silk fabric. It was the most amazing, bright, colorful silk she'd ever seen. The fabric was bright blue, with bright yellow and pink flowers, and green leaves. She touched it and could not believe its softness.

"I'm told it is of very high quality," the sergeant explained. "I hope you will enjoy it."

Anna was speechless as she watched the sergeant head back toward the truck.

And just as quick as they had come, the truck pulled away with the soldiers waving as they drove away from the farm.

The families went back to their planting after the Americans left. The little ones were excited, already eating a second bar of chocolate. Anna dug into the dirt and planted, remembering her days in America. She remembered going to the opera with her father and sister. She remembered swimming at Jones Beach, working long hours in the clothing district, and saving all the money she, her sister and father earned. Her father did, on occasion, splurge, and take them to a good restaurant and the theater.

On their time off, they would walk in the parks, and visit all the monuments and museums. She also remembered how protective her father was of her and her sister. He never allowed them to go anywhere without him. He was very strict and protective of them. Now that she had daughters of her own, she understood why he had been that way. If she or her sister were stained in any way, they couldn't marry in their station.

Innocenza interrupted Anna's thoughts, asking for a drink of water. Anna looked at Innocenza's smile, walked over to bucket, got her a cup, and filled it with water. She handed her daughter the water and looked at Franco. She recalled, while watching him, that it had been some time since Saverino's death. Anna was grateful that Franco had started to become himself again. He had stopped drinking and was acting more like himself. Anna had prayed for his mood to change, and it seemed that her prayers were being answered.

Vincenzo and his family went back to their field after the Americans left and were working hard at planting. The DiGorios now lived on the farm all year round. They occupied an apartment in the same quarters behind Franco and Anna. With the families working together, there was enough food for them for the winter, with a little extra for the monastery, and food to sell to pay their rent.

Franco shared his milk with the DiGorios and the nuns. Vincenzo had recently acquired chickens and his boys brought fresh eggs to the monastery every morning. The combining of the families' efforts made for abundances, and what was left was traded for cloth and other needs. Life was good, except for the constant threat of the lingering war.

That night, there was time to rest. The work day was cut short because they had accomplished their goal. The children were enjoying their play time, even though they were confined to the house, while Lucia and Anna prepared the meal together, for it made the workload easier.

Lucia had given birth to a baby girl over the winter. How pretty this child was, with her deep, dark, smooth skin and black, curly hair. Everyone adored the new baby girl. Her older brothers fussed over her, Lucia was delighted with her new daughter, and Anna was enjoying having another little female to sew for. Even though Anna was very busy, she always found time to sew for the baby. Many of the dresses were sewn from Maria's leftovers. Of course, when Anna finished they looked brand new, with sweet little pockets and a touch of lace on them.

Earlier than usual, the family was able to enjoy the evening, having finished work for the day. The dishes were done, the younger children were playing, and the older ones were resting, when there was a knock on the front door. Everyone looked up as Teresa got up from the kitchen table to carefully answer the door. Standing in the doorway on that cool spring night was Sister Maria, out of breath. She came into the house, which was rare, and shut the door behind her. "Mussolini has been captured!"

The family was in shock and flocked to her to get more news. Franco said, "What? Are you sure?"

"It's the Italian partisans; they captured him and hung him," Sister answered.

"Franco, what do you think this means to us?" Anna asked.

Franco looked lovingly into his wife's eyes, hugged her, and said, "Maybe we will sleep a little easier tonight."

And wonderful, much-needed, sound sleep did come easier on that night, April 28, 1945, for both families and to most of the Islanders, as well as to the people that lived on the mainland.

Two days later the Gennusas and the DiGorios received word that Adolph Hitler and his long-time mistress Eva Braun, after their marriage ceremony, had committed suicide.

The next morning the families got up early and went to the monastery to attend Mass and receive Holy Communion. They thanked God that Adolph Hitler and Mussolini were no longer on the earth.

On May 2, 1945, all German troops in Italy surrendered, and on May 7, 1945, all German forces surrendered to the allies. May 8, 1945, was declared Victory Day in Europe.

World War II was finally coming to an end. The Americans were still at war with the Japanese, but after the first atomic bomb was dropped on the city of Hiroshima in Japan on August 6, 1945, it was evident the whole war would be ending, leaving its survivors to clean up the horrendous destruction.

Chapter Fourteen

Fall and the harvest were just around the corner, and the Gennusas and the DiGorios looked forward to the work which seemed so much easier now that the threat of war was over.

Franco and Anna's daughters were promised by their parents that they could return to school after the harvest. With so much to look forward to, there were many wonderful smiles on the faces of all the people, all over the island. The older Gennusa daughters worked happily, picking olives from the trees, not caring about the cold rainy weather.

At night, after dinner was done, both Teresa and Pina helped their mother sew new clothes for school. They had to wear uniforms to school and the uniforms had to be handmade.

Anna loved watching her older daughters as they helped with the making of their new clothes. She loved teaching her daughters, and hoped they would learn to be better at sewing.

"Remember daughters that your father and I can't give you all the clothes you want for school, but we will provide what we can. Please don't be selfish and ask for more than we can offer, because there is no more. It will hurt your father very much if he feels he can't provide. The war is over, but it will take us several years to recover. Do you understand?"

Teresa leaned over, kissed her mother on the cheek, and said, "Mamma, I don't need any of the things you're making. I'm happy just to know that you and Pappa are allowing me to go back to school."

"Mamma, me too," Pina chimed in, "Teresa and I won't disappoint you."

"You girls will have to make up your farm work when school isn't in session," Anna said.

"Of course, Mamma," Teresa said, "Pina and I will do more than our share."

"And, of course, your grades will be at the top of your class," Anna said.

The two looked at each other with big smiles on their faces and then looked at their mother, more than willing to comply, and replied, "Yes, Mamma."

One day, toward the end of November, Teresa was in the center of the small city of Corleone, a short distance northeast of Bisacquino, in front of the Catholic Church. She was attending Mass with her schoolmates before classes, and while her schoolmates ran ahead of her and quickly entered the large structure to get out of the cold, Teresa enjoyed the sun shining on her face. She was happy to be going to Mass as she did every morning. She was finally where she had prayed for so long to be.

Her short hair from war time had started to grow out and now almost reached her shoulders, falling in soft waves. A hat which was part of her uniform, and which she thought was ugly, covered her hair. Looks didn't really matter to her anyway. Standing on the church steps, she took a minute to reflect on one of the experiences she'd had with her father in front of the church before for the war, in 1943.

Teresa and her father had heard Mussolini speak to his people, encouraging them to unite. He promised, with the help of Germany, a better life for all of them. She shuddered when she thought of the frightened young child that she'd been back then, facing that monster. She thought of what would have happened, not just to her island but to the rest of the world, if Germany had taken over Europe.

Pictures and words appeared in the news of what had happened to the European Jews. It was devastating. The classes she attended on history explained the recent events of the war. The Nuremberg war crimes trials had started and were being studied. It was hard for her to understand that some of the German people who supported Hitler were not aware of what was going on in the death camps.

Teresa shook her head at her thoughts and looked toward the sun, smiling at its brilliance and knowing how blessed she was to be starting another productive day. Her favorite part of the day was attending Mass in the morning.

Teresa opened the large, heavy, varnished door of the church with its metal door handles and entered the sanctuary. She put her finger in the small bowl of holy water by the door and blessed herself. Standing by the door she looked ahead, knowing that Pina was already there praying, and walked down the aisle to sit with her classmates.

Chapter Fifteen

The winter of 1945-46 was long and cold. Anna missed her older daughters while they attended school and spent more time with Vincenza and Francesca. They'd never gotten as much attention as her other daughters because of the world's situation. These two girls just happened to be middle children, caught in the middle of the family and also in the middle of a world of danger. The two eager and vibrant creatures helped Anna with the cooking and care of the two little ones—when they weren't at their grandparents' house being spoiled.

Anna enjoyed them and started to see them in a different light. She'd never noticed Vincenza's intelligence, the way she could easily calculate numbers, and her astonishing common sense. One night, during that long winter, Anna approached Franco and said, "Vincenza came to me today and said that she's been doing a lot of calculating. She figured that if we invested in a small scale, we could save and sell more wheat. By accurately weighing the wheat, we would have better control. By controlling our wheat better, we could save and have more to give to the nuns and to my parents. Franco, I think she has something there. What do you think?"

Franco looked surprised and replied, "She's a female. What does she know about such things?"

"Franco," Anna said, "The sex of a person has nothing to do with their ability to think."

"I will talk to her and see how she came up with that idea," Franco answered.

"Franco," Anna said, "Vincenza gives me so much advice without knowing that she does. You should take her with you to market to sell your vegetables."

"How about Francesca—has she given you any insight as to why she cries and what makes her happy?" Franco asked.

Anna said, "That one is easy. She's happiest when she's at the farm digging in the dirt like you. As far as those tears, I think she'd rather live at her grandparents' home than with us; but if she thinks that I'm giving her up to my sisters and parents to spoil, she is wrong."

Franco started to spend more time with Vincenza. He took her to the market to help sell vegetables and to vendors where he bought goods. She weighed vegetables and grains on her newly acquired second-hand scale, bought from one of the town vendors. It was evident to Franco that they were saving by using the scale, and he watched with amazement and pride as Vincenza smartly negotiated with their customers. She almost always got her items sold at her price.

Vincenza said to her father, as they were heading home one evening with their empty cart, "Pappa, I've been doing some thinking. I think that if we traveled to Giuliana we could get a better price for our vegetables. I know we have relatives there, your sister and a few cousins, but there are too many people in our village that we know, and we give too much away. I know it's hard for you not to give food to the poor people in the village, but we need to feed our family first. If we went to a village where we don't know as many people, we wouldn't feel obligated to give so much of our food away."

"Yes," Franco said, "I still have several cousins there. It would be nice to see them and see how they're doing since the war has ended."

"If we go to Giuliana it would take one hour a day traveling time back and forth, but we will make a better profit," Vincenza said.

Franco asked, "Would you like to see your Aunt Maria?"

"Yes," Vincenza answered, "it would it be nice to stop and see her. Maybe she will cook for us."

"Oh," Franco said with a smile, "I think my sister would love to see us and cook your favorite meal of pasta and green beans."

That evening, when Franco was alone with Anna, he told her of the conversation he'd had with Vincenza. Anna asked, "What do you think?

"She's right," Franco said. "Today she had a bunch of basil left in her basket, and she was upset because she hadn't sold it. She convinced one of our last customers to buy the basil. The women didn't want to buy it until Vincenza gave her one of your recipes."

"She sold the basil?" Anna said,

"Our Vincenza is very clever," Franco said. "Tomorrow we're going to Giuliana to sell the rest of the vegetables and see how we do. When we go to the farm, I'll talk to Vincenzo about some of her ideas to help there, too." Franco looked at Anna with such pride, talking about his daughter. He continued, "And on my trip I'll take Francesca to help me pick the ripest of the vegetables, for she knows which ones are ready for market."

The Gennusa family was almost at peace, like the rest of the people on the island since the war was over, and the cleanup was under way. Franco felt safe leaving Anna and his younger daughters at their home while he traveled and spent much-needed time working on the farm.

With the oldest girls happy in school, and the middle girls with their father at the farm gathering vegetables for market, Anna was alone in the village home with her two youngest daughters—Innocenza, now four years old, and Maria, two.

The summer days of 1946 were hot, but the nights were cool and comfortable. Anna's days were busy with her little girls by her feet, and her sister and her mother visited often. The days went by quickly, but at night, after the little ones were fast asleep, Anna thought a lot about Franco.

Franco hadn't come near her sexually since their last encounter. She missed him so much, his smell and his touch. She knew better than to approach him again. Her last rejection had been very hurtful to her. Anna thought about their incomplete lovemaking, which left her feeling undesirable.

That undesirable feeling also left her feeling empty. She understood that Franco didn't want to have another child. It would be easier if she felt that she could discuss it with him, but she didn't feel that she could.

It was evident to her that Franco would never touch her again, and it hurt her very deeply. Knowing there was nothing she could do, she worked hard to put it out of her mind and accept it. During her lonely nights, it was hard not to think about her feelings. Anna loved Franco no matter how he treated her. Their affectionate feelings for one another were still there, but nothing more.

The next fall's harvest was even easier for Franco and Anna because they had the help of their oldest daughters and the DiGorio's boys, who were growing larger and stronger. The older daughters didn't mind helping with the olives; they were excited knowing that school was just around the corner.

It was almost time to think about Vincenza's education and the very thought of sending her off with her older sisters saddened Franco. He had come to rely on her, not only for her good business sense, but for her strong physical abilities. Vincenza's strength and never-ending energy amazed Franco. He thought that she seemed to be interested in the work she had done with him, but wondered if she really enjoyed it or if she was just doing what she felt had to be done. The situation weighed heavy on Franco's mind because he needed her.

Vincenza had full breasts and a larger build that her older sisters, but she was slim. Her long, curly, blonde hair was always tied back in a ribbon and held in place with a scarf she wore on her head. Her hair and scarf never distracted from her lovely blue eyes, her thick, light brown eyebrows, and smooth white skin. Vincenza had a wide smile with perfectly straight teeth; she was beautiful, even when she was hot and her face flushed as she worked. Vincenza's appearance never mattered to her, though; she was confident in her abilities and focused more on her work than her looks.

Sweet, tearful Francesca had a different personality altogether. Though cute, and happiest when she was covered with dirt, she would rather be at the farm or at her grandparents' house. She never talked about attending school. When the subject was brought up by her aunts, she would start to cry. The thoughts of teachers and four walls around her made her irritable and claustrophobic.

After the harvest of 1946 was finished, and the olives had gone to market with no interruptions by German soldiers, the farmers visited with each other as they had done before the war. The older daughters were in school in Corleone; and Vincenza and Francesca spent their days with their father, planning for next season. At night, the daughters loved learning how to sew and be creative with their mother.

After dinner, Franco would go out to the barn and take care of his mule, and clean and organize his barn. One cold December night, as Franco walked out to the barn to tend to his chores, he heard a familiar sound coming from the corner. He waited a few minutes, pretending that he was tending to his mule, and then looked around the barn to see that no one was behind him. He went to the corner and there, hidden behind some hay, was Mario. Shocked, Franco asked why he was hiding. Mario answered, "I am sorry that I have to impose on you, but I must spend the night here, for it is the safest place I can think of. I will leave as soon as I can."

Franco said, "Son, are you hurt?"

"No, I'm fine," said Mario.

Franco looked seriously at Mario and asked, "Who are you hiding from?"

"I can't say, but you must not tell anyone that you've seen me, and I promise not to come back to your house again."

Franco started to speak when Mario interrupted him, "Signore Gennusa, it's safer for your family that you don't know."

Franco turned toward the door of the barn and went out to his backyard. He sat on the wall of his well and lit a cigarette, trying to imagine who Mario could be hiding from. As he lit his cigarette, he heard a soft voice call his name. He looked toward the next yard in the moonlight, and saw Deanna standing in the bushes between their properties, bundled up in her long winter coat.

Franco got up from the well and quickly walked over to Deanna. He walked into her yard and stood in front of her, worried, not knowing what she wanted, but wondering if she knew that her oldest son was in his barn.

"Franco," Deanna said as Franco held his breath, "I saw you come out of the barn and sit on your well wall. The cigarette you lit looked inviting. Do you have one you can spare?" Franco was surprised at her wanting a cigarette; he took one out of his pocket, lit it, and gave it to her.

Deanna took the cigarette and put it into her mouth. She took a long drag. Her skill with smoking was also a surprise, for women didn't smoke; and if they did, they didn't do so in public.

Deanna blew out the smoke and looking at Franco said, "I wondered why you haven't been to see me or my sons since Saverino died. Are you avoiding us?"

Franco, shocked and uncomfortable with her question, asked, "Why do you think I'm avoiding you?"

Franco held his breath in anticipation of her reply and she said, "Oh, now that I am alone, I thought you might be afraid to be with me."

Franco looked at her and asked, "Why would you think that? I had nothing to do with Saverino's death."

Surprised, Deanna said to Franco, "I never thought you did. Why do you imagine I would think that?"

Franco was happy that it was night out so that Deanna couldn't see his facial expressions while carrying on this conversation. Franco knew that he had a guilty look on his face. He didn't want to carry out this conversation any further. He replied, "It was the war. It made us all feel unsure about so many things."

"Yes, you're right. It has left its scars on all of us." Deanna took another deep drag of her cigarette, blew out the gray smoke, and said, "If you ever need quiet time away from your house, you can come here to me."

"Your house is quieter than mine?" Franco asked.

"Yes," Deanna replied. "My youngest boy is in school and my oldest is never home."

Franco's spine stiffened at Deanna's mention of her oldest son.

"I never know where he is. He leaves home for days at a time. Ever since his father died, he acts like he's responsible for his father's death."

Franco, puzzled, asked, "Why do you say that?"

"I hear him at night crying for his father. He says to himself that he's sorry he didn't save him."

Franco was getting more uncomfortable. "Do you have any idea why he feels he is responsible?"

"No," Deanna replied.

Franco was relieved to hear that Deanna didn't know.

She continued puffing on her cigarette and started to move closer to Franco. She crossed her arms around herself, shaking, and said, "It is a cold night tonight."

"Yes," Franco took a deep breath and continued, "It is."

Deanna put her cigarette on the ground and crushed it. She stepped closer to Franco and opened up her coat. She pressed her lightly dressed body next to Franco and said, "You're so warm."

Franco stood still and slightly stiff, as Deanna wrapped herself around him. He smelled her sweet, clean hair and her perfume. Relishing her scent for a few minutes, he closed his eyes. He could feel her full breasts as she pressed them against his chest. He tried to control his sexual desire for her body, but it was evident that she was stirring up desire in him. Franco reached down, and ran his fingers through her long, dark hair. Deanna bent her head slightly back and on her tip-toes, stretching as high as she could, she reached his lips and kissed them deeply. Franco returned the moist kiss and held Deanna for a long time.

Deanna whispered in a soft sexual voice, "Come into my house. There's no one there. No one will ever know."

Franco was brought back to reality with Deanna's words that no one was home, which reminded him of Mario hiding in his barn. Franco pushed Deanna away from him, looked at her, and said, "No that will never happen. Saverino was my friend."

Deanna looked angrily at Franco and said, "Saverino is dead and buried. I am his widow and I don't even know what happened to him!"

Deanna was angry as Franco walked out of her back yard.

Chapter Sixteen

The winter of 1946, like all winters, was long and cold on the island of Sicily. The older Gennusa daughters were home from school for winter vacation. Anna loved to have all her daughters close to her, and Franco was just as happy. The older daughters took over the care of the little ones. While at home, the middle two sisters were earning respect from their older sisters for the things they did and took care of while the older girls were in school. Franco and Anna were surprised at how mature their older daughters were becoming.

"Anna," Franco said one night after dinner, "our daughters seem to like each other and respect each other for their own talents. That is nice to see! Even in my own family there was bickering going on between my brothers and me when we were growing up."

"Yes," Anna replied, "it looks like our daughters are good friends and will always be good friends. I think that says a lot for us." Anna smiled with pride.

That same night, when the daughters were in their bedrooms, Anna was sitting by the fireplace in her rocking chair mending. Teresa came and sat next to her on the floor. "Mamma," Teresa said, "I'd like to talk to you about something I've been thinking about for some time. I've been thinking of maybe going to the mainland after I finish school."

Anna stopped mending and looked at her oldest daughter, patiently waiting for her to continue.

Teresa cleared her throat, unsure of herself, and then went on to say, "I want to continue school there."

Anna looked at her daughter and said, "I don't think—"

Teresa stopped her mother, "Before you say no, I'd like to explain to you my plan. Please, Mamma, hear me out."

"Okay, Teresa, tell me." Anna said.

Teresa cleared her throat again and began, "When Innocenza got sick and I took her to see Dr. Capetti, you were giving birth to Maria; and that was when I became very interested in medicine."

"Medicine?" Anna questioned.

"I know that it sounds ridiculous but I want to become a medical doctor. I've talked to Dr. Capetti and he wants to give me a job during summer vacation. He says that I can work for him when you and Pappa don't need me at the farm. I promise I'll still work at the farm in the fall during harvest time."

Anna was shaking her head while Teresa continued, "Dr. Capetti wants to help me. He has a cousin I can live with on the mainland. I'll work by taking care of her children when I am not in school. His cousin is very wealthy and works for the hospital in research. Mamma, please, help me. At least think about it, please."

Anna shook her head and said, "I have to do a great deal of thinking about this. The chances of you continuing your education…I just don't know. Why the mainland? There's a university in Palermo."

"Because, Dr. Capetti has relatives that I can stay with, and they can help me there," Teresa answered.

Anna tossed and turned in bed that night, not knowing what to think of her oldest daughter's request and how to present this idea to Franco. The next morning Giuseppa came to visit as she often did, walking carefree into Anna's bright sunny kitchen. As she walked past Anna to get a good cup of rich coffee, she asked, "Are you worried about something? I can see it in that pensive expression on your face. Does your husband know that you're worried?"

Anna sighed and responded, "No, it's Teresa."

Giuseppa poured a second cup of coffee and handed it to Anna. "Oh," Giuseppa said, "that oldest daughter of yours. That one with ambition! She has many needs and the energy to fulfill her many desires, just like you at that age. Remember?"

"Yes," Anna said, "I remember. But what she asks is nearly impossible. I don't see how it can happen."

The sisters sat down across from each other at the kitchen table, drinking their coffee in silence for a few minutes. Finally Anna said, "Teresa wants to go to medical school on the mainland after she's done at Corleone."

"Well," Giuseppa opened her eyes wide, "that certainly is a large request. Your daughter has large expectations for herself, just like her mother did. Is it possible that she can do it?"

"That's the problem. It sounds like she has it all figured out, and it's a reasonable plan, but—"

"Oh, but, could that be Franco?" Giuseppa asked.

"We need her here to help with the younger girls and to help do her part to bring in food for all of us. Giuseppa, why does she want to go? She knows better," Anna said.

"Anna, what if your daughter got married after she got out of school?" Giuseppa asked.

"Well, her husband would be expected to help provide for us. We would provide for each other," Anna commented.

"But suppose her husband didn't want to work next to you and Franco and suppose her choice was a city boy who didn't like farming?" Giuseppa asked.

"When the time is right, Franco and I will choose a farmer husband for her," Anna said.

"You can't do that," Giuseppa exclaimed. "Remember how frightened you were before your wedding and how upset you were that Mamma and Pappa chose your groom? You were lucky that you fell in love with Franco and never had any regrets. What are the chances that Teresa would be happy with your choice of a husband for her? As it was, you and I were the only ones happy with the husbands our parents chose for us. Our other sisters are not. There is time before any decision has to be made. Maybe Teresa will change her mind," Giuseppa said.

"You know Teresa is stubborn. She won't change her mind," Anna replied.

Chapter Seventeen

S pring came to the island again in its exquisite form and was appreciated by all the islanders. It had been two years since the end of the war, and the island had again begun to sparkle. The houses in the city were clean with newly painted windows and doors. The pots around the houses started to show the promise of bright and bountiful flowers sprouting, soon to grow into larger blooms. The people of the island also looked better since the war. The worry lines had begun to fade from their faces and they were rosy and tanned from the sun.

Life on the island was returning to the way it had been before the war. Anna worked the land next to Franco, but worried about approaching him to discuss Teresa's desire to go to medical school. Anna had prolonged the inevitable, but knew the subject would have to be brought up soon, for Teresa was coming home for summer vacation.

The days rolled on as summer vacation came near and the older daughters came home for the summer. The girls walked into their village home with their arms open to the family they loved. Teresa said, "Pappa, I was able to get you the latest newspapers. The priest at the school saved as many as he could for you."

"Thank you, my sweet daughter, for thinking of me. Have you had any time to read any of them?" Franco asked.

"No, Pappa, I haven't, because I took another class this term. It's on medicine."

Anna looked at Franco to see if he'd caught what Teresa had just said, but he was already absorbed in his newspapers. Anna looked at Teresa disapprovingly.

Teresa then realized that her mother hadn't spoken to her father about her attending medical school, which disappointed her. Anna approached her oldest daughter and told her quietly that she hadn't talked to Franco about medical school.

"Go to your room now with Pina and unpack. Dinner will be

ready soon."

"Pappa," Teresa said after she helped herself to a second dish of pasta at dinner, "did you ever hear of a man called Marco Verno?"

Franco had his mouth full of pasta, chewed it slowly, then swallowed and asked, "Who did you say?"

Teresa was reading one of the newspapers she brought back from school, "Apparently, according to this newspaper, there was a Mafia leader here in our town. He had connections to a Mafia leader that was largely in control of the activities on the island while the war was going on," Teresa answered.

Franco stopped eating and put his fork down on his plate. His back stiffened as he looked at Teresa and asked. "What are you talking about?"

"Pappa, there was a Mafia member who helped with the war on our island, and was located somewhere in Bisacquino. This person was linked with Don Calogero, who helped the Americans get through the hills of the island to capture the Germans with no resistance. I was wondering if you knew him."

Franco didn't reply to Teresa's question. She walked over to her father, her hand was shaking, and handed him the paper. Franco read the paper and exclaimed, "Oh, my God!" He dropped the newspaper on the floor and went to the fireplace and then fell into a chair in front of the fire.

Anna picked up the newspaper and then handed it to Teresa. "Francesca," Anna said, "Take the little ones to the bedroom and stay there until I tell you to come out. Teresa, your reading is better than mine. Read the article and tell me what it says."

Teresa, standing with Pina and Vincenza looking over her shoulders, read to herself, and then looked at her mother, "Mamma, this Mafia leader was murdered in Palermo two weeks ago, and the body of a young boy was found next to him, also murdered. Apparently, this Marco Verno was heavily active in the Mafia organization here on the island." Teresa finished the article and then looked up at her mother with tears in her eyes.

Anna looked at Teresa and inquired, "What, Teresa, what's wrong?"

Pina took the newspaper from Teresa and finished the article. Her face turned white and she dropped the paper to her side. Vincenza picked up the paper and started to read the article.

"The body of the boy was Mario, Mamma," Teresa said. "He's dead."

Anna looked at Vincenza, puzzled. She couldn't imagine to whom she was referring when Franco said, "Anna, it's the Marconi boy."

The burial of Mario Marconi was extremely difficult for many people. Mario's younger brother and his mother stood next to each other holding flowers in their hands as Mario was put into the ground, right next to his father, to rest. After prayers were said, Deanna and her youngest son threw flowers into the grave on top of Mario's casket. With tears in their eyes, they walked arm in arm through their back yard and into their house. Their guests followed them into the house where the kitchen was filled with food donated by the neighbors. Anna and her older daughters hosted the mournful affair with grace and quiet dignity. Franco sat alone in the corner of the kitchen drinking wine.

Anna brought a plate of food to Franco, but he refused it. He lit a cigarette and wondered if he could have prevented the death of the young boy. Holding his glass of wine tightly, he thought about this young life cut short and the promise he'd made to Saverino to tell his sons how much he loved them. Franco never told the Marconi boys because, after their father's death, out of guilt, he couldn't look at them. Franco carried a burden on his shoulders and now the death of Mario only made the burden heavier. In solitude, he tried to comfort himself but could not.

The days went by and it never seemed to be the right time to approach Franco about Teresa attending medical school. Franco was taking Mario's death very hard. He was drinking to forget the boy's death, but no matter how much he drank, he couldn't forget.

"Mamma, I need to know soon about attending medical school," Teresa said.

"I know, Teresa, I will talk to your father tonight. You have your heart set on this education. The chances are so slim for you to attend. I wish you would change your mind."

"Mamma, please just try," Teresa pleaded.

That night the girls were all in bed when Anna walked over to where Franco was sitting in the rocking chair by the fireplace drinking wine. "Franco," Anna said, "I need to talk to you about Teresa."

Franco took a drink from his glass and asked, "What about?"

"Franco, our daughter has been taking extra classes about medicine at school. She was hoping that you'd let her go to the university on the mainland after she finished high school."

"No," Franco said.

"Can we discuss this?" Anna asked.

"I heard Teresa and you talking about those extra classes she had taken in school. I am not oblivious to what goes on in my house, Anna, although you may think so. When she's done with school, she will come home and take care of the younger children so you can help me work. Then, maybe Vincenza can to go to school, when I can spare her, to learn math. Vincenza, with a little more knowledge, will be able to help us better with our money. Teresa has got to learn that she can't have whatever she wants. She has responsibilities and obligations to this family."

"But, Franco, she has it all planned out; and it won't be hard on our family," Anna said.

Franco looked at Anna, downed his glass of wine, got up from the chair and said, "There will be no discussion on this again. The answer is no." He walked over to the pantry, took out his large bottle of wine, poured some into his glass, and walked to the barn.

The days ahead for the Gennusa family were quiet. Franco continued to drink, and Teresa was disappointed and cried to herself. The decision was made that there would be no further education for Teresa. She was told by her father that she needed to be less selfish and think of her other sisters. They also deserved a chance to get a high school education, especially Vincenza, who had a bright future in business which would benefit the family. "This is about family, Teresa," Franco said. "Sometimes I think you forget you have one."

It was time to come together and enjoy a festive holiday to celebrate a bright, peaceful future.

During the war all festivals had sadly been canceled. Centuries of celebrations on special occasions, festivals with brightly-colored work carts, were a thing of the past during the war. Previously, plain wooden working carts had been transformed into works of art. Each owner put his own creation on his cart, showing family origins and historical events. These brilliant, yellow, pale blue and red-colored carts had shone in the sunlight, decorated with fresh flowers, ribbons, and flags that swayed in the breeze.

During past celebrations, the decorated carts had paraded around the fountain in the center of town. A great citizen like Dr. Capetti, in his little town of Bisacquino, felt it was time to bring old customs back to the land that he loved. Dr. Capetti, along with many of the town's people who wanted to spread cheer, organized a festival for the beginning of the following month.

When the news spread that the festival was going to be held, the Gennusa family prepared for the exciting, colorful occasion. The daughters gathered at the kitchen table at night after dinner and shared their ideas about how to decorate their cart. Anna and Franco sat quietly as their excited daughters talked.

Even Teresa forgot her disappointment about not having an educational future and got into the spirit of the occasion. She decided that if they used a little bit of red dye with a touch of yellow and a touch of white on white fabric, they could create a bright pink flag different from anyone else.

"We could take the dyed fabric and hang it from the side of the cart. Mamma, what do you think?" asked Teresa.

Pina said, as Anna turned to her, "We could take some of Papa's baskets and wrap them in that colorful fabric."

"Mamma, I think we should paint the whole cart in bright yellow and print our family names in blue. I was thinking of Pappa's family on one side, and on the other side, your family," Vincenza said.

"Well," Anna said, "those are great ideas and certainly different. What's the matter, Francesca, why are you crying, again?"

"Mamma," little, tearful Francesca sobbed, "I want to ride in the cart."

"Mamma," Vincenza said, "that's a good idea. We could dress

the little ones in colorful dresses, put them in the Pappa's baskets, and they could wave to the crowds."

Franco delighted at listening to his daughters and said, "How about if Mamma makes us all dress up alike and walk by the side of the cart to dedicate the cart to our ancestors. With all our family names on the cart, we could have a family theme."

Anna and the girls got excited with all the ideas. Anna turned to look at the Innocenza sitting quietly on her sister's lap. She asked, "Innocenza, what do you think we need for the cart?" Innocenza, in her quiet manner, handed her homemade doll to her mother and everyone laughed.

When the day of the festival came, the Gennusa family was ready. Their cart was painted yellow and wrapped in colorful fabric hanging from the sides. The sun shone down on the cart and made it even more beautiful. The fabric was woven into large baskets, with the youngest Gennusa girls sitting in them, holding their homemade toys. Anna, with the help of her older daughters and her sisters, had everyone dressed alike. Even Franco and Anna's father had matching shirts. Altogether, there were three of Franco and Anna's daughters in the baskets, along with three of their male cousins. The boys had on matching shirts like Franco and Anna's father. The cart had sixteen children and young adults. Included in this parade was a small gray-haired grandmother, walking beside the side of the cart.

Some of Anna's sisters had thought the whole process was silly. Anna had pleaded with them to participate for her children's sake, especially for Francesca. None of them could say no, because of their extra affection for Francesca and her big tears. The aunts agreed to participate that day and enjoyed the event.

The families gathered at Anna and Franco's house to prepare the cart. The mule was harnessed, and covered with bright pink fabric. Franco and Anna's father walked on either side of the mule to lead him. As the family paraded on this beautiful bright day, the people of Bisacquino stood in their doorways and on their balconies and watched and cheered. The birds sang, the people cheered, and it was a wonderful world-peace day in the village where finally everyone could celebrate together.

As the family headed toward the center of the village they passed many people who wanted to share in the joy of the parade. Without an invitation they gathered behind the cart and soon the crowd had multiplied by many children who joined in the festivities. Their happy faces were gleaming and they were laughing and giggling as they ran behind. There were several violinists, guitarists, and even a harmonica player who joined in and started to play.

The cart made a loud and musically cheerful entrance into the center of the village with the large crowd that trailed behind it. All other cart owners looked toward the noise and the music and watched as the Gennusa family approached the judges. Most of the carts moved out of the way as the parade pushed their way toward the judge's stand. Dr. Capetti laughed with delight, amused as he watched one of his favorite families approach him and the other judges. He looked at this family, especially the little ones in the baskets, with affection. He shook his head and applauded as they reached the stand.

The judges stepped down from the podium and walked around the cart. One of the judges asked about the names on the cart and Anna's father explained the names and the family theme. Then another one of the judge's walked around the cart, whispering the names to himself, such well-known village names, as Rosato, Campisi, Scavotto, DiGregrio and Gennusa. The judge recognized his grandfather's name, Campisi, and read it out loud with a tear in his eye. That judge also cried because his family was spared from the hard war that had just ended. He was comforted knowing that there would be many more of these festivals shared with his countrymen.

The judging was done. It was unanimous. The Gennusa family won first prize, not for the colors or the fabrics, but for the theme on their cart and its tribute to the island's ancestral heritage. The delight of the family was exhilarating. They all kissed and hugged each other and the people that had paraded with them. The town's people congratulated the family members by grabbing them and dancing around the fountain.

Franco and Anna, happy with the outcome of the competition, grabbed their small children, and twirled them around, dancing together to the music. There was food and lots of wine shared with those who participated in the event. It was a day for the islanders to forget their catastrophic past and look forward to a fresh, new start.

The day rolled into night, ending in exhaustion and excitement for the Gennusa family. Anna kissed her husband goodnight and left the kitchen to go to bed after her daughters were tucked away for the night. Franco, still drunk from the day's festivities, went to the barn to undress his mule of the brightly colored fabric around the harness and to feed it. After he was finished caring for his mule, Franco rambled around the barn for a short time and then decided to have one last cigarette on the quiet wall of his well. He sat on the wall on the warm pungent night, still enjoying the adrenaline left over from the day's victory party.

Franco lit a cigarette as he enjoyed the moment; he felt that a glass of wine would be perfect. He was annoyed when he heard rustling over by the bushes in his yard, wishing for a moment of peace. He looked over to see Deanna's silhouette in the shadows. Franco knew it was her because he could smell her—even from a distance. He didn't want his day spoiled; he hadn't had such an enjoyable and peaceful day with his family since before the war. And there she stood, bringing back the reality of the loss of her son and husband.

Franco was starting to feel less guilty for the loss of his neighbors. He wanted to forget and move on with life, like most of the people on the island who had been caught up in an ugly war. But reality stared him in the eye once again. Franco tried not to be insensitive to her; but he needed to move on with his life, not only for himself but for his entire family.

"Franco," Deanna's said, "congratulations on winning first prize on your cart today. I bet your daughters and Anna had a great day."

"Yes, thank you, Deanna," Franco said. "This village needed a few minutes to forget the past."

"I guess…" Deanna said coldly. "I guess it's easy to forget the past for those who haven't lost a husband and a child."

"Maybe it's time for all of us to pray that we can heal and continue on," Franco replied.

"I guess," Deanna said. She turned away from Franco, walked back into her yard, and disappeared into the night, leaving her only fragrance behind.

Franco, left alone to smell her perfume, sat on his well in agony. She had left him feeling full of guilt. Selfishly and uncaringly, she was in pain from her loss and wanted someone else to suffer, too. Deanna slipped away into her sad world, leaving Franco with many upsetting memories of his dear, beloved friend and his friend's son. In this upset state, he promised himself and God that he wouldn't allow her to do this to him again. He didn't have control of the war. He didn't have control over her son. He only had control over his family, and he promised himself and his Superior that he would protect them.

Franco walked back into his house, angry now and carrying his burden once again. Franco walked into his kitchen and went to the shelf were he kept his jug of wine. He poured a glass full and drank it thirstily.

Chapter Eighteen

Fall came and Franco's family, along with the DiGorio family, worked hard in the olive groves gathering their harvest. It was a long fall, and winter was going to be long and emotionally hard once again. But Franco thought little of the current season and looked forward to prosperous seasons ahead.

Anna liked the winter months because it gave her more time to create and sew. It was her time to bring in money from her work for the family. She loved the work and never felt overwhelmed by it. Her older daughters helped with her sewing, and Anna loved working with them. It was a good time for the family for they spent a lot of time together instead of going their separate ways, like in other seasons.

Teresa was in her last year of school, and nothing had been said again about her going to medical school. She was allowed to work with Dr. Capetti when needed, and when she could give some time to him. Keeping her hand in helping people seemed to compensate for not going to the university the following fall. Teresa was growing into a self-assured young lady, and her maturity gave her the ability to know her place in the family. She wanted and needed that place. Teresa became Anna's best friend, and the friendship was shared with her beloved Aunt Giuseppa. Anna and Giuseppa watched Teresa growing into a responsible young adult and respected her as a peer.

The spring of 1947 wasn't as bright on the island. The Gennusa family worked on the farm, but Franco was concerned because the land was drier this season than it had been in the past. He worried that he wouldn't be able to produce what he had in the past. Even Vincenzo and his sons were concerned about the dryness of the season. Trying to figure out what to do, they prayed hard for rain, but little rain came that spring, which yielded smaller and fewer vegetables.

Anna and Lucia assured their families that they would manage and would work to make up for the small crops. Anna said that doing more sewing was not a problem, and Lucia told her family that she had no problem with cleaning houses, if needed. Destitution was not an option for either family. The wives felt confident in their convictions to work harder for their families, but the husbands had some problems with it. They knew their wives were capable, but were there enough hours in the day to accomplish so much?

Fall came, and the olives on the trees were few, due to lack of rain. When the harvest was almost over, Vincenzo sat by the fireplace with Franco one night, and stated his concern about the lack of olives. "Franco, I don't know how we're going to make ends meet this winter with no olive oil to sell."

Franco looked at Vincenzo as they each drank a glass of wine and said, "I'm so sorry that you and your family will have to endure a hard winter this year."

"Franco, I'm so grateful for all your help in the past. It hurts me to think that I may have to move my family into the city to find work. I wish so much to stay here. My wife and sons feel safe and happy here, but we need to work."

"Vincenzo, I'm grateful that you're talking to me now about our work. I'm worried that I will not be able to provide for my family either if we have another dry season," Franco lamented.

"What will you do, Franco, if you don't farm?" Vincenzo asked.

"I don't know. This is all I know to do," Franco answered in a worried tone.

It was painfully obvious to Franco and Vincenzo that the harvest hadn't gone well. The olives that the trees yielded were small and dry. Franco carried his concern on the way to his village home. He thought of Vincenzo and his family and felt responsible for their care. He thought of the nuns and the people they cared for at the monastery. He wondered if they would be able to survive the winter ahead without his help from the food that he gave them. Franco wondered about Anna's parents. They were getting older, and some of their other sons-in-law refused to help support them. It was impossible for him to give them as much as he had in past winters. Franco wondered if he would have enough olive oil to trade with Dr. Capetti if one of his family members got sick. Franco's head started to throb. He kept wondering what he was going to do to get through the winter.

Anna could see and feel Franco's worry. She was quiet, because small talk only made matters worse. Anna stayed close to Franco to let him know that he didn't have to carry his problems alone.

Franco, while traveling back to his village home, turned around to look lovingly at his daughters sleeping soundly. He saw his oldest, Teresa, and felt proud. She was strong and had taken over some of Anna's responsibilities.

He looked at his lovely, long-legged Pina, with her long, blonde, curly hair. She never asked for anything but to be part of this family. She always did her part.

Franco turned slightly to look at Vincenza with much admiration. He thought how lovely she was, with her long, blonde hair. It was hard not to notice her perfectly framed angelic face. Her eyes were large, with long, thick eyelashes. He took pride in her physical strength and intelligence. He was so proud that she belonged to him. She should have been the son he never had. Yes, Franco thought to himself, breathing hard, all this would be easier if he had sons.

Franco turned around to look ahead of the cart, unable to look at his young daughters any longer. He became weary. As he looked straight ahead and commanded his mule to continue their journey, he wondered if he had the right to put such a burden on Vincenza; she didn't seem to mind. *Does she know how much I depend on her? How will we survive this winter?* Feeling old, he wished the trip would be over quickly because he was extremely tired.

The olives that Franco brought to market only yielded half of the normal oil. Franco drove home that day feeling very anxious. He pulled up to his house, unloaded his oil, and stored it in the mezzanine until it was needed. He walked into the house to find Anna humming to herself, as she often did when preparing a meal. The younger daughters, seeing their father, ran to him and hugged him. Franco returned their hugs and then picked up Maria and looked into her shining, round blue eyes. He felt like a failure. He needed to do more for his family but he didn't know what more he could do.

That evening, after his family was asleep, Franco wasn't ready to retire for the evening because of his troubled thoughts. He put on his heavy winter jacket and walked out to the barn where he noticed that the hay was askew. His heart started to beat fast, wondering why the hay was in disarray. He walked over, slowly praying hard that no one was in the hay, hiding from the law. The war was over and the Mafia was now doing business in the larger cities. Responsibility for the safety of a person at this time would be difficult for him to endure. Franco put his head in his hands and prayed softly, "Please God, don't let there be anyone there."

Franco approached the hay and bent down. He listened to hear breathing, but heard nothing. He held his breath and pulled the hay back, but there was nothing. Franco shook his head and got very angry. He knew that his young daughters had been playing in the hay that morning while he had gone to market, even though they'd been told many times not to. Franco got up from his knees, shook his head, and decided that the little ones would be punished for disobeying him.

He walked over to the other side of the barn and loosened a wooden board from the wall. He placed it on the table, reached into the wall and grabbed a glass and the jug of wine he'd hidden. He poured wine into the glass and drank the cool, tangy liquid. He poured another glass and downed that one, too. Franco sipped his third glass and felt less stressed from this day. He finished the third glass, poured his fourth, and then put the jug back into its hiding place.

Carrying the glass of wine, he headed out to the back yard and walked to his well wall, feeling the cold air on his face. He put his glass of wine on the ground, reached into his pocket, and pulled out a cigarette. He lit it and took a deep drag. Relaxing in his favorite quiet spot, he looked at the brightly lit starry night, and took a deep breath. The night was so bright that the house and barn could be seen clearly. The air was cold and crisp. His lungs tingled from breathing it and he began to feel better, drinking his wine and smoking his cigarette.

Halfway through his cigarette, Franco heard a noise from next door. He became irate, thinking to himself, *Why can't I have one moment of peace?* He knew it was Deanna. He needed to be alone, and he was tired of being watched by her. She watched him at the market, she watched him with his family at Mass on Sundays, she watched from the background, morning, noon and night. Franco was tired of her watching him. The loss of Saverino and Mario were constantly on his mind and Deanna's watching him only made the thorn dig deeper into his side.

Franco looked in her direction and sighed, not saying a word to her. She said, "Alone again, Franco? Is there trouble in your house? Anna not able to satisfy you anymore? It's hard not to notice that Anna hasn't given birth lately."

Franco got angry at the mention of Anna. He didn't want to continue this conversation. He picked up his glass and got up from his wall. He started to walk toward the house when Deanna continued, "I know that you could have saved Saverino, and you called him your friend?"

Franco froze at the mention of Saverino's name and turned to look at Deanna. "What?"

"I know that Saverino and you were in the Resistance Party. I know that you helped the Mafia during the war. I know that my son joined the Resistance Party before his father died. Someone brought Saverino home that night to die. I know it was you, because he trusted you."

Franco threw his cigarette on the ground and said, "You don't know what you're talking about."

"Oh, but I do. You had the perfect setup. The innocent farmer with all those daughters. What harm could you do, and why would you be involved. I get lots of information these days, being the lonely widow. It's amazing what men will tell in bed. You have no secrets, Franco, I know everything."

Franco started to lose control. He rushed at Deanna and exclaimed, "You're crazy!"

"No, Franco, I'm not crazy. I also know the reason why, and how, you and your family were not harmed during the war," Deanna said. With Franco now standing in front of her, Deanna reached out and took his glass out of his hand. She sipped the wine. "Mmmm, that is good. You better drink sparingly, for it will be a long winter, and your rations are sparse."

Franco said, "Why are you doing this to me? Why can't you leave me and my family alone? Have I been a bad neighbor or friend to you and your family?"

"Franco, you have always been a good neighbor, and were there always for us. But now my family is almost gone and I miss what I had. Why should you have it all?" Deanna said.

Franco reached out, took his glass of wine and drank it all. Angrily, he threw the glass to the ground. Deanna opened up her coat and stood there with the bright stars shining down on her naked body. Franco looked at her full breasts and stepped back from her. Deanna took two small steps toward Franco and reached for his hand. Holding his cold hand in her warm one, she rubbed it with her other hand to warm his skin. She placed his hand on her breast and moved it softly in a circular motion. Franco didn't stop her as she let go of his hand and stepped closer. She reached down to his loins. After rubbing and gently squeezing it, she let go. She undid his belt and his pants fell to the ground, leaving him standing there half naked. The cold air rushed at him. His manhood, raised in its glory, longed to be touched again.

Deanna bent down and put him into her mouth. She worked him with skill, and with determination to have him. Several seconds later, after letting him go, she reached for his lips. She kissed them roughly. Franco, stupefied, could not respond to her kiss. He took a deep breath and moved slowly away saying, "Why are you doing this?"

Deanna moved close to him and again kissed him roughly. She pulled away abruptly and said, "Because you owe me."

"Deanna, what is it that I owe you?" Franco asked in a low, defeated voice.

"You owe me Saverino," Deanna said.

Upset, Franco asked, "Why do you say that?"

Deanna, with hate in her voice said, "Because you brought Saverino home to me and my sons the night he died. If you hadn't thought only of yourself and your family that night, and had taken him to Dr. Capetti instead of here, he would still be alive. Don't think I cared much for Saverino. He was a disappointment to me in bed. But if he had lived, my beloved Mario would still be with me. Mario never would have joined the Resistance Party and then the Mafia organization after the war if his father had lived. My son was all I had in my life that I cared for. My beautiful, loving, handsome son is gone, and you, Franco, killed him."

Franco felt the energy drain from his body. "No," Franco said, shaking his head. "No." Franco stood in the cold night half naked and felt numb. Then he grabbed Deanna by her shoulders. He looked at her and tears welled in his eyes.

"Tell me, Franco," Deanna whispered, "your daughter Innocenza—she's so different looking from your other daughters; who is her father?"

Franco became enraged, found his strength, shook her violently and threw her on the ground. As she fell, her coat opened wide and showed her naked body. She said, "Yes, Franco, you killed my Mario and I will never let you forget."

Franco screamed, threw his body on hers and started to hit her face. Her face immediately swelled, as blood gushed from her nose, and when Franco stopped, she raised her bloody face to his ear and said viciously, "You killed my boy."

With these painful words, Franco plunged his penis as deeply and as hurtfully as he could inside of her. She screamed and then laughed. She finally had him. Franco continued to force himself into her. He could not stand her laughing at him. Out of hate, he grabbed her throat and squeezed hard. He continued into her, and then he finally let go of her throat.

Deanna grasped for air, put her hand to her throat, and rubbed her neck. She yelled, "You bastard!" Franco was completely out of control and continued, hurting her, over and over again. Deanna lost control and stopped resisting. She let Franco continue doing it to her. After reaching his climax he lay on top of her for a few seconds. Then, he let her go.

Deanna lay there for a few minutes, trying to get control of her senses. Franco got up and sat next to her on the cold ground. Taking deep breaths, Deanna touched and rubbed her vagina. Her face was completely covered with bruises. Blood was running from her nose, and she tried, with her other hand, to stop the bleeding. She said, in complete control, in a deep loathing voice and with great satisfaction, "Here, on this cold earth, next to my dead husband and oldest son, I have conceived your son, the son that you desperately need, and Anna could never give you." Deanna hesitated for a second, moaned, and then continued, "This son of ours, you will never be able to claim him as yours, because society and God will not let you do so. This son of ours will have your blue eyes, but the rest of him will belong to me."

Franco, with disgust, watched Deanna groaning in pain as she struggled to stand up. Blood was running down her legs as she wrapped her coat around her bruised body. She had difficulty walking as she stumbled into her house. Franco sat for a few minutes, in shock at what he had done. He lay down on the cold ground, curled into a fetal position, where he spent the remainder of the coldest and loneliest night of his life, alone.

— *PART IV* —

Chapter Nineteen

"I've made a decision," Franco said one night, three weeks after his encounter with Deanna. It was at the dinner table, but Franco wasn't eating. He was drinking wine and was inebriated when he said, "We're going to go to America."

Anna looked at her husband, confused, and asked, "What did you say?"

"I've purchased tickets for a trip, and we'll be leaving at the end of November," Franco said coldly.

"Franco!" Anna exclaimed. "What are you saying?"

"You heard me," Franco said. "We are going to New York City."

Anna was shocked and enraged. Red faced, she stood up from her chair. With vengeance in her eyes, she said, looking at the drunken stranger across the table, "I'm not going."

Franco looked at his wife, brought his glass unsteadily to his mouth, and took a drink. He looked at her and said sternly, "You will do as I say. We are going to America."

The girls sat in their chairs, shocked. Teresa sat straight up and asked, "Pappa, but why?"

Franco looked at his oldest daughter and said, "I don't have to explain to you why I make decisions. You will do as I say."

Franco got up from his chair, went to the sink, poured himself a large glass of wine, spilling some, and walked out of the kitchen and into the barn. Before he left the room, he turned to his family and said, "We won't be able to take much with us, so choose wisely, Anna."

Anna sat in her chair for a few minutes.

Pina said to her mother, "I won't go to America, Mamma. My life is here. This is where I belong."

"Mamma, what is this all about? What about Pina and me finishing school?" Teresa asked with deep concern.

Vincenza had a tear in her eye and said, "Well, Pappa must have a good reason. We should find out before we get so upset."

Pina, very upset, looked at Vincenza, "You are always so practical; just once, don't be. It's irritating."

"Pina," Vincenza said, "do we have any choice if Pappa has made up his mind?"

"That's not the point," Pina said. "You're always compliant. Can't you just—"

Before Pina had a chance to finish, Anna said, "Okay girls, bickering isn't going to change the fact that your father has made up his mind."

With large tears streaming down her face, Francesca said, "Mamma, you must talk to Pappa and change his mind. I can't leave Grandmother and Grandfather. They need me."

At that comment, Anna felt a sharp pain in her stomach. She told the girls to clean the table and get to bed. Anna took her heavy winter coat from the hook, put it on, and went to the barn. Franco was nowhere to be seen in the barn. She went to the back yard and found Franco sitting at his favorite spot on the well. She approached him slowly, standing in front of him at a distance and said, "Franco, I need to know why we are going to America. I know you don't have to tell me the reason why you made this decision, but please, do tell me. Let me know what you're thinking, so that I can make this transition easier for all of us. You're asking us to leave our home, our families, and our country. Please tell me why."

Franco slowly took a gulp of wine and reached for a cigarette from his pocket. He put the cigarette in his mouth, lit it and took a long drag. He blew out a cloud of smoke and sat in silence as Anna slowly approached him.

She sat next to him on the well. She could feel the distance between them, a distance that had been noticeable to her for the past few weeks. She knew that something was wrong, because he wouldn't look at her and wouldn't come near her. Her heart ached as she carried her worries alone, not knowing what to do. Softly she said, "Please, don't shut me out. Let me know what you're thinking."

Franco sat quietly for some time, with Anna waiting patiently, when he finally said, "In America we can go to work and put the older girls to work. We will live there for a few years, work, and then can come home after we have money. We will have money for our daughters' dowry, for when we choose husbands for them."

"Franco," Anna said, "it is not as easy as you think."

"Don't tell me that. I heard your father brag over the years how much money he brought back when you and Giuseppa came back from the states, after working in the factory. We will put the older girls to work and save our money," Franco said angrily.

"Franco, you don't understand," Anna said. "It is hard work. I don't know if I can do that kind of work anymore. I'm too old, and what will you do? There are no farms in New York City. There are fabulous stores, with big windows that show all the newest fashions that our girls will never be able to have. There are theaters and restaurants that all the New Yorkers go to that we will never be able to afford. Our lives are simple here, and what about the girls' education? There will be no money for them there. Franco, do you understand what I am saying? We will never be able to come back. We will never be able to save enough money."

"If you want, I'll go with Teresa and Pina to New York and work. We will save our money and then come back. You can stay here with the younger girls. I understand the burdens you have. Let me help take that away from you. Think what you are doing to us."

"Anna," Franco said roughly, "we are going to America and there will be no further discussion on the matter. This whole family is going together. This conversation is closed."

"No, Franco, this conversation is not closed." Anna put her head down in her hands in despair. She looked up at Franco, and then continued, "I will not go to America. My life is here. I will not leave my parents and Giuseppa. How can we afford to move? We used most of the money that we were given by the Steins. I know there isn't enough left to buy passage for all of us. How will we do this?"

Franco thought of the ruby ring he had hidden in the attic, and the large amount of money he had received for it. With the sale of his livestock and some small farm tools, there was enough money for their tickets. The only thing he didn't sell was their home. He knew he and his family would need it when they returned. He thought about going to Palermo and how he had secretly arranged for sponsors on the black-market to get them into America. These people would meet them at the dock the day of their arrival, show identification, and sign for Franco to enter into America. He even had a little extra money to spare, to start their lives in the new world. He said softly to Anna after finishing his wine, "You will go."

Anna stood up in front of Franco and said softly back to him, "No, Franco, I will not go."

Franco looked at her and frowned. In a deep, nasty voice he said, "Why do you think I married you?"

Anna was surprised. With little resistance, she took a deep breath and said, "Why?"

"I married you because you are an American citizen. I took you into my home and have supported you all these years because you had your American citizenship. That citizenship belongs to me. I could have married anyone, a woman with money of her own, a woman with land of her own to grow crops on, and a woman—not a child,—not a child-wife whom I had to teach everything."

Franco was slurring his words when he said, "A woman who could have given me a son." Anna lowered her head and tears fell from her eyes with Franco's last words. He continued, "I was wanted by many women, but they were not American citizens. That was why I married you. We will go to America."

Anna felt pain in her heart that she had never felt before. She had been betrayed by the one person she deeply loved. With all her strength, raising her tearful face, she looked at her betrayer and said, "No, I will not go."

Franco stood up and threw his glass across the yard, where it smashed against the house. He took his fist, clenched it and with all his strength, punched Anna in the face. Anna fell to the ground and stayed there for several seconds, semi-conscious. Franco said angrily, "Tell me, Anna, who is Innocenza's father? You will go to America."

The next day, her sister Giuseppa ran into the kitchen to see Anna standing by the kitchen sink, looking down at the dishes she was washing. The girls were crying in different parts of the kitchen. As soon as the door closed, Anna said to her sister, "I suppose Francesca told you. She ran out of the house this morning when I told her we were leaving for America."

Giuseppa stood at the door for a few minutes with her hand on her mouth. Her eyes filled with tears and she was having trouble breathing. Finally she said, "He can't do that. He promised he would never take you away."

"Yes, he can," Anna said without emotion. "Giuseppa, he has made up his mind. We will be leaving at the end of November." She was still standing at the sink, her back to her sister. Giuseppa walked over to the sink, put her hand on Anna's shoulder, and turned her around. She looked at Anna's face and saw the huge bruise around her eye. Giuseppa gasped at Anna's face and said, "I'll tell our father. He'll take care of you."

"No," Anna said, "Pappa is too old and you know he would never interfere. We will be leaving soon. If you could make this as easy as possible for me, I really need you to do so. Please," Anna sighed, "Giuseppa, please."

Giuseppa put her arms around her sister and cried hysterically. Anna stood with her arms at her side, no tears in her eyes, because she only felt numb.

The weeks ahead were extremely hard for Anna as she prepared to move to another world. She was constantly worried; she knew that the streets in America were not paved in gold, as most people believed. She knew life would be hard for her and for her daughters, and she wouldn't be able to provide for them what they needed to live comfortably in a complicated society. Anna did her best to console her daughters, and tried to explain that it would only be for a short time, although she knew they would never return. She hoped that maybe a miracle would happen before their departure.

Anna packed only necessary belongings, and was grateful that

Maria was now three years old and easier to handle. The two younger girls were quiet, which was normal for Innocenza, but with Maria quiet too, everyone felt the strain. The two little girls sensed something was wrong and didn't play; mostly, they sat quietly in the corner of the kitchen. The older girls cried, not understanding; and Francesca spent all her time at her grandparents' house, crying hysterically. Anna worried that Francesca would make herself sick before the trip. Anna allowed her to spend as much time at her grandparents' house as she wished, and hoped the separation wouldn't be too hard. Vincenza, although distraught by this move, looked at it as a positive and a practical adventure, which was her attitude regarding every aspect of her life. She cried, but only when she was alone. She knew that she was the strong one, and that she had to be in control. It was her station in life, and her intelligence guided her to do the right thing for her family.

The day came when the family was in Palermo, saying their goodbyes to their friends and family. Anna's family was all there, except Giuseppa who couldn't bring herself to go to the docks for their goodbyes. Her anger was evident, and she had such hate for Franco. The night before departure, she went to him in tears and asked him not to go. Franco was drunk and only pushed her away. She left the Gennusa house in tears, never to say goodbye to her sister and best friend.

Vincenzo was there with his family, and he hugged Franco and Anna goodbye. Lucia looked sad as Anna said, "I never say goodbye to a good friend. I will see you again someday." Lucia hugged her friend and could not say a word in return. She only cried.

The hardest thing was watching Francesca say goodbye to her aunts and her grandparents. The tears flowed profusely from all of them, as they hugged and kissed her dimpled cheeks. The separation was harder than Anna ever imagined.

Franco took the whole affair in stride. He had lots to drink before boarding the ship, which made his transference easy. His daughters' and wife's tears did not faze him. Franco walked up to the ship with his head high, not looking back at Anna's parents.

The Gennusa family boarded a ship called the *Marine Perch*. This twelve-thousand ton American Warship had been converted into a passenger transport. This ship served as a passenger ship between 1946

and 1949. It had made several runs back and forth to the States after the war, and was known to be sturdy, but not comfortable. The Gennusas, like many other families, carried their own belongings aboard the huge vessel, because they were traveling third class.

They stood on the ship's deck and waved to their families as the ship was pushed out of the dock by a tugboat. The *Marine Perch* headed its bow toward the great waters of the Mediterranean Sea, and toward the United States of America.

Freezing from the cold wind, Franco went to show his tickets to a porter who directed them to their cabin. Franco and Anna, along with the older girls, carried their bags down several flights of stairs. Vincenza and Francesca took the hands of the smaller girls and descended the narrow stairs where the porter instructed them to go. The closer they got to their space, the more the children started to complain about the smell. The heat from the ship, and the strong smell of disinfectants, made the entire family queasy.

They entered a room full of empty, narrow beds stacked on top of each other. The bunks were three layers high and each bed was numbered. The sheets and blankets looked clean, but were stiff to the touch. The walls of the ship were gray and dull, which made the room uninviting. The family took in their surroundings and felt lost.

Each member of the family had a bed, but there was no number that matched Franco's ticket. Puzzled, he spoke to a family next to them. They were from Palermo and were getting settled in their bunks. Franco asked if they could help find his bunk. The mother of the family said that Franco's bunk was on the opposite side of the ship, which confused Franco and so he asked the woman to repeat herself. She explained that her husband wasn't with her because all men slept on the other side of the ship. Franco assured Anna that there was a mistake and he would check with the porter. It was some time before Franco came back to his family, saying that he was told that all the men on board were placed on the other side of the ship. He could, however, share his day with his family and eat meals with them. Franco was very upset, and started to feel the effects of the wine wearing off.

Anna took control and said to Teresa, "You and Pina get the children settled in their bunks and I'll help Pappa with his bags and get him settled. We'll be back soon."

"Stay together. Francesca, this is not the time to be crying. I need you to be a big girl and help your older sisters get settled in." Anna reached down to Francesca and kissed her cheeks and the girl stopped crying.

Anna and Franco left their daughters and headed toward Franco's quarters. They entered a large room, a duplicate to Anna's, with men and young boys only. This room was large, with lots of bunks crowded in layers on top of each other. The walls of this room were the same dreary gray color, and the sheets and blankets on the mattresses were the same also. There were numbers on the end of the bunks. Anna found the number of Franco's bunk and place his bag on it. Franco had not had a glass of wine since early that morning, and longed for its rich taste. Not feeling well from the smell of the room, Franco sat on the bed and said to Anna, "Go back to our daughters. As soon as I'm settled, I'll come to you."

"Yes," Anna said, and quickly left her husband, worried about her daughters being left by themselves.

Franco tucked a small satchel under his head. It gave him comfort to know that the embarkation papers were safe as he lay down on his bunk. When Anna was out of sight, he held on to his stomach, shaking from withdrawal, from lack of alcohol. He felt uneasy, and needed to rest for a few minutes. Alone for a short time, Franco was grateful for a moment to himself to rest on his bunk.

That evening at dinner the family was very hungry. They hadn't eaten the lunch that was served in the cafeteria that afternoon. A strange-looking, long log-shaped meat product was served to them, wrapped up in a soft bun. The family later realized that they had been introduced to an American hot dog. They sat in a cafeteria, a large room with gray walls and several large picnic-style tables and benches. The little ones thought it was fun, because it looked like they were having a picnic outside of their grandparents' house, in the back yard.

Teresa stared at some bright yellow, smooth stuff which had a sharp smell that she did not recognize. She looked at it, felt nauseated and pushed it away. Later, it was reintroduced to the family as mustard. They were served cold glasses of milk, which they all drank willingly. The milk they usually drank was warm, directly from the cow. Although cold, the rich whole milk tasted good and felt good in their stomachs.

At the evening meal, they were served meatloaf with a large bowl of mashed potatoes covered in gravy. The meatloaf had a thick, red sauce on top of it. The girls looked at this meat and couldn't put it on their plates. Anna was worried that her daughters weren't eating. She took the large bowl of mashed potatoes, dug below the gravy and put a large amount in her mouth. The potatoes were delicious. She took a spoonful of the potatoes, placed them on the children's plates, and demanded that they eat. The potatoes were creamy and the girls ate heartily. Anna asked the server in English if they could have more potatoes and soon another huge bowl was given to them.

The server saw the children eating the potatoes happily, and brought back a bowl of a creamy, light yellow substance. Anna was told it was butter. The server told Anna to put the butter on the potatoes because it would make them taste good. Anna placed the creamy, rich butter in a mound of hot potatoes and watched it melt. She placed a spoonful in her mouth and was surprised at how delicious it tasted. She told her daughters and Franco to try them, and all enjoyed their first American dinner of mashed potatoes and butter.

After their dinner of mashed potatoes, the children were full and tired. It was dark outside and the girls only wanted to go bed and sleep. Franco went to his family's cabin, helped put the children to bed, and wished them a good night. After giving his girls hugs, he hugged Anna for the first time in many weeks. He asked that she take care of his daughters.

Anna asked, "Franco, why are you carrying that small satchel?"

"I have our passports and some important papers in it."

Anna didn't reply, but started to tuck her daughters into bed.

With a severe headache, Franco left Anna with the responsibility of the family and went to his own cabin. He too was filled with mashed potatoes and butter. The potatoes made his stomach feel better, and he stopped shaking, but unlike the girls, he didn't sleep sound that night. He laid awake in his bunk for the duration of the night, holding the satchel close to him.

The next morning, the ship was in open sea, heading toward the new world. In the cafeteria, lower class guests were served scrambled eggs and toast with butter and jelly. The eggs were dry, and the toast was burnt, and made from limp white bread. The coffee was weak in comparison to the dark, thick coffee the Gennusa family was used to, and mixed with the strong smell of the disinfectants being used to clean tables and dishes in the cafeteria, the aroma of hot food and coffee didn't even smell appetizing. The Gennusa family was used to daily fresh farm eggs, and the only bread they ate was homemade and thickly sliced. They tried to eat the eggs but ended up only eating toast for their breakfast.

Anna was tired from all that had happened over the last couple of days, and just wanted to be with Giuseppa, who would put her arms around her for comfort. She tried very hard to hide her sadness and disappointment about this trip. Whenever she felt misplaced, she would look at her beautiful daughters, and felt a love and joy that helped her to forget her true feelings.

Chapter Twenty

Soon a week had passed since the Gennusa family boarded the ship and they were beginning to look pale. The girls couldn't eat the food served to them, because it looked and smelled so strange. The stuffiness of their cabin, and the smell of the disinfectants used daily made the family sick. Franco and Anna took their daughters to the deck of the ship several times every day to get fresh air, but the air was bitterly cold, even on sunny days, and it was hard for the girls to stay on deck with the cold wind rushing through.

Franco and Anna tried to play games with their daughters, but they too were becoming weak from lack of food and water. Their diet consisted of milk, butter, and any kind of potatoes that were served to them. The chicken dinners, filled with strange spices, were not appetizing, and the red meat was served very bloody, which made the family feel even worse.

As the ship continued into its second week of travel, many things were happening in the world, of which the Gennusa family was unaware. The Europeans and the Americans were dealing with the aftermath of a hard-fought war that would continue to affect people all over for years to come. The Gennusa family didn't realize that these events would continue to be a part of their lives in the new world.

Most influential to the older girls would be a young actor, Marlon Brando, making his electrifying debut in Tennessee Williams' "A Streetcar Named Desire" during their second week of travel. The play was performed in New York City; Brando showed his exceptional talent mumbling and cursing in a tight sweaty undershirt, dominating the stage. Little did the older girls imagine that they would soon fall in love with this brilliant and handsome actor, and swoon at the mere mention of his name.

The Gennusa family was too sick to keep up with the news of the world. The children got sicker as the ship traveled into the high waves, and the waters were rough for several days. Many of the passengers were sick from the ship's rolling as it traveled.

The days passed slowly and remained long, cold and windy. Unable to stay out in the bitter cold and feeling weak, the Gennusa family stayed indoors. Anna was worried, because her daughters had begun to refuse even water. Once she tasted the water for herself, it was no surprise that her girls wouldn't take it; the water tasted moldy. Teresa and Pina understood the need for water and drank it, even though they were used to fresh spring water. No matter what Anna did, she couldn't get the youngest girls to drink.

By the end of the third day, the waves had settled down and Anna discussed the girls' condition with Franco, but he didn't need to be told; it was obvious they were not well. "Franco, our daughters are dying. We need to do something. I can't handle this on my own," Anna cried. "Please do something."

Franco, heart sickened, said, "I'll talk to the porter again and tell him it's urgent." In dismay, Franco left Anna to seek the porter in charge of the third-class passengers and found him working in his stateroom. Franco, with his satchel tucked under his arm, waited politely at the doorway until the porter looked at him.

The porter's small cabin had a desk with several telephones on it. Several small black and white pictures of what appeared to be the porter's family hung on the wall in black frames. The walls of the cabin were a dull gray, just like throughout the rest of the ship. Water outside the ship splashed against a small porthole high up on the far wall. The porthole, although not very large, let enough sunlight into the room for it to be cozy.

Finally the porter noticed Franco at the door. A tall slender man with light brown hair, of about Franco's age and weight, he put his writing instrument down on his desk and stood up from his chair. He stretched out his right hand to greet Franco who also extended his right hand and quickly began telling the man about his concern for his daughters.

The porter looked at Franco and said, "Signore, I'm sorry but, as I told you before, there's nothing I can do. There is plenty of water and food for all the passengers on this ship. There are many passengers at the ship's hospital right now because they are seasick. The rough weather we have experienced the last few days has affected many of passengers. The staff and I are doing our best for all our guests. If your daughters refuse to drink and to eat...." The porter stopped and said, "Are you all right? Signore, you don't look so good."

Franco wiped his brow with his sleeve, looked at the porter in annoyance and said, "No, I'm not fine. I need help. My wife and daughters are dying. They need help."

"Yes," the porter said, "I can see your family is not doing well, but there's nothing I can do if they refuse the food and liquids that we serve. I can only do so much, Signore. You must get them to eat." The porter was annoyed at Franco's persistence. "I'm sorry, but the problem is yours."

Franco sighed and wiped his forehead again before leaving the porter's cabin. He walked up to the deck where the fresh, cold air made him feel better. His stomach didn't ache as much when he breathed the cold air. Franco noticed many other people standing by the railing, looking up at the sky. Some of them looked very ill and they were shaking from the cold, brisk wind blowing on them, but he could see that the fresh air was making these people feel less seasick. He walked to the railing close to the bow of the ship and looked out to the ocean. He didn't feel cold, but was soothed by the brisk wind. He opened his coat and welcomed the sun that shone on his chest and face.

He could feel his pants down low on his hips for he, like the rest of his family, had lost weight. He needed his wine, and needed it badly. For just a moment, he forgot about his family and their needs while standing on the deck trying to control his shakes.

It came as a surprise to Franco that his wine had this effect on him; the mere thought of the warm liquid made his body ache and crave it even more. If he'd known he was going to feel this way on this trip, he would have brought wine with him. He would have snuck it on board, if he had only known how much he would need it. When he was with Anna, he kept his hands in his coat pocket so she wouldn't see his hands shaking.

Franco looked into the bright blue sky and took in several deep breaths. He looked down at the wide barren ocean, longing for the smell of the warm air of his homeland. He thought of his family dying down in the bow of the ship in their stuffy quarters, and his inability to do anything about it. He closed his eyes and imagined the coolness of the rich dirt in his hands; he envisioned himself working his magic when planting. He dreamed of being in the fields looking at the bountiful food that grew on his fine farm. He opened his eyes and looked again out into the open space of the blue ocean and longed for the only home he had ever known.

He shook his head and thought to himself that life in America would only be for a few years, and then they would go home, rich. American streets, he knew, were lined with gold. Together, he and his family would all work hard, get some of that gold for themselves, and return to Bisacquino, to their home. Trying to convince himself he said out loud, "I have done the right thing." He repeated himself as he touched the bulk in his pocket, "I have money to get us started. We will establish ourselves and save our earnings"

Franco reached into his pocket, looked around to see if anyone was watching him, and then pulled out a large roll of American dollar bills. After paying for passage for himself and his family, there was plenty of money left for their future in America. Franco never told Anna about the money; there was no reason to tell her. He had control of the situation. Franco returned the money deep into his pocket and felt secure.

With his hand on the money in his pocket, Franco thought about Anna and his daughters, and how much they needed him. He knew he should get back to them, but he hesitated; he felt terrible, tired and achy in his lungs.

Franco looked to the bright sky and again thought of Anna. A pang of guilt ran through him as he thought of the night he had raped Deanna. It made him sick to his stomach knowing she was carrying his child. Before he and his family left for America, Deanna had made it known throughout the village that she was expecting a child.

Franco felt incredibly guilty standing there on the ship's deck. He didn't want to be confronted with his family's crisis and stayed out a while longer, avoiding having to face them. He took his satchel off his shoulder and pulled out a pack of cigarettes and lit one. He put the pack in his pocket and dragged deeply on the cigarette. The smoke swirled in his lungs and made him feel dizzy and made his stomach feel worse. But he didn't care; the soothing effect of the smoke outweighed the pain in his lungs. He finished his cigarette, threw it into the salty water, and turned to go to his family.

Franco took his first step into the hatchway and felt a sharp pain in his chest. He stopped and held his breath until the pain stopped, but as he proceeded to the door, he started to cough. He drew a deeper breath in his lungs, trying to control the cough, but he coughed even harder. A thick, dull, heavy fluid filled the back of his throat and he turned back to the edge of the ship to spit the fluid into the water. He stood for a few seconds, waiting for his dizziness to subside, and once he felt better, headed back toward the door that led to his family.

Franco entered his family's cabin and looked helplessly at his sick children. Little Maria wasn't only lethargic, but her sweet perky smile was gone, and Pina didn't even stir when he approached her. He was becoming desperate but didn't know what to do. For the first time, he acknowledged to himself that they were truly dying. Franco swallowed hard.

At that moment a small, gentle, elderly Italian woman from a bunk close by approached him and said, "I see your family is not doing well. I have some fresh oranges that I can share with them. Please take them, for I have plenty. I am traveling alone. I'll be meeting my husband in New York."

The woman continued, "My husband knew about the food on these passenger ships, for he has traveled several times from Palermo to America. He warned me to bring fresh fruit with me and I have more than I need. Come, I have plenty to share."

Franco gratefully walked to the woman's bunk and she handed him a large bag of fresh oranges. He offered her money but she refused, saying she had plenty, so he thanked her instead. He thanked her over and over and offered his service if she ever needed it.

Franco brought the oranges to his family, peeled them, and handed sections of the juicy, fresh fruit to his daughters. They ate willingly and it was obvious that they were feeling better with every bite. Anna smiled at her husband, because she knew he wouldn't fail her and their daughters. Franco had taken matters into his own hands and had found a way to take care of them. Everyone was feeling better already thanks to the sweet, juicy oranges. Franco told the girls to put on their coats, for it was a cold but clear day, and they were going to go out into the sun to get fresh air. The girls rose up from their bunks and headed toward the deck, into the brightness of a cold, crisp day. Franco and Anna spent most of the afternoon outside, watching their daughters at play.

Franco held on to the railing because he was feeling weak, but he did smile at Anna when she looked his way. Anna never suspected, and she was too completely involved with her daughters, to see that Franco was very sick.

Several days passed, and the children were getting better. With one fruit a day, the nourishment was getting them by, but Franco no longer wanted or desired any food. He refused the fruit that Anna tried to make him eat. Anna could see that Franco was losing weight, but her focus was on her children. They had begun to force themselves to drink the water and took the fruit, knowing it was keeping them alive. Anna felt that Franco could take care of himself as he had several times in the past when she wasn't there to take care of him.

The chef, after talking to Franco about the problem of his daughters not eating, cooked French toast for them at breakfast one morning. He sneaked the girls into the kitchen to sit with the kitchen helpers and he served them bread dipped in a sugar, cinnamon, and a mixture of milk and eggs, fried in butter to a crisp, golden brown, and served hot with more butter. The whole family, even Anna, enjoyed this unusual meal. Some of the girls loved the thick, brown syrup served on the side.

The chef, seeing how much this breakfast was enjoyed by this delightful family, fell in love with the little ones. The family was so gracious and appreciative that he saved some of the French toast for their dinner that night. He also saved applesauce, and homemade thick biscuits with jelly, that were only served to the upper-class passengers. Because the chef had fallen in love with these beautiful children, he even gave them sweet sugar cookies when he could. Franco and Anna thanked him many times, but the thanks were not needed. The chef was truly delighted by these unselfish and well-mannered children.

The long, boring days finally led into the third week, and the third day before the end of the trip. The Gennusa family got up joyously that morning, knowing that they were going to be served hot French toast as promised the night before by the chef. Their mouths watered for this delicious food, and they looked forward to their breakfast. Franco didn't eat the fried toast, because he couldn't adjust to this strange food and still didn't feel well enough to eat.

The chef also promised the children vanilla ice cream after dinner that evening. This too was usually served only to upper-class passengers, but the leftovers were saved for the girls. This special event was going to be shared that evening with the kitchen help, who kept the gathering a secret from the other workers.

Those days of the voyage were the longest and, in some ways, the hardest on the family. The children still hadn't entirely adjusted to the ship, and even on the last day they felt sick. But knowing that sweets were waiting at the end of the day made the trip a little easier and happier. Anna, knowing that her daughters would survive the trip in fairly decent health, was able to relax a little.

The captain of the ship announced over the intercom that it was going to be a warm and perfect day. He made a report every day, but this day was very special for the Italian passengers. The American military was leaving Italy after having occupied the country since the first troops had entered Sicily in 1943. The American flag was taken down and replaced with the Italian flag. There was a loud cheer from the passengers as the captain reported this historic event.

As the cheering continued, the captain reported that President Truman promised to help Italy if her freedom was ever threatened again. That statement was welcomed by the Italian government. The American captain, who spoke English and Italian perfectly, reported the news in both languages. The captain also related to the passengers that it would be a sunny day, which made the news even better.

Each day, during the captain's announcements, Franco and his family sat in the cafeteria and listened. Franco admired Anna as she'd translate the English. Their daughters waited anxiously every day, and loved hearing their mother speak words in a different tongue. When the captain spoke Italian, the girls understood because Anna taught the language at home, though they normally spoke the Sicilian dialect. The girls had to know how to speak Italian correctly in order to attend school.

The morning of the third day, before arriving at their destination, the family was gathered on the deck, sitting in the sunshine. Anna was translating to her family as the captain told of the day's events.

Teresa said, "Mamma, I never realized how well you had mastered the English language."

"Well, there is a difference, but there are many similarities in both the Italian and English languages," Anna said. "If you listen, you'll hear similarities to Latin. Most languages are derived from Latin." Anna explained to the younger girls. She continued, "I can read and speak a little Greek language, too."

Franco looked at Anna and felt surprised and then angry at himself for not knowing these things about his wife, that she was not only bilingual, but also spoke and read two other languages. His anger passed and he looked at Anna with great pride.

Anna saw him watching her. Their eyes locked and they were brought back to their younger days—those days when they got lost in each other's arms and made love with such intensity. They looked at each other and shared a moment that was only theirs to share. Both were lost in that moment, and that is where they wanted to be.

They traveled together, each of them, silently but knowing they were thinking the same thing, forgetting about their present demands. Anna's eyes swelled with tears for her lost love. She felt loneliness and longing for her husband. Franco's eyes filled with tears as well. Looking at his wife, he longed for her, and his longing made him feel even sadder. The hot tears on his face brought him back to reality and he looked away, into the vast blue sea, suddenly feeling enormous guilt.

Anna felt as if her skin had been torn, like a knife had punctured her heart. Franco had rejected her again, turned away, and reminded her of the man she had fallen in love with so long ago, the handsome young stranger with piercing blue eyes. He had handed her a pouch with a gold charm and vowed his deep love for her.

All these years later, the charm still hung around her neck. She raised her hand to her necklace and rubbed the charm, recalling her wedding night, how nervous she'd been but how she'd looked into his tranquil blue eyes and fallen totally in love. She remembered how she had given herself to that man. At that moment she had believed that he would always be there for her, that they would always be together. The memories left her as quickly as they had come.

Anna turned to her daughters who were standing around her. Teresa came to her mother's side, and put her arms around her. Anna drew her oldest daughter to her and felt all her other daughters' love surrounding her. Their existence kept her warm from the cold wind that was blew around them. She felt nothing else—no pain, no love for the man standing nearby, who had become a stranger to her; she felt nothing.

Franco turned to the open ocean and breathed in the cold air. He thought to himself how much he wanted his life back with his wife. But his past sins—and the one in particular—plagued his mind. He couldn't stop replaying the image of the night he spent with Deanna. He had asked himself so many times how he could have been so naive as to fall into Deanna's trap. How could he have been so violent that night? He never realized that there was so much hate built up inside of him. This unexplained deep hate drove him to be that destructive to Deanna and it was this hate that he battled constantly within himself.

He tried very hard to get rid of the image of that horrible night, but couldn't. Franco hung his head, looking out to the horizon, trying to be taken in by the alluring blue waves. He tried to concentrate on their whitecaps, but couldn't. All he could see was Deanna's swollen, bruised face. He couldn't forget watching her as she turned and stumbled into her house, blood running down between her legs.

After that night with Deanna, he felt dirty and unworthy. Because of his guilt he could not, to his tremendous regret, ever touch his wife again. His shame was too much for him to bear. He knew he could never be trusted and loved by Anna again if she found out what was tormenting him. She would never forgive him. He also knew, especially after Maria was born, that no matter how much he longed for Anna, their sexual life would never be the same. He couldn't live with himself if Anna died from giving birth to another child.

Franco was getting weaker. Holding on to the side of the ship, he excused himself, and physically exhausted, headed back to his bunk. Franco no longer had the strength to be around Anna. His guilt was draining him even more than his physical illness. With the little strength he had left, Franco reached his cabin and stumbled into his bunk. He lay as still as he could and then he gave way to deep, heavy coughing.

The girls waited patiently at their bunks for their father to have lunch with them. They wanted to talk to him more about the ice cream the chef was saving for them for that evening's dessert. The whole family was invited to this special quiet last-night party in the kitchen. The little ones were so excited that they forgot that their tummies were upset.

Anna told Teresa and Pina to take their sisters to the cafeteria for lunch "Your father and I will meet you there."

The daughters left for lunch, and Anna headed toward the men's sleeping quarters.

For the second time on this voyage, Anna entered the large, gloomy room where Franco slept. She looked for Franco's bunk in the middle of the room, but was surrounded by so many other bunks that his could not be seen. She stood in the doorway, hoping that someone would help her, but no one came to her assistance so she walked boldly into the large room and made her way to Franco's bunk.

The stale smells of disinfectants and male body odors were strong were strong in the room, especially since it was so warm. She found Franco in bed, lying on his side with his eyes wide open.

Franco realized that someone was standing by his bunk and turned his head. He touched his satchel under his head to make sure it was still there, and then looked around and saw his wife. Anna bent down to him, to touch his head, but he pushed her away before she could touch him. "Franco, what is wrong?" Anna asked.

Franco summoned all his strength, and lifted himself up, not letting on how very sick he felt. He looked at her and said, "I'm not feeling well today. I have a pounding in my head. The ship's doctor gave me some medication just before you came so I should be alright in a little while. Go have lunch with our daughters, and I'll see you at dinner. I just need to get rid of this pounding in my head."

Anna again asked about his health and, annoyed, he said, "Go away, I'll be alright."

Anna left, angry at him for his attitude toward her when she had been trying to help him.

Franco lifted his head long enough to watch his wife leave the room. When she was out of sight he started to cough violently until his coughing produced blood. He reached weakly for a container hidden under his bed and spit into it and then pushed it back under his bed. He fell back into his bunk and groaned from the pain in his lungs. He lay still for some minutes, feverishly hot, and then turned ice cold. He knew that he was not well and was waiting for the ship's doctor to see him again and to get medication. Franco broke into a high fever after the doctor left him; and that was just a few minutes before Anna came to see him. He didn't tell the doctor about the blood he'd been spitting up the night before. Like his youngest daughters, Franco couldn't drink the brackish-tasting water. He lay back on his bunk, glad that Anna was not near him. He closed his tired eyes and slipped into a coma.

Anna walked to the cafeteria, upset and angry, thinking life had not been good for her and Franco in a very long time. She entered the cafeteria and saw that her girls were eating heartily, which made her feel better. She smiled as she approached them, and Teresa gave her a plate of mashed potatoes with butter floating on top of them. The mashed potatoes were saved from last night's dinner by the chef. Anna ate the potatoes, but pushed most of the butter to the side of the dish, for she found it too rich.

It was the next to the last day of the trip, and Anna got up early and went to the men's cabin to see how Franco was doing. Finding him sound asleep and not wanting to disturb him, she decided not to wake him. He looked at peace for once. She touched his head and found him a little warm, but not as hot as the day before.

She noticed that his satchel was under his head and wondered what important papers were there. She never dared to ask about the papers, and how important they were. She knew she had no right to ask, and that Franco wouldn't tell her anyway.

Anna checked on Franco several times a day, and he was always asleep. Each time she checked on him, his fever seemed to be going down. By the end of the night his fever had subsided completely.

The next day after they had finished eating, Anna said to her daughters, "Come, let us go up to the deck and get some fresh air. Today will be our last day on this ship. Let's make it a memorable one."

As they walked to the deck Vincenza said, "Mamma, is Pappa alright?"

"Yes, darling," she said sweetly, touching Vincenza's shining, long, blonde hair. "I just checked him, and he's sound asleep. I know he has taken some medication that the ship's doctor gave him. I think it is best if Pappa just rests."

"Mamma," Vincenza said, "I'm worried about Pappa." Anna looked surprised at her daughter and asked, "Why, my daughter?"

"Pappa looks sick to me," Vincenza said.

Anna said, "Pappa assured me that he was alright, and that the ship's doctor is looking after him. You must stop worrying. You worry too much about everything."

Anna climbed the stairs with her family and went to the deck. She felt the cold, fresh air hit her face, and the air felt good. Vincenza worried her, because she took too much to heart. This daughter continuously worried about everything. Her great intelligence and sensitivity, plus her common sense, were a great burden to carry for such a young person. Vincenza had never been young. She was born old and wise, and carried the responsibility of this family with a heavy heart.

Anna's little ones ran when their feet hit the deck and the rest of the family followed. They found a sunny spot, and the little ones started to play tag. Vincenza and Francesca found chairs and sat down. Vincenza had a worried look on her face, as always, but Francesca's mind was elsewhere, as it had been since the beginning of the trip. Anna walked closer to the ship's side. With her older daughters next to her, and the younger ones within sight, she put her back to the side of ship. Facing her children, she put her foot on the back of the rail and slumped a little in a relaxed position. She turned to one side to find Teresa standing next to her, diligently protecting her sisters. Watching for a few minutes, Anna glanced to her other side, to see Pina looking out into the ocean. Pina was pensive, as she had been since she came aboard the vessel. Anna turned to her, placed her arm around her shoulders, and hugged her. Pina placed her hand on her mother's arm, put her head on her mother's shoulder, and returned the hug.

Anna held Pina tightly and said, "My dear, sweet daughter, you grow more like a sleek graceful swan every day." Anna raised her hand and in a circular movement said, "I can see you on a fashion magazine someday, in America, for you carry your beauty so well. Your legs are so thin. Amazingly, they continue to grow longer every day. You keep stretching and reaching to a new beauty every time I look at you."

Pina couldn't help but smile at her mother's compliments. She looked at her and said, "Ever since I was a child, you have always overstated my looks, Mamma. It's very nice, and I thank you, but my looks have not given me what I really want."

Sighing, Anna asked, "And, what is it that you really want, Pina?"

"I want to be back in my home in Sicily. I want to feel the land under my feet. I want to feel and see its history, and to be a part of it, Mamma. I want to help cultivate its future. I need the island to know where I belong. I want to help make it a more modern place for my children to live," Pina said sorrowfully.

"I'm sorry for taking you away from what is so important to you. I never realized you were so passionate about Sicily," Anna said.

"Mamma, I never felt there was a need to express how I felt about our island, for I never imagined that I would live anywhere else."

Anna, still holding her daughter said, "It will only be for a short time, and then we will return to Sicily. Look at this as an adventure, and that someday you will be able to share with your children. America is so different. It's full of magnificent new buildings and new streets. It has many different types of cultures, all mixed together. These cultures live together in harmony, and it's amazing. It will be an education that, otherwise, you would not have gotten.

"Your father is greatly concerned about us not having dowries for you girls. You know that if we cannot give wealth to a family that we feel is worthy for you to marry, you'll marry out of our station. That is unacceptable to both your father and me. We will work hard, save our money, and you girls will learn the way of Americans. We will go back to Sicily when you're ready to marry well."

Pina said, after taking a deep breath, "I love you, Mamma. You always know how to make me feel better. I promise I won't be a burden to you on this trip and I will do my share and work hard, so we can go back to our home."

Anna smiled and said, "Pina, I never doubted that you would do your part. Come and look at your sisters, my daughter, and look at how beautiful they are. How lucky we are to be a part of a wonderful family like this. Think of tomorrow—and stepping into this new world that will be home to us for only a short time—as a place for a challenging adventure."

Without responding to her mother, Pina put her arm down, turned with her mother, and looked at her sisters whom she loved deeply and with such pride.

Chapter Twenty-One

The day wore on, and Franco never came to meet them for lunch. Anna didn't worry because she was still angry at him for rejecting her during her visit yesterday.

It was late afternoon and the girls weren't feeling well so they were resting in their bunks. Anna told Teresa and Pina to watch the girls while she went to check on their father.

Anna walked slowly toward Franco's quarters, not knowing what to expect from him. She stood in the doorway of his cabin and felt unwell at the smell of heavy body odor. She stopped, turned around, and walked up several floors and out to the deck.

The day was ending and daylight was giving way to the night sky. It was only four-thirty in the afternoon, but night was evident. Anna walked to the side of the ship, holding her coat, for it had become bitter cold without the shining sun. She noticed that there were only a few people on deck.

Most were couples looking out into the water. They were cuddling together to keep warm, or just as an excuse to be close to each other. She looked at these couples and wondered what their lives were like. She too looked toward the water, out onto the dark horizon, and wondered what lay ahead for her and her family. She took a deep breath and for one moment selfishly enjoyed the solitude.

After a short time, Anna faced the metal door, and walked toward it feeling very tired. She walked down several flights of stairs to Franco's cabin and waited at the door again, hit by the heavy, pungent smell of the stale odor in the room. A handsome, short, stocky young boy with big brown eyes and dark, curly hair came to her and asked if he could help. She told him that her husband was in bunk number 222 and she would wait for him to meet her at the door. She asked the young man if he would mind getting her husband for her. The young boy smiled and skipped away in Franco's direction.

Anna waited only a short time, scanning the room filled with men and young boys, noticing that the stale smell was strong in the room, but it didn't seem to bother the men. They seemed happy— probably because they'd be reaching their destination the next day. Anna noticed that some of the bags were packed, and other men were busy packing. A few minutes later the young boy came back to tell her that bunk number 222 had been sent to the ship's hospital.

Without a word, Anna headed toward the medical facility. She walked quickly, and had no trouble finding it. A small, thin nurse in a white uniform and a starched white cap came to her and asked Anna her name. After Anna gave her name, the nurse led her past many beds filled with sick people.

The smell of disinfectant, medication, and death was very strong. The nurse stopped at the end of Franco's bed, and told Anna that he had been in the ship's hospital since late that morning.

Anna was shocked.

"I'll send the doctor in to speak with you," the nurse said.

Anna walked to the side of the bed where Franco lay, half dazed. She approached him slowly and then bent down to him. "Franco," she said, "What's wrong?"

Franco could barely focus as he turned his head and looked at Anna. He didn't recognize her. He turned away and looked straight ahead, and then closed his eyes.

Anna touched his head, noticing that his small satchel was being used as a pillow. She was shocked to feel that his fever was much higher; his face was flushed, and sweat was running down his forehead. Anna reached over to the side of the bed and dipped a cloth in a bowl of cold water. She placed the cloth on Franco's forehead and he moaned at her touch.

"Signora, I am Dr. Travazanno," Anna lifted the cloth from Franco's head and turned. The doctor was surprised to see a petite, very beautiful women looking back at him. He had to compose himself, and then continued to speak in broken English talk. "I have been taking care of your husband for the last couple of days."

Anna looked up to a large balding man with a soft, gentle face, around the age of fifty.

Shocked, Anna responded to the doctor, "What do you mean—you've been taking care of him for the last couple of days?"

"Your husband has been very sick but refused to get medical care, not wanting you to know he was sick. He didn't want to spend money on medication."

"But I don't understand...I saw him this morning and his fever was gone. He was asleep when I checked him. What's wrong with him?" Anna asked.

The doctor looked at her, and said sadly, "Your husband has developed a very severe case of pneumonia. Because his body is weak, he has also developed a high fever. I haven't been able to get his fever under control."

Anna sat slowly in a chair and put her head in her hands. She stayed quietly for some time and the doctor continued. "I pleaded with your husband to let me get you, but he was adamant that you not be told. It wasn't until just a short time ago that his fever spiked. He's gone into a coma."

Anna lifted her head and said confidently, "He will be fine."

"Signora, your husband..." the doctor hesitated, sighed and then proceeded to say, "Your husband is really very sick. He will not make it through the night. He hid the fact that he had been throwing up blood for several days. My nurse, after your husband was admitted, went to his bunk to get the bed number so she could locate you, and she found a container hidden under his bed, full of bloody fluid. Your husband is bleeding internally. I've been unable to locate the source of the bleeding. When he urinates, which is not too often because he refuses to drink the water, his urine is mostly blood. Unfortunately, I don't have the means on this ship to help him."

Anna sat up, leaned back in the chair, and put her hand to her mouth. She listened to the doctor intently and asked, "What are you telling me?"

The doctor looked at Anna and said, "I'm sorry, but your husband is dying. It's only a matter of hours. I've done all I can for him but I'm unable to help him. He insisted he didn't need help. If he would've let me take care of him when he first became sick, I might not have been able to help him, but I would have done my very best to try. I am so sorry. Your husband is dying, and there is nothing I can do. As you can see I have many patients here and we are short-staffed. I didn't have the time to argue with him." The doctor, feeling guilty, continued, "I'm so sorry. I just don't have that kind of time. If he had only come to me sooner."

"I have no money for his care. What shall I do about keeping him comfortable?" Anna asked the doctor quietly.

The doctor looked at Anna in sorrow and said, "Don't worry, Signora. I may not be able to save your husband's life but I will keep him comfortable and free of pain."

Anna swallowed hard, looked at the doctor and said, "My daughters need to see their father. I need to bring them here."

"How many children do you have, Signora?"

"I have six daughters."

It was hard for the doctor to believe that a woman so young-looking and with such beauty could have given birth to six children.

The nurse came in just then, after overhearing Anna say that she was going to get her daughters, "I'm sorry but—" the nurse began to say.

The doctor stopped her, "It will be fine. I'll take full responsibility for the family being together. Please make sure that when these children come, they see their father; and please be as helpful as you can."

"Yes, Dr. Travazanno, of course I'll help the family,"

The doctor left the side of the bed to take care of his other patients and the nurse followed. He felt guilty for not having contacted Anna; he was overwhelmed with all his patients and with practically no staff, but still he felt guilty.

Anna got up from her chair and stood next to Franco in disbelief. She couldn't comprehend how sick he was. In her state of shock, looking at him, she whispered, "Franco." Then, a little louder, "Franco." And, in a deep, agonizing voice, "Franco." She turned from him without touching him and walked out of the ship's hospital room.

Anna knew that her daughters would be outside on the deck, getting fresh air. She stumbled and tripped several times as she climbed the several flights of stairs to the deck, and then opened the door to the deck and looked to the bright, star-filled sky. Still in shock, when she opened the door to the deck and looked to the bright, star-filled sky, she didn't feel the cold air hit her face. She tried to find solace in the great sky, but not finding it, she scanned the deck and spotted her daughters. She watched, momentarily relieved that they were safe, and admired their beauty. Their hair blew in the swirling wind as they played and the sound of their laughter comforted her.

The girls' joyful laughter brought on a feeling of sorrow for Anna and she began to feel weak. She caught herself before she fainted and forced herself back to reality. She thought to herself, *Where will we go from here?*

The four little ones were playing with each other, while Teresa and Pina watched them diligently. Life had demanded they grow up quickly and Anna knew how lucky she was to have such mature and strong older daughters. Their strength would be a help to her in the days ahead.

Anna's body felt heavy and weak. Needing a minute more to compose herself, she turned again to the sky and she prayed, "God, please help me."

Pina turned and saw her mother standing close by, her face up toward the sky. She smiled and went to her mother.

Teresa watched as Pina spoke to their mother and then the two embraced. Teresa instantly knew that something was wrong. She called to Vincenza to watch the younger ones while she walked toward her mother and Pina with a heavy feeling in her heart.

In her heart, Teresa didn't want to think the worst, but she was scared to find out what Pina and her mother were saying. Still, she demanded to know what was going on.

Anna looked at her oldest daughter and said, "It's Pappa. He's very sick."

"Has the ship's doctor seen him?" Teresa asked. "Yes," Anna said.

Teresa demanded to know, "Well, what did he say?" Teresa knew by the pale look on her mother's—and Pina's—face, that what was coming next was not good. She waited for Anna to finally answer, "Your father has pneumonia."

Tears welled up into Teresa's eyes, "How serious is it?"

"Very serious," Anna answered. She put her arms around Teresa and said, "Your father has gone into a coma." Anna hesitated, sighed and continued, "He's dying."

"No," Teresa said, backing away from her mother. "Mamma, no!"

Anna tried to put her arms around her oldest daughter, but Teresa wouldn't let her. She put her hands to her eyes and sobbed. Finally, she melted into her mother's arms, letting Anna comfort her. Anna held her tight and rubbed her back to console her as Teresa continued to sob loudly. When Teresa's tear had begun to subside, Anna let her go and held her at arm's length. "We're going to see your father now," Anna said. "You must be strong—not for me, but for your sisters."

Anna turned, moved closer to Pina and said, "I need you to be strong, too. We need each other and especially today. We will keep one another strong and do what we have to in order to make it through this day. Now, let's get your sisters and go see your father."

Anna turned back to Teresa and wiped the tears from her face. Anna said, "I won't tell the others that Pappa is dying. I want them to be happy when they see him, just in case he comes out of his coma. If your father comes out of his delirious state, we can be a family again, if only for a short time.

"Do you girls remember the day that the farmer and his son were murdered in front of you in the village?"

The two girls nodded their heads yes.

"Do you remember how that horrible situation stays vivid in your mind today?"

The daughters nodded yes again.

Anna continued, "Well, I want your younger sisters to remember these last moments with your father for the rest of their lives, and I need them to remember him with happiness and love. I need their father's last minutes vivid in their minds so that they can carry on with love in their hearts and minds forever. Now, let us go to the young ones."

Anna turned, and together with her oldest daughters, walked over to the children. The little ones were excited to see their mother and innocently skipped toward her. "Come girls, gather around me. I need to talk to you," she softly said.

The younger girls stopped playing and gathered around their mother. Anna looked at each one of her daughters and took a deep breath. She was no longer shaking, because she knew she had no choice but to take control of the situation, and to be strong.

She cleared her throat and told her daughters that their father wasn't feeling well, and that he was in a room with lots of sick people. They were going to see him but it was important that they be very quiet. Vincenza, normally intuitive, started to ask one of her many questions when Anna stopped her by putting her finger to Vincenza lips. "Vincenza," Anna said, "take my hand and let us go see Pappa."

Anna took Vincenza's and Francesca's hands. The older girls led the little ones, as Anna started walking toward the door that led to the ship's hospital. After entering the door quietly and quickly, they walked down many stairs, and went around many corners. While they waited at the door of hospital room for the nurse to come for them, Anna again reminded them to be very quiet.

The nurse saw them and waved them into the room. They walked by many beds filled with sick patients, and the girls looked in wonderment at all the faces. They stopped in front of their father's bed and waited for their mother to instruct them to approach their father.

Anna walked over to Franco's side. She bent down and whispered in his ear. "Franco can you hear me? I have our children here. Can you open up yours eyes to see them? They need to see you and they need you to recognize them." Anna was talking to Franco, repeating herself over and over again when the doctor came to Franco's bed.

The doctor stood among Franco's quiet daughters, surprised at their beauty. Most of them had light hair and light eyes, but each was unique. He couldn't help but notice the darker-skinned little girl. She, too, was as lovely as her sisters, but different. He admired this attractive family. The doctor was glad that he had allowed the girls to be with their father.

He walked to Anna's side, and then turned to look at the girls. He was again astonished by each one's beauty and thought to himself, *What a rich man Franco is, to have such an extraordinary family.* He looked at Franco and felt pity for his patient, because he wouldn't live to enjoy these children. The doctor turned to Anna, bent down and whispered in her ear, "Signora, I don't think he can hear you. I don't think he will wake up."

Anna turned to speak to the doctor in a low voice, so her daughters would not overhear, "Dr. Travazanno, he must wake up. He needs to acknowledge his children. Our daughters need him to see how much he loves them." In a determined voice she continued, "He needs to do this for them. It will make the process of being without him easier. I will give him no choice." She continued, determined, "He will wake up."

The doctor, knowing that he couldn't reason with Anna, didn't say another word, but backed away. Anna turned back to Franco and talked to him persistently. The girls watched the doctor back away from their mother and then parted to give him some space. The doctor stood in the middle of this family for just a moment, and, knowing they needed some private time, moved away from them.

The doctor hung his head in shame, disappointed in his lack of medical knowledge, and walked away from the family. He was angry for not being able to save and give his patient back to his remarkable family. He walked to his next patient, feeling despair, and hoping he could forget his failure by saving another man. The doctor hoped that getting involved with his next patient would lessen his burden of the oncoming, inevitable loss of life. Franco's death would stay with him, he knew, for a very long time.

Dr. Travazanno saw the long hard road ahead for this family, and tears welled in his eyes. As he stopped by the bed of his next patient, he said to himself that he must not get involved with this family. He was a medical doctor, and doctors don't get involved in their patients' private lives. There was nothing he could do for them. Although he knew he was helpless, he was still filled with guilt.

"Franco," Anna bent over and whispered in his ear, and said

firmly, "you must open your eyes. Your daughters are here in front of you and they must see you again. Franco, you are dying. You owe me this much. I have to carry on without you. I need you to look at them and let them know that you care. That will make this whole process easier for all of us."

Persisting, Anna continued to speak, "Franco, are you listening? I don't know why you have been so far from me the last few months, and at this moment." Very coldly, Anna continued, "I don't care. You are solely to blame for our not being together, and that is something you will have to take to your grave. As far as I know, I have done nothing to put this wedge between us. Open your eyes, Franco. If you have done something I need to forgive you for, I will not."

With no movement from Franco, Anna was now becoming desperate. She could feel a burning in her stomach. She was having trouble breathing, but she wouldn't stop until she got what she felt was needed. She continued to talk urgently to Franco. "That guilt, whatever it is, you will have to carry alone. I will not forgive you, ever. I know you well enough to know that whatever has kept you away from me is so horrendous that I could not, and will not, forgive you. What has happened between us should not reflect on our daughters. They need to have good memories of us as a family. Wake up, Franco, because if you don't, and there is a God in Heaven, you will have to explain this to him." Anna reached for Franco's shoulder and started to shake him.

Teresa and Pina watched in horror as their sickly father was handled roughly by their mother. Teresa said out loud, "Mamma, stop, you're going to hurt him." Vincenza put her arms around Francesca who was confused and began to cry. The little ones, not sure what was happening, watched their mother in silence.

Ignoring her oldest daughter, Anna lifted Franco up for a second. Then she stopped shaking him and angrily put him down on his pillow. She continued talking, bending toward his ear. She said, "If you expect me to feel sorry for you, I don't. Franco, you owe it to me to wake up. Are you listening to me? Do you hear me?" Determined, Anna said harshly, "Now wake up."

At that moment, Franco opened his eyes and looked straight ahead. The nurse, who had come to the other side of the bed while Anna was talking privately to him, was amazed when Franco opened his eyes, and went to get the doctor.

Franco turned his head to Anna and looked at her.

"Franco, your daughters are here to see you. If you can't talk, at least try to let them know that you love them. Can you do that?"

Franco opened his eyes wider to let her know that he would comply with her wishes. Anna called each of the girls to see their father. Each went to their father's side, and Franco looked at them after they kissed him. He reached out and touched their faces, lovingly caressing and rubbing each of their cheeks. He lingered his touch on each one of his daughters' faces as long as he could; but when it came to Innocenza's, he raised his hand and brushed her hair. Anna watched in silence, outraged at Franco's rejection of Innocenza.

Upset, Innocenza quickly moved away from her father. Anna held Innocenza close, and then turned and handed her to Teresa. Anna quickly picked up Maria and put her youngest child in front of her father. Franco looked at his beloved youngest daughter, smiled at her and reached for her. Anna, holding Maria, brought her closer to him. Franco kissed her and touched her cheek for the last time as a tear rolled down his face. The older girls were crying. They went to their father again and put their arms around him as he fell back into a coma.

The doctor stood at the end of the bed. He went to Franco and listened to his weak heartbeat. Anna got up from her chair and escorted the girls out of the area. They walked slowly to the door, passing many patients but not acknowledging any of them. The older girls were crying and Vincenza had assessed her father's condition. Knowing that he was dying, she cried harder than the others. The three younger girls were confused by the way the adults around them were carrying on.

Anna told the girls to go to dinner, and that she would see them after dinner, before they were ready for bed. Anna reminded Teresa and Pina to attend the ice cream party after dinner. She gave orders to her oldest daughters to stay close to the little ones. The older ones started to argue with their mother, wanting to stay, when the nurse told the girls they weren't allowed to stay, and that rules had been broken to allow them to come to be with their father. The older girls, still crying, headed out the door.

Anna went back to Franco and sat next to him for hours. His condition didn't change, so later that night, well into the evening, Anna approached the nurse and told her she was going to check on her daughters but she would be right back.

Anna went to her daughters, confused, disoriented, and afraid of what was ahead for them. She found them curled up in each other's arms. Teresa had Innocenza with her, Pina had Maria, and Vincenza and Francesca were asleep in Vincenza's bunk.

Satisfied that her daughters were safe, Anna started back to Franco when her neighbor, the woman who had shared her oranges, stopped her. She said the older girls had come back from dinner crying and had told her about their father. They had attended their ice cream party but came back very sad. The neighbor told Anna that she had consoled the girls and had helped put them to bed. She told Anna to go back to her husband, and not to worry about her family, because she would sleep in Francesca's bunk for the night to keep an eye on them for her. Anna was grateful and thanked her many times before she left to be with Franco.

Anna walked quietly to Franco's bed and found the nurse checking on him. Franco was still in a coma; his condition hadn't changed. His heart rate was very slow, barely beating. Anna sat by the bed for many hours, even though she was tired and stiff.

It was getting close to morning when the doctor came and asked to speak to her away from Franco. Anna straightened up slowly, feeling the pain of sitting so long in one position, and walked in small steps away from Franco's bed to Dr. Travazanno.

"Signora," Dr. Travazanno said, "I need to know what you would like me to do with your husband if he should not survive this trip."

Anna looked at the doctor surprised, because she hadn't thought that she would have to make such a decision about Franco. Anna had only thought about the moment and she responded, "Oh God, I don't know." She repeated, questioning herself softly, and said again, "I don't know."

The doctor explained that in the morning, Anna could hire a mortician to take Franco to the funeral home, and they would find a plot for him. "They will bury him."

Anna felt a pain in her stomach and put her hand there. She said to the doctor, "How much would this cost?"

The doctor said he didn't know for certain, but it could be inexpensive if she chose a coffin of cheaper wood. The funeral homes varied in price, depending on the type of funeral. The doctor, talking to Anna, noticed that she had become pale. He hesitated for a moment and said, "Signora, are you alright? You look like you're going to pass out."

The doctor summoned his nurse and told her to bring a glass of water. The nurse handed Anna the water, which she drank, and some of the color came back into her face. The doctor asked Anna, "How can I help you, Signora?"

Anna said, "I don't think you can. I have no money to bury my husband. I have no family in New York. I have nothing."

Dr. Travazanno dismissed the nurse, and then looked at Anna with compassion, and said, "There is one thing that I can do, but it will depend on when Franco dies."

Anna, puzzled, asked, "What can you do?"

"I don't normally get involved with my patients, but it's been hard not to, with you and your family. If your husband should die before morning, I could notify the Red Cross, and they'll take him off the ship. They will have the city of New York bury him."

"But my husband has a passport. Won't they check to see if there are relatives aboard the ship?" Anna asked.

"No," the doctor said. "By the time the Red Cross takes his body with his medical and release papers, and he gets to where they will bury him, there will be few inquiries made. There are other bodies that will be picked up by the Red Cross. They don't usually ask if the people have families on the ship."

Anna looked at the doctor. "Where will they take him?"

The doctor said that Franco would be taken to a mortuary, and the body prepared for burial in a cemetery owned by the city of New York. The section of the cemetery for these unknown people was called Potters Field.

The doctor saw concern on Anna's face and said, "The city has many people to bury in one day. They are understaffed; there isn't time to check every body that they get. They will give him a number and put him into the ground. I'm afraid that if I ask for his plot number, they may ask questions. It's best that we don't inquire about him after they have taken him.

"Signora, it is up to you what is done with his body, but I can tell you, it would be the best solution for you since you have no money. If your husband dies tonight, the city will take care of him. You think about it. I will be here for the duration of the night."

"Thank you, doctor," Anna said. "Dr. Travazanno, where is Franco's shirt? I see that his pants are still on him but not his shirt."

"That's a good question," Dr. Travazanno said, "When Franco was first brought here sick, he fought with the nurse when she tried to take off his clothes to put him in a hospital garment. My nurse insisted on getting his shirt off because it was soaking wet. He fought very hard to keep his pants on, so the nurse gave up the fight because his pants weren't as wet as his shirt. It was a surprise to her that he had the strength to fight. She couldn't understand why he was so determined to keep his clothes on."

Anna looked puzzled at what the doctor had just told her. She replied to him, "I would like, if he should die before morning, to bury him in his own clothes. Is that too much of a problem for you or your nurse? It will be my only request."

The doctor told Anna that it would be no problem to bury him in his clothes. The doctor said, "Signora, you need to take the satchel that your husband is resting on. I am sure there are important papers you will need to get off the ship. Your husband is too sick to know that the satchel is gone. I'll need his passport, if he dies before morning, to give to the Red Cross."

As the doctor walked away, Anna placed her hand on her head wondering why Franco fought about his pants. With so much on her mind, it never occurred to her to look in his pockets.

Minutes became hours, and morning drew near. Anna sat quietly and listened to Franco still breathing, but barely. She looked toward the window, and saw the sun starting to peek through, bringing on a new day. It was December 15, 1947. She was becoming frightened and torn, not wanting Franco to die, but concerned about what to do if he was still alive when they docked that day. How could she afford to bring him to a hospital to die? How would she find the money to bury him? What was she going to do?

Anna was becoming desperate when she looked at Franco's frail, wet face. She got up from her chair and moved her stiff body to the end of his bed. She picked up a dry blanket and replaced the wet blanket that covered Franco with the fresh, dry one.

For several minutes she looked at Franco, contemplating what to do next. She put her hands together in prayer, brought them to her lips and whispered, "Please God, give me strength for what I am about to do." She bent down to his ear and whispered, "Franco, I have one last request of you. The sun is shining, and soon the ship will be docking. I have no money to take care of you after you die. It is best for you, and for us, if you die before we dock today. The doctor has assured me that the city of New York will bury you. There is no way I can afford to do it. Please, Franco, I need you to die, and I need you to die now. You owe me, Franco, to do what is right for me and for our daughters. Can you find it in your heart to give me my last request?"

Anna moved away from Franco and took a deep breath. Franco instantly lifted his head and opened his eyes wide, looking straight ahead. He had come out of his coma. He held up his head for just a second, put his head down on the pillow, and closed his eyes for the last time. Franco was dead.

Franco was unable to tell his wife before he died how much he loved her. He was unable to tell her how sorry he was for causing her so much pain. He was unable to tell her to check his pockets, for there was a roll of money in them to help her and his daughters. Franco was gone, granting the only woman he had ever loved her last request.

Anna got up from the side of Franco's bed, never touching him, and took the satchel from under his head. She threw it on her shoulder and walked out of the hospital room. She never looked back at Franco. She never acknowledged the patients in the room when she passed by them, never said goodbye to the doctor standing by the door when she passed him. She walked up several flights of stairs to the ship's deck and then looked out into the ocean.

She saw in the distance what looked to be an uneven horizon. She watched, and knew it would be sometime soon that the ship would enter the New York Harbor. She watched, stared. She didn't feel the cold, brisk, morning wind that hit her face. She didn't feel the early morning sun softly shining on her face. She saw nothing, felt nothing.

Chapter Twenty-Two

~~~~~

Anna wasn't sure how long she'd been on the deck when the hustle and bustle of the morning crew brought her back to her senses. She left the deck to go to her daughters. She walked down the stairs and through the hallways for the last time. She entered their large room and found her daughters packing their belongings, and getting ready for their last breakfast aboard the vessel. The passengers were warned ahead of time that breakfast would be their last meal served on their voyage, and because there would be no lunch, breakfast would be served late.

Anna dreaded meeting with her daughters. She stood for a minute to gather strength and then slowly approached them. Teresa saw their mother's face and knew her father was dead.

Pina asked, "Mamma, is father all right?"

Anna looked at her tall, thin daughter. She sighed and said to her softly, trying to keep the others from hearing, "No, my sweet child, your father has passed away."

Anna left Pina's side, to give her daughter a few minutes to herself. She went to her other daughters and said, "We must go to eat our last meal on this ship. We must see the chef and the kitchen crew before we leave, to say our goodbyes, and thank them for all they have done for us. Make sure you girls say goodbye to all our bed-neighbors before breakfast. Okay," Anna said trying to be cheery, "Let's go to breakfast."

Her daughters walked toward the door, with Teresa and Pina crying. Vincenza lingered behind to speak to her mother. "Mamma," she said, "tell me about Pappa."

Anna looked at her daughter, knowing that telling her the truth was more acceptable than not doing so. She took a deep breath and said, "Vincenza, Pappa has passed away. He died early this morning."

Vincenza, the practical daughter, said, "We have no money, how will we bury him?"

Anna proceeded to tell Vincenza about the Red Cross, and that her father's body would be properly taken care of. She explained how the city of New York would take care of him.

Vincenza did not cry. She simply said, "That's good. We won't have his burial to worry about. All will be okay. We will manage." Anna took her daughter into her arms, grateful for her encouraging words and gave her a hug.

After breakfast, the Gennusa family was packed and standing on the deck of the ship, waiting and watching among all the rest of the passengers as they sailed by the Statue of Liberty. The anticipation of seeing the extraordinary monument had been talked about constantly by the other passengers during their voyage to the new world. The children knew the Statue of Liberty's history, for it was told to them by the kitchen crew at night, while they were eating ice cream. The children learned that Lady Liberty was a gift to America from the French, for their friendship, and with admiration for their American democracy.

Anna forgot her anxiety for a short time, and turned to look in a different direction, toward the New Jersey shore. The sky was bright and clear, and it was easy to see that Ellis Island was a short distance from the Statue of Liberty. She thought about the island's history, and knew that the immigrants who wanted to come into America had to stop at this huge building to be processed. She knew there were records of multitudes of people who had passed through from Greece, Ireland, Germany, Italy, Russia, Scandinavia and many more nations.

"Look," Francesca said, "there she is." Anna turned back to see the huge copper and iron figure slowly appearing before them.

The people on the ship ran and gathered on the side of the ship where the Lady Liberty stood, to get the best view of her. They shouted and waved as they cruised up the Hudson River by this stately figure. Quiet and easy-going Innocenza, who barely spoke, said, to Anna's surprise, as they glided past her, "Mamma, she has such big feet." Anna turned to her daughter and sighed with a smile. She picked her up and hugged her.

Anna said, "Very soon we will be going over the Holland Tunnel. Did I ever tell you about the tunnel?" Before Innocenza had a chance to respond, Anna continued. "It's located on at the end of Canal Street in New York City and extends under the river, to the state of New Jersey."

Innocenza looked at her mother, puzzled, and asked, "Mamma, what is New Jersey?"

Anna explained to her daughter that it was one of the American states. She continued to tell her daughter some of the tunnel's history, and how her grandfather had worked on it while they lived there.

The tunnel, she said, is a long road that connects one part of land to another, under water. It was built so no water can get into it. It took seven years to complete. Anna looked at her puzzled daughter, and knew the information she was giving meant nothing to her. But talking helped Anna stay focused, and she felt some comfort in holding her daughter warmly next to her.

The closer the ship got to its destination, the more anxious Anna became. She tried to stay calm as the ship eased slowly up to the dock. Anna and her family, with all the other passengers, watched with amazement as this mammoth piece of iron was steered into its designated spot with style and grace. After the *Marine Perch* was in its proper position, the enormously loud engines stopped. The silence of the ship gave the passengers an eerie feeling. It was some time before a wide plank from the ship was connected to the dock and a large rope rail was attached to the side of the open walkway for the passengers' safety as they exited. The passengers held onto it when they exited.

It was hours before the upper- and middle-class families had exited and it was time for the lower-class passengers to leave the ship. These upper- and middle-class passengers were led off the ship, with their luggage carried by porters and some of the ship's crew, while the lower class carried their own baggage.

When it was time for the lower-class passengers to depart the ship, it was late afternoon and already getting dark. It was cold and the winter wind was blowing. Anna's daughters shivered from the cold, but to Anna's relief, they were brave, even the little ones, and did not complain.

Finally it was time for Anna and her daughters to leave the ship after weeks of being at sea. The family had to walk quickly, because of the surge of people pushing behind them. As soon as they touched firm ground with their meager belongings, they all felt better. It took a while for them to feel like they weren't rocking on the sea anymore, but soon her three younger daughters' color came back to their faces. Anna instructed her daughters to stay close to her and Vincenza held on to Maria's hand while Francesca held on to Innocenza. Her older daughters helped their mother carry the bags.

It was difficult staying together in such a large crowd but Vincenza and Francesca pulled and pushed their way through the crowds and Anna constantly looked back at her daughters, worried that she might lose them in the bitter cold.

The spectators who waited for the ship to be emptied were happy to find their relatives and loved ones. Groups formed as friends and families were reunited, making the process even more difficult for having to navigate around the groups of people, especially for a mother with six children. But somehow, the family stayed together.

Finally, Anna reached an exit table where she stopped to collect her thoughts. She looked at her daughters, shivering from the cold, blowing wind, and was relieved that they were all together. She thought to herself that everything would be okay. *Don't worry. The next minute will take care of itself. Just get through this one. You will find a way.*

Hoards of people behind Anna and her daughters pushed, for they wanted to get to the tables quickly. Anna and her daughters had their passports and travel tickets were inspected quickly, for the first time, and were then hurried to their next stop where an inspector asked Anna for her sponsorship papers.

Anna looked puzzled and said, "Sir, I'm not sure what you're asking for." The inspector asked again, and when he saw that Anna didn't understand, he explained. Anna, still puzzled, started to shake, but Vincenza, seeing her mother struggling, suggested that they look in Pappa's satchel.

Anna took the satchel off her shoulder and opened it. Inside she found a few of Franco's personal items and a large envelope with legal-looking papers inside.

The inspector recognized the documents and took them from Anna's hand, verifying that they were the correct papers. He checked the papers thoroughly and stamped them and then handed them back to Anna and told her and her family to go to the building down at the end of the dock.

Anna took the documents and put them back into the satchel and then walked with her daughters to the building. While walking, Teresa inquired about the papers, and Anna told her she didn't know what they were.

Anna and the girls were grateful to be out of the bitter cold wind and inside a warm building as they entered the next checkpoint. Just then, a middle-aged couple approached them with opened arms, calling out their names and speaking Sicilian. Anna looked at these strange people, not sure what to make of them as they kissed and hugged her and the girls.

The man, speaking in Italian, whispered into Anna's ear after his hug, saying to pretend she knew them, because they were posing as their sponsors. The man asked Anna where Franco was and Anna was forced to tell him about Franco's death. The man looked at her coldly, "The price of our sponsorship will not change, even without your husband," he said.

Anna looked at the man and said, "Sir, I'm sorry but I don't know what you're talking about."

The man took the family's passports and the sponsorship papers, walked over to the desk, and showed the passports and signed papers. The signature was approved, stamped, and the documents given back to him. His wife signed the same papers. The inspector gave carbon copies to the sponsors.

The sponsors had the signed papers in their hand as they escorted Anna and her daughters out of the building. They went back into the cold, bitter wind, and the couple asked for their money. Anna explained that she did not understand.

The man said that he and his wife had received a partial payment by Franco to sponsor the family to get them into the country. He told Anna that he would not give them their passports and papers unless he and his wife were paid in full.

Anna was now nervous and said, "Sir, my husband never told me about this."

Vincenza, who was listening to the conversation, said, "Mamma, maybe there is money in Pappa's satchel."

Frightened, Anna took the satchel off her shoulder, bent down on the ground, and emptied out the contents. All that fell out of the satchel were Franco's personal items—his comb, shaving apparel, a framed picture of his parents, a small inexpensive medal of the Virgin Mary, and a small bundle wrapped in cloth and tied with string.

The man bent down and quickly grabbed the bundle. He stood up and Anna stood up, too. As the man untied and unwrapped the package, Anna was shocked to see money. The man looked at her and said, "This is the payment for our services. The money is mine." He handed the money to his wife, and she put it into her handbag.

"But, sir, that money is for my family. I have no money to feed them. What am I to do?" cried Anna.

"That's your problem. Our work is done. You can get through customs with these papers that are signed."

After the man stopped talking, Anna watched the man and his wife disappear into the crowd of people. Anna stood in shock. She couldn't believe two strangers had just walked off with the only money she had, even though she didn't even know she'd been carrying it. Anna looked around for help, but there was none.

Teresa told her mother, "Mamma, I'm very cold. What should we do?" Anna looked at Teresa and then she heard Maria crying. She bent down to pick up Franco's personal items and placed them back into the satchel. She stood up, threw the satchel on her shoulders, and picked up Maria. She led her family to the next stop.

Chapter Twenty-Three

A nna and her daughters were in awe as they entered a huge, impressive, warm building. The children had been in large buildings before, but never in a new building on American soil and their innocent minds were overwhelmed. Inside the building, the structure of the ceiling was supported by large exposed iron beams. Huge lights hung from the middle of the beams and a large American flag hung above the huge front door. The girls turned their heads to look at every inch of this place, while Anna guided them to their next stop. This enormous room had many officials in uniforms instructing people in which direction they needed to go.

Anna didn't stop for help because she remembered the process from her last trip here when she was a young woman. She looked for a table with a sign on it with a big "G", since her last name started with the letter "G." She walked quickly in that direction, with her daughters following, passing long rows of other lettered tables. Anna kept an eye on her daughters, making sure they were still behind her and keeping up with her pace until they reached their table. She got her girls into the back of a long line of people and waited to get their passport inspected for the second time.

Standing in line, Anna tried not to think about what would happen next. She knew it would be some time before their passports and papers would be inspected and she tried not to think too much about her worries for fear she would break down in front of her daughters. She was very troubled by the sponsorship papers she held and didn't know why a sponsor was needed to get into the country. She wondered where Franco had gotten the money to pay these people to sponsor her and her family. *Stop thinking,* she told herself. She didn't have the luxury of worrying right now. She wouldn't let her children see her fear and reminded herself that in life there are times when there are no choices and this was one of those times. She had no choice but to stay in control. She repeated this to herself over and over again. "I have no choices."

Maria started to cry hysterically and Anna realized that her youngest daughter had to go to the bathroom. Maria was too frightened and confused to tell her mother that she'd wet her pants and didn't want to be punished. Ashamed, the child put her arms around her mother's neck and put her head down on Anna's shoulder to hide her face.

Anna was upset at herself for not tending to her daughter's needs. She assured Maria that it was alright. Maria let go of her mother and rubbed her eyes. Anna sighed, disturbed that she had no clean clothes for any of her daughters, especially now, when Maria needed them. She shook her head and thought to herself, *This matter is not important.* Anna looked at her little daughter, kissed her cheek, stood up and told her older girls that she was going to take the little ones to the bathroom. When she came back, they could go to the facilities. She ordered her daughters to stay together in the line and move with it.

Anna stood on her tip-toes, stretching her body, and trying to see over people's heads for a restroom sign. She looked down one end of the building and then turned to the other side. She approached a uniformed person who was busy helping other passengers, but was happy to direct Anna to the restrooms at the end of the building. She walked with the two little ones, holding their hands, toward where the gentlemen had told her to go.

Anna found the bathroom marked Female, and then entered it. She gasped at the smell. The small room was stuffy, and it smelled urine and disinfectant. It was repulsive. The little ones stopped at the door, not wanting to go in. Anna said that it would be okay, but to hurry.

Anna's daughters instinctively held their breaths and Anna ordered them not to touch anything. She held each of her daughters up away from the toilet seat while they urinated. After they were done, and came out of the stall, where trash was strewn over the floor, Anna wouldn't allow the girls to wash their hands because the sinks were unclean.

When walking back to the others, Maria said, "Mamma the bathroom was stinky."

Anna looked down at her daughter, very upset, sighed, and said, "Yes, little one, it was."

Anna and the girls walked back to the table, the little ones now more comfortable.

Maria said, "Mamma, I am hungry."

Anna stopped and looked down at Maria. She felt a knot twist in her stomach and said in her gentle way, as anxiety built up inside, "Yes, I know you are. Please be patient."

While talking to Maria, she reached down to Innocenza, always so quiet, and touched her head. She rubbed her hair gently to let her know that she was safe. As Anna walked toward her older daughters, she looked anxiously at the large clock hanging on the wall—the day was slipping away. She took her eyes away from the clock and quickly walked to her daughters. Her heart was pounding and she had trouble catching her breath.

Anna told her daughters where the restrooms were, and like she had told the younger girls, told them not to touch anything.

As the girls started to walk away, Pina said to Teresa, without the others hearing, "I am afraid. Where do you think we will go from here?"

"I don't know," Teresa said. "I think Mamma is very afraid and trying not to show it."

Pina asked, "Who were those people that took Mamma's money?"

Teresa, walking a little faster to keep up with Vincenza and Francesca, said, "I don't know. I'm not sure, but it seems to me that these people signed for us to get into this country. Apparently, Pappa paid them to be responsible for us, and to provide housing for us."

"It looked to me like Mamma didn't know who they were or what they wanted." Pina continued, "Teresa, should we talk to Mamma about this and how afraid we feel?"

"Yes, I'll ask Mamma," Teresa responded. "I'll talk to her about this situation. Maybe we can help her."

The girls came back from the restroom and joined their mother and the little girls in line, but it took a long time before Teresa finally got the courage to say to her mother, "Mamma, the young ones are complaining that they're hungry, and we are all getting tired."

"Yes, Teresa," Anna said, taking a deep breath with a heavy heart. "I know but I can't do anything about that right now. Please be patient."

"Yes, Mamma, but what will we do when we leave this building?"

Anna looked at her concerned daughter and said sternly, "Let us get through this first, and when the time comes, I will know what to do next. Don't worry, Teresa, I will know what to do."

Teresa turned to Pina who was listening to the conversation. Teresa, slightly afraid, didn't want to press her mother for any more information. She just shrugged her shoulders at Pina.

After several hours of waiting in line, and the strain of standing on a hard cement floor, Anna's lower back was hurting. She took a deep breath and felt the anxiety deepen in her chest as she reached toward her back and started to rub it. A large group of people standing in front of them were now finished with inspection, and then it was their turn. Anna inched up to the inspection table with all her girls, took out their passports from her purse, and handed them to the authorities.

The sunshine had completely disappeared, and the building, with its bright lights, was almost too bright. Anna was getting a headache from hunger. She'd forgotten how cold it could get in New York City, and was annoyed at herself for not having the insight to pack hats and mittens for her daughters. But under great distress, Anna had forgotten many things she could have done to make the trip more comfortable, like bring food for her family. She hadn't wanted to leave Sicily. She'd had so much on her mind that she forgot what her last trip to the United States had been like. She couldn't think of the things she needed for her and her family to survive.

A long time had passed, waiting in all the lines and Anna had been thinking too much about the things she hadn't done for her family while getting ready for this trip, especially not having money of her own. It made her feel sick and ashamed. She never thought that she would lose a member of her family on the trip, especially her strong and healthy husband. Finally, reaching the inspection table for the second time that day, they waited as the authorities closely examined their passports.

The whole family's picture, except for Franco's, was in the one passport book. Because Franco was not an American Citizen, he had his own passport with only his picture, and there was no indication that he had traveled with them. Because he had carried his own passport, there was no question of his whereabouts. To the authorities, he did not exist. The authorities did not question, and were not concerned, that Anna was traveling alone with her children.

The inspector looked closely at the passports, looked closely at each child, and compared them to their pictures. Then the inspector checked the family's ticket, and each birth certificate, including Anna's. Although the girls were born in Sicily, they were American citizens through Anna's citizenship. Because they carried an American passport, it made the process of getting through inspection easier and faster than most of the other passengers.

After the inspection they were quickly directed to another station where the inspectors opened their bags and checked them quickly because there were so many people waiting their turn.

The inspectors hurried the family along. Anna and her girls walked a few feet from the inspector's table, where Anna stopped and stood in the middle of the huge room, watching the activity, not sure what to do next. She looked in all directions.

"Mamma," Francesca tugged at Anna's coat and said, "I'm hungry. I want some mashed potatoes."

Anna felt the tug on her coat and looked down, startled, and said, "What?"

Pina heard her sister saying to her mother that she was hungry. She picked her up and said, "Francesca, as soon as Mamma can, she will get food."

Pina kissed Francesca on the cheek and put her down, keeping her close and holding her hand.

Anna looked more intense, and she felt strong anxiety as she looked at her surroundings. She knew that Eleventh Avenue was just outside that door. She knew where she was. She knew what door to go through, but had no idea what she would do after going through that door. She didn't know what waited outside for her and her daughters. She stood in the middle of the large room, quietly thinking, for a long, long time, and felt very alone. Fear filled her and she began to sweat. She could feel the perspiration dripping down her armpits. She kept saying to herself, "Don't lose control. You will be okay. God will watch over you and your daughters. Just don't lose control!"

It was completely dark outside, and the building was emptying out. There were only a few passengers left waiting by their baggage. These people, Anna could tell from their luggage, were lower-class passengers. The upper and the middle classes were gone. Transportation outside of the building had been waiting for them after they cleared customs. A gentleman in an official uniform approached Anna and her family, and told her that they would have to vacate the building; the building was closing, and all passengers had to leave.

Anna swallowed hard, and looked around the room one more time, hoping that somehow an inspiration would come as to where to take her family. She started to breathe heavily when no answers came. The girls were tired and restless.

"Mamma," Vincenza said, "may I make a suggestion about what to do next?"

Anna looked at Vincenza angrily, and said, "No, I don't need any suggestion from you. I need you to be very quiet while I think."

"But, Mamma, I think—"

Anna grabbed Vincenza by her coat, pulled her up and, losing her patience, exclaimed, "I said to be quiet, Vincenza, and I mean it. Quiet!"

Anna let go of Vincenza, and Vincenza landed on her feet. She started to cry, which was unusual. Anna looked at all her children and yelled at them, "Be patient, all of you. Do you understand?" Frustrated, Anna looked away from them, as Teresa went to Vincenza and put her arms around her sister. She pulled her away from their mother.

Teresa said, "Don't, Vincenza. Mamma needs just a few minutes."

"But Teresa," Vincenza said, "I know what to do." Meanwhile, Anna looked to her left and saw the uniformed gentlemen heading toward them. She took her luggage and directed the girls toward a large heavy door that led to the outside world. Anna hesitated when she approached that door. From hunger and fear, she felt weak, as she knew she could no longer avoid the inevitable. With a heavy heart she opened the door.

Anna led her family into the cold night. The wind was blowing hard and the cold was sharp on their faces. She stood in front of the building, frightened, knowing she and her daughters were destitute. She didn't know what to do next. She stopped at the edge of the sidewalk and looked up to the West Side Elevated Highway and took a deep, anxious breath, hoping it would release some of her tension. She felt the bitter cold air enter her lungs and her lungs ached. The cold didn't make her feel better; and as the air came out of her mouth, icy steam came with it.

Anna looked up and down the street and then felt a wet sprinkle hit her face. She looked at the bright street lights and realized it was snowing. The snow's large flakes started to come down heavy and fast. Behind her, the lights were bright from the building which gave Anna a clear view in front of her.

Teresa, shivering, said, "Mamma, the little ones are freezing. What are we going to do?"

Anna looked at Maria and picked her up.

Maria started to cry and said, "Mamma, I want my Pappa. Where is my Pappa?"

Anna started shaking and opened her heavy winter coat to protect her baby from the snow and cold. She brushed the snow away from Maria's hair, trying to relax the baby as much as she was trying to relax herself.

Anna heard Innocenza whimpering. She reached to touch Innocenza and pulled her very close. Anna looked at the sky and said a prayer. She put her head down to look away from the falling snow and asked God to help her. Anna gently let go of Innocenza and put her right hand into her pocket for warmth.

The snow was coming down harder now, developing into a blizzard. The girls' hair and coats were covered with this heavy, wet, white snow. Anna dug deep into her pocket for warmth when she felt a familiar form. Remembering what it was, she put her fingers around it and squeezed it. Then she pulled it from her pocket and held it up in the street light.

The snow was accumulating around Anna and her daughters. She stopped shaking, took another deep breath, and her anxiety was gone. Anna smiled for the first time in a very long time. She looked again at the object in her hand, closed her hand around it, and placed it to her heart, while thanking God for answering her prayers.

She opened her eyes and said to her daughters, "We will be fine." With more conviction she turned to the object still closed in her hand and repeated, "We will be fine."

Anna opened her hand and looked lovingly at her spool of pure-white thread. The fear, anxiety, anger, and confusion left her body. Again, she said out loud with strong conviction to her daughters, "We will be fine."

The End

About Mary B. Patterson

Mary B. (Gennusa) Patterson was born in a small village, Bisacquino, on the island of Sicily off the shore of Italy. She came to this country as a small child and grew up in Thompsonville/Enfield, Connecticut.

Raised in an ethnic Italian family, Mary's parents said she was "always old enough to get married but never old enough to date." Trying to fit into American young society, Mary found creative ways to balance her ethnic home and American backyard life.

Mary moved to Maryland to help in her sister's restaurant, the Topside Inn, in Galesville. There she met her husband; and after three weeks of dating, he asked her to marry him. It took her one week to say yes, and they were married six months later. Together they raised three remarkable sons in Crofton, Maryland.

CPSIA information can be obtained at www.ICGtesting.com
Printed in the USA
BVOW11s1124020314

346386BV00011B/208/P